Also by Gareth L. Powell and available from Titan Books

Embers of War
Fleet of Knives
Light of Impossible Stars

Stars and Bones
Descendant Machine

GARETH L. POWELL

FUTURE'S EDGE

TITAN BOOKS

Future's Edge
Print edition ISBN: 9781803368634
E-book edition ISBN: 9781803368641

Published by Titan Books
A division of Titan Publishing Group Ltd
144 Southwark Street, London SE1 0UP
www.titanbooks.com

First edition: February 2025
10 9 8 7 6 5 4 3 2 1

A CIP catalogue record for this title is available from the British Library.

Printed and bound by CPI Group (UK) Ltd, Croydon, CR0 4YY.

For Dianne

CONTENTS

PART ONE:
MASS EXTINCTION

PART TWO:
THE FUNDAMENTAL THINGS APPLY

PART THREE:
INTO THE DARK

PART ONE

MASS EXTINCTION

CHAPTER ONE

A TREE FALLS

"Guv?" My barman was a mechanical, multi-limbed lifeform from a system in the vicinity of Arcturus.

"Yes, Siegfried?"

"You'd better get in here."

I sighed. "What are we dealing with?"

Siegfried looked like a football thrown through a cutlery drawer. "Attempted shakedown."

"Another one?" I rolled my eyes. "What's that, like three this month?"

"Four."

"Where are they?"

"Standing at the bar. You can't miss them. They're the ones that look like geckos in sweatpants."

I pulled open my office door, to be greeted by the buzz of a dozen conversations in half a dozen languages. The place smelled of desperation and black mould. The only illumination came from a row of lights hanging above the counter. Tonight's would-be gangsters were standing in a tight group at one end, trying to look simultaneously menacing and inconspicuous.

"For goodness' sake," I said. "They can't be much older than hatchlings."

I walked around the counter to face them. The tallest only came up to my chest, but they had pointed snouts filled with sharp teeth, and scalpel-like claws on their three-fingered hands.

"Are you the owner?" one of them asked in the Common Tongue. Judging by the length of the spines protruding from between his shoulder blades, he was the oldest of the bunch, and probably their leader.

"How can I help?"

"We have an offer for you."

"Let me guess." I folded my arms. "Does this offer have something to do with me paying you a percentage of my takings in return for protection?"

Eyelids flicked back and forth across large, black reptilian eyes. "Uh, yesss."

"Sorry, kids. Not interested."

The leader pulled himself up to his full height. "We could make thingsss very difficult for you."

"I don't doubt it, but I'm still going to have to say no."

A hush fell as the patrons smelled a confrontation. Some of the smaller reptiles in the group looked around, unnerved to suddenly find themselves the centre of attention. The tall one didn't seem to have noticed. His attention remained fixed on me. "This is your lassst chance," he hissed. "A place like thissss, with a lot of wood and packing materialsss. Very flammable. Anything might happen."

I uncrossed my arms. "You boys must be new in town. I assume you're trying to carve out a little territory for yourselves. A little notoriety?"

"What of it?"

"You think you're the first to try something like this? I've been here two years, and there are always parasites about, looking to take what they haven't earned. I've seen gangs come and go. You're no different."

Claws flexed. "Are you going to pay or not?"

I shook my head. "The thing is, kids; if I needed protection, I'd already have it. There are plenty of hoodlums to choose from, and a lot of them are tougher than you."

The leader held my gaze for a few seconds, then he held out a three-fingered hand. One of his henchmen produced a stolen emergency flare and passed it to him. "How about we torch the place now?"

"I wouldn't recommend it."

"Oh, really?" The leader twisted the flare's base, igniting it. For a moment, the only sound in the bar was the roar of the red flame.

I sighed. The flare was designed to be seen through rain and fog by search helicopters. It probably contained a mix of strontium nitrate, potassium perchlorate, and an energetic fuel such as aluminium or magnesium. Which meant it had a burn temperature of at least a thousand degrees centigrade—certainly hot enough to set fire to anything in this place. I couldn't let that happen, so I reached out and snuffed it with my hand.

The reptiles looked at me aghast. The leader said, "How did you do that?"

I smirked and held up my hand. In the overhead light, my palm glistened with an iridescent rainbow sheen.

"Alien nano-virus," I said. "I picked it up on an archaeological dig, a long way from here." I slapped the extinguished flare from his hand. "It makes me very, very hard to kill." I hauled back and punched him across his scaly face. His jaw snapped shut and he crashed back into his little entourage, who fled, leaving their fallen leader sprawled unconscious on the concrete floor. "And a lot stronger than I look."

Scattered applause broke from the tables around the room. The locals always appreciated a show. I ignored them, turning instead to where Siegfried hovered like a rotund Swiss Army knife. "Drag that outside, would you?"

"My pleasure, guv."

As the conversation among the drinkers turned back to the latest reports from the front line, I stepped out to the small concrete yard at the back of the ramshackle bar. Leaning there against the corrugated iron wall, nostrils filled with garbage fire smoke from the surrounding refugee encampment, I gazed up at the vast foam ships being constructed in orbit and wished I had the guts to book a berth.

Beyond the lamps and circles of firelight, the night was very dark, and a cold breeze ruffled up from the salt marshes to the southwest to flutter tent walls and fluster laundry. Like everyone else, I had come here fleeing the war; but unlike the majority in the camp, this was where I had stopped, too scared and too stubborn to cash in my chips and leave altogether.

From the campfires, I caught snatches of competing songs; the crackle of burning plastic; children crying; food cooking. From further afield, the brine stink of the marshes and the occasional echoing thunder of a shuttle lifting from the civilian port. I kicked aside a tin can. Once, a lush grass analogue had covered the ground here; now, the passage of thousands of refugees had worn it to a bare, hard-packed dirt, strewn with the detritus of their half-abandoned, makeshift lives. Beyond the sea of tents, barbed wire gates marked the camp's entrance. The wire wasn't there to keep the refugees from leaving; it was there to deter the local wildlife, especially the nocturnal Komodo-jackals that prowled the edges of the salt marsh and picked off the occasional incautious security guard.

Whenever a completed foam ship broke orbit, which happened about once a week, the entire encampment looked up. Some of them muttered blessings and good wishes, kissed prayer beads or raised their hands to the skies in the knowledge that another ten thousand sleeping souls had cast themselves into the abyss in the hope of finding sanctuary among the uncharted stars on the far side of the gap. Others shook their heads and cursed at the sight, lamenting a missed opportunity. They knew there would only ever be a finite number of foam ships, and never enough to take every refugee. Eventually, the Cutters would find their way here along the tramline network.

The tramlines were a web of furrows in the undervoid, which a correctly positioned ship could use to glide from one star system to the next, expending very little energy. Every known species employed them. They had been arteries for colonisation, conflict, and commerce, the roads of empire; but now the enemy were using them against us.

That was the part I didn't want to think about.

I pulled a joint from behind my ear. Smoking wasn't one of my customary vices, but one of my regular customers had slipped the little hand-rolled cylinder to me in lieu of payment and it seemed a shame to let it go to waste. I cupped my hands and lit the end with a borrowed lighter. The first drag made my head feel light. The second brought a surge of nausea. I managed two further inhales before coughing, giving up, and flicking the butt over the fence. If I wanted to feel sick, I could huff the toxic smoke from the garbage fires. I stood for a moment, letting the wooziness subside. The bar was a familiar presence at my back, its conversational weight sensed rather than heard. It had been mine since I'd taken over from its former owner when he shipped out. He had left it a stripped-out derelict mess and I'd been the only one interested in fixing it up and reopening. It didn't really have a name, but under my stewardship, it had become one of the few places on the planet where people said the beer came cold, and the gin didn't taste like a reactor leak.

Sparing a final, rueful glance at the orbital construction platforms, I turned back through the door into the storeroom where, between the stacked kegs and cases of spirits, I kept a small bed made from pallets.

The one thing I had in common with every other lifeform in this stinking camp was that I'd left somebody behind. The trouble was, I didn't know how to move on. At first, owning a bar had seemed like a good survival strategy. If I was going to be stuck in a place where everybody else was just passing through, it made sense to have something permanent. But now, after two years of waiting, the novelty of it all had worn thinner than a twice-used tissue. I sat down and regarded my palm. Closing my hand over the flare had been momentarily agonising, but now there wasn't even so much as a scorch mark. My knuckles, which should have been torn to shreds where they'd impacted the rough hide covering the kid's jawbone, were similarly unscathed.

I should get out of here, I thought. *I should just throw my clothes into a bag without bothering to fold them and apply to be on the next foam ship out.* It didn't matter what waited on the other side of the gulf, it would be preferable to a life spent rotting here.

"Guv?" Siegfried drifted into the storeroom like a spiky balloon.

"Don't tell me those lizards are back?"

"No, but someone's asking for you."

"Who is it?"

"I didn't catch his name." The barman moved two of his tool-tipped metal limbs in an approximation of a shrug. "But he says he's your ex-husband."

CHAPTER TWO

ON THE BEACH

I stepped through the connecting door and immediately clocked Jack. He was sitting at a table, leaning on one elbow and watching the front door as if expecting someone. He'd shaved the nearest side of his head, and a silver earring gleamed from the exposed lobe. His long black coat hung loosely from his shoulders. He hadn't noticed me yet, so I picked a bottle of gin from the shelf and sidled up behind him.

"Freshen your drink, sir?"

His shoulders stiffened. "Ursula?"

"Who else were you looking for?"

He swivelled on his barstool, and I caught my breath. I'd forgotten how striking he was, in a hard, square-jawed kind of way. A dancer's body with a sword-fighter's poise. He said, "Charming place you have here."

I wanted to tell him it was a shithole, but my regulars were within earshot, so I just nodded, and said, "Coldest beer in the whole camp."

He tapped a fingernail against his glass. "And roughest gin?"

"I'm told it does the job. The first one numbs your taste buds, and after that, you're golden."

He laughed. "Oh, Ursula, I've missed you."

"I've missed you, too."

"They told me you were still here," he said. "But I couldn't believe you really would be."

"I told you I'd wait."

"I'd hoped you wouldn't. I wanted you safe."

"I'm as safe as anyone here."

He looked up at the corrugated iron ceiling and exhaled.

"What?"

"Nobody's safe." He leant across the bar and seized my free wrist. "Nobody here's even remotely safe. You know that."

I thumped the bottle down on the counter. "Keep your voice down."

He pursed his lips. "You could try to be civil."

"You could just tell me where the fuck you've been."

Jack shook his head. "Trust me, you really don't want to know."

"The hell I don't. You left me—"

"I told you." He rubbed his forehead. "I told you why I had to go."

"I'm not an idiot."

"Then why are you angry?"

I leant my hands on the bar and took a long breath. "Why on earth do you think?"

"Less than a minute, and we're back to this?"

"What do you expect? You got us berths on the last freighter out. I abandoned everything and everyone. And you never showed."

"I had my duty."

"I thought you had my back."

"And I thought you understood. My comrades were counting on me. Our world was counting on me."

"Yeah, and how did that turn out?"

He scowled. "You know what happened."

"Everyone died. Earth fell, and you being there made no difference."

"That's not entirely fair. Some transports got away under covering fire from our forces."

"How many?"

He picked up his glass and glowered into the amber centimetre of spirit at its base. "Maybe two dozen. Yours among them."

"You should have come with me."

"I had to stay."

"You knew you couldn't defeat them."

He swigged down the dregs of his drink and managed not to cough. He pressed his lips against the back of his hand while the burn passed, then whispered, "We had to try."

•

Those final hours in London had been nightmarish chaos. With the interstellar tramline network collapsing like a broken spider's web, confirmation of attacks on other worlds arrived only hours before the routes connecting them went down completely. The damaged ships that limped through to spread the alarm were often the last to make it before those tramlines decohered altogether. And yet somehow, the Cutters still advanced.

When the shit hit the fan, I was in the process of being discharged from hospital. I'd been in there for months and knew most of the nurses by name. Since picking up the alien parasite, I'd had every scan and test you could imagine, and a few you'd probably rather not. Suffice to say, I'd been prodded and poked in places you'd usually not get anywhere near unless you'd at least bought me dinner.

"Whatever it is," the doctor had said, "it seems to have adapted and fused with your DNA."

I sat back in my chair. "So, you can't get it out of me?"

He looked apologetic. "We wouldn't know where to start. We're not even sure where you end, and it begins."

"I'm stuck with it?"

"If it's any consolation, it doesn't appear to be contagious, so we'll be able to release you from quarantine. Nor does it seem to be doing

you any harm. On the contrary, all indications suggest it's going to great lengths to keep you healthy."

I looked at the back of my hand. The skin seemed smoother than I remembered, and the nails were hard and glossy, more like carbon fibre than keratin. But nothing had burst out of my chest or turned me into a terrifying blob of fleshy protoplasm, so I guessed I should be grateful.

"We will, of course, be referring you for further tests."

"I thought you might."

Once the paperwork had gone through and I'd been officially released, I collected my things and left. Outside, the sky and the Thames were the same shade of brutalised steel. I started walking towards the tube. I wasn't up to raw-dogging reality, so I had my earbuds cranked to eleven, blasting out the playlist I'd been putting together in preparation for this day. Around me, dead leaves fell from the trees, car tyres hissed on the wet roads, and I watched the advertising holograms flicker and strut above the glass towers on the river's far bank. They looked wan and insubstantial in the overcast light. The news about the parasite wasn't what I'd hoped, but I couldn't let it slow me down. I had to convince Doctor Vogel to select me for his next off-planet expedition. I'd been a fucking idiot last time out, taking off my glove when I did, but at least I hadn't brought back anything infectious. That had to count for something, right? With my hands firmly wedged in my pockets, I dodged around an elderly Korean woman and her umbrella drone. If I didn't get on another mission roster, I could effectively kiss my PhD, and perhaps my entire future career, farewell.

My phone buzzed for attention. I blinked up the call and frowned as I saw Jack's number. He was on shore leave and had been looking after my flat while I'd been in hospital. I'd been hoping he would be here to meet me, so I was kind of annoyed he was nowhere to be seen. I tapped the side of my eye socket to answer, and saw his face overlaid on my vision.

"Ursula?"

"Jack, I thought you were coming to meet—"

"Ursula, listen to me. You need to get out, right now."

The signal glitched, then reasserted itself.

"Out? Out where?"

"Get to Heathrow," he said. "There's a transport called the Mango Feedback. It's evacuating the families of serving crew. I've told them you're my wife."

"You told them what?"

More static. I heard sirens in the streets.

Jack said, "New York's gone. It's just gone. And Mexico City's under attack." People were slowing their pace, holding their hands to their ears as they absorbed the breaking news reports. The lady with the drone umbrella let out a cry and collapsed into a sitting position on the wet pavement. When Jack came back through, he was gripping the sides of the camera and shouting into the lens. "London might be next. You must move. I'm sending you the flight details. There's a berth waiting for you. Don't stop to think or pick up luggage; just get to the airport. There isn't much time."

"You're not coming?"

"I need to report in. My ship needs me."

"I'll wait for you."

"Just get to Heathrow. Let me check with my ship, and I'll find you. I promise. Get to the transport and I'll find you."

●

I refilled his glass.

"Do you know how hard it was to get from Chelsea to Heathrow while civilisation literally collapsed around me?"

"You made it, though."

"A lot of people didn't."

Jack lowered his eyes. "I know."

He was silent for a moment, and I looked away, trying not to remember. As the self-driving networks broke down, the cars had choked the streets. There were fights. I got caught in a few scuffles. If I hadn't had the protection of the alien infection, I doubt I would have made it through the gridlock alive.

"It was a surprise attack," Jack said, and I honestly couldn't tell if he was talking to me or himself. I watched him scratch the label from the bottle, scrunch up the paper, and flick it away across the tabletop. "We didn't have time to warn everybody. We did what we could."

I reached over and touched the back of his hand with my fingertips. "I chose you over everybody. I didn't go back for anyone. I fought my way through crowds of people who are all now dead, just to be with you."

"And also, to live."

I glanced around at our surroundings. "You call this living?"

•

I stood at the hatch.

"Please," I said, "we have to wait."

The naval crewman shook his head. "We got orders, ma'am."

"But he'll be here. He said he'd find me."

The guy glanced out at the overcast sky and the other transports lifting from the tarmac. Sirens wailed in the distance. Armoured hovercraft patrolled the airport's perimeter. "I don't reckon he is."

"Just a few more minutes?"

"Sorry, ma'am, we got incoming." He touched a control and the hatch lowered into place with a heavy metallic thud.

"No, please, I—"

My phone rang. It was Jack. Judging from the noise and vibration, he seemed to be in some sort of vehicle. He said, "You made it?"

"Where are you?"

"Don't wait for me."

The crewman was trying to guide me towards the passenger compartment. He made an I-told-you-so face and reached for my arm, but I shook him off. "Why not?"

"Because I'm not coming."

"What—"

"All leave's been cancelled. I'm shipping out with the Crisis Actor."

"No, you can't."

"I'm sorry. I must."

"But I need you."

"And if I'm going into battle, I need to know you're safe."

"No!"

"I love you."

"Then don't do this. Come with me. I need you."

"I'm sorry."

•

"Are you still with the *Crisis Actor*?"

We were at a corner table now, in the intersection between two corrugated iron walls, the bottle of gin between us. Jack had opened his coat, revealing the tarnished scabbard at his belt.

"She's a bit banged-up," Jack said, "but still flying."

"The crew?"

"We lost a few." His thumbnail worried the scraps of label still clinging to the bottle.

"And for the last two years?"

"We've been fighting a guerrilla war in Sol system, trying to slow the Cutters' spread into the network."

"That must have been tough."

"It wasn't easy. We ran out of a lot of supplies and ammo. We took a lot of casualties." His expression hardened. "For a time, we thought we might be trapped in the system for good." He drained his glass and wiped his mouth on his sleeve. "Then we saw a chance. The last remaining tramline connection. We had to fight hard, but we got through just before it lost all coherence."

"And now?"

"Now can wait." He reached across the table and took my hand. "Will you have a drink with me?"

I pulled my hand away. "I don't drink."

He looked surprised. "You're running a bar. I assumed—"

"You assumed wrong."

"You used to."

"I used to do a lot of things."

"So, what happened?"

"The world ended. I lost you."

"So, you stopped drinking?"

"No, I started. I spent the first six months here getting blackout, falling-down, puking-up drunk." I glanced towards the bar. The place was quiet now the excitement had died down. Siegfried was more than capable of handling the drink orders by himself. "Then the guy who ran this place up and left, and I needed a project and I needed to get sober, so I took over, and I've barely touched a drop since."

Jack sat back and rested an ankle on the opposite knee. Straps and buckles covered his boots. "Are you still angry?"

"I don't know what I am." I pushed the gin bottle aside. Its base made a harsh scraping sound on the wooden tabletop. "I think I blamed you for staying behind, because it was easier to be angry with you than deal with losing you."

"And now?"

"I guess I'm relieved you're not dead."

"That makes two of us."

"And now, you're here. 'Of all the gin joints in all the towns in all the world…'"

"Yes." He looked away. "About that."

I felt a stir of disquiet. "What is it?"

Jack sighed. "We have an ulterior motive for coming to find you."

"We?"

He looked me in the eye, and the skin prickled at the back of my neck. "There's a possibility you might hold the key to slowing the Cutters' advance."

•

24

Before the war—if you could really call it a war, rather than a constant, desperate rear-guard action—Void's Edge had always been considered a dead-end at the farthest extremity of the tramline network. As such, it had never required a military presence. Not until the Cutters' onslaught caused ships to start falling further and further back. Now, the docks at the military port were a series of twenty fresh pits dug into the tundra floor and lined with sandbags, containing vessels from half a dozen different species and civilisations. We descended a flight of metal steps into the one that held Jack's ship. When I saw her, I stopped in my tracks.

"Holy shit." The *Crisis Actor* had been ugly to start with; now, she looked like hell.

"The old girl's been through a lot." Jack sounded defensive.

"I don't doubt it."

Parts of the hull had been scorched and buckled. Antennae were missing. A whole section had been replaced using parts scavenged from a completely different class of ship. The result looked like something you'd get if you asked a blindfolded drunk to build a submarine out of boiler parts and military scrap. She was asymmetrical and sported lumps and bulges where no ship had any business sporting lumps and bulges. Her days as a stealth warship were over. Fly her into a hostile atmosphere and she'd light up the radar screens like an oil rig dropping from the heavens. God alone knew how she had made it down from orbit without shearing apart in at least half a dozen different places.

"Whose idea was it to paint her with yellow and black stripes?"

"Some creative soul at the Foss Repair Station. Apparently, they were all out of battleship grey." Jack leant close. "Don't mention it when you get aboard, though."

"Why not?"

"Cris was furious about it."

"Who's Cris?"

25

"It's what I call her for short."

"The ship?"

"Yes."

He led me across the blasted soil of the pit to the base of the *Crisis Actor*'s embarkation ramp. As we approached, ground defence gun turrets swivelled in our direction, and then swivelled away again as the onboard intelligence recognised us and deemed us friends rather than potential invaders.

"Trust me," Jack said. "If she wanted us dead, we would have been atomised the instant we entered this pit. Probably even before that."

His pride in the ship shone through in his voice, but there was also an uncharacteristic shyness about the way he wouldn't meet my eye when he was talking about her.

Puzzled, I said, "I'll try to be on my best behaviour."

"Thank you."

I followed him into the shadow of the misshapen vessel. Overhead, sections of the hull shimmered with the energies barely contained within. I could almost feel my skin blistering from the radioactive overspill. A ramp lowered on squealing hinges, and we ascended.

The *Crisis Actor* didn't look any better from the inside. Cables, tubes, and wires hung from the ceiling, lashed together with plastic ties. Maintenance panels hung unfastened, revealing the jury-rigged electrical repairs within. Patches of steel welded to the bulkheads marked where shrapnel had scythed through the walls. Everywhere I looked, I saw evidence of the two years she had spent on the run in Sol system, waging a desperate running battle against a relentless and lethal enemy.

"It's quieter than I remember."

"We lost a lot of people."

"I'm sorry."

Hands in pockets, Jack shrugged. "It wasn't your fault."

"Nevertheless."

"Forget it." His lips hardened into a tight line. "We all knew what we were signing up for."

"Did you, though?" I couldn't help it. The Cutters' attacks had been as swift and brutal as they had been unexpected. Before them, the navy's main peacetime duties had involved preserving communication links with extrasolar colonies and offering humanitarian need where required; maintaining diplomatic relations with neighbouring civilisations; and patrolling trade routes and tramline termini to deter pirates, terrorists, and traffickers. Nobody had ever seriously expected an interstellar war.

Jack sighed. "We did our duty."

I couldn't argue with that. I could see the rusty bloodstains on the walls; holes like stab marks in the bulkheads; the dirty yellow smears where shrapnel had depressurised a corridor and been hurriedly patched with sealant foam.

The *Crisis Actor*'s bridge and power plant lay close to the core of the vessel, where they were safest, shielded from projectiles and blast effects by the rest of the ship. But even down here, there were signs of damage.

Jack noticed me looking. "They don't fire bullets," he said. "More like shards. And those shards slice clean through armour, deck plates, and human bodies alike. They don't care what's in the way; they just don't stop."

"Shards of what?"

"I have no idea. Bits of themselves, maybe. They look like coloured glass, but they go through ships and people like hot knives through snow."

"Shit." I didn't want to picture *that*. "How do you defend against them?"

"You don't." He scrubbed a hand across his brow. "You just have to try to get out of the way."

We entered the bridge. It was a dome-shaped room ringed with workstations. The captain's seat occupied a rotating platform in the centre, kind of like a Lazy Susan, or one of those revolving serving trays you sometimes see in Chinese restaurants. It could be turned to view any of the other stations.

"Where's Captain Avion?"

"She's dead."

"So, who's in charge now?"

Jack turned and placed a hand on my shoulder. "I am."

"You?"

He released me and shrugged. "Well, me and my wife."

I heard the words but my brain wouldn't parse them. "I'm sorry, your *what*?"

"My wife?"

"Your *wife*?" I glanced around the almost-deserted flight deck. "And which one of these assholes is that?"

Jack looked up at the dome and spread his hands. "You're standing in her."

•

The *Crisis Actor* used a synth body to communicate with her crew. She chose that moment to slouch over and greet me.

"Oh look," she said. "It's the *archaeologist*. Long time, no see. I'm so glad you could join us again." She resembled a woman in her late twenties, with shaggy hair, an askew tie, and tight-fitting blue business suit. "I trust our journey hasn't been in vain?"

I crossed my arms. "You tell me."

She smiled. "Do you remember when you were careless enough to contract that alien virus?"

I felt my cheeks grow hot. "As if I could forget."

"Well, I hacked your medical records and we've been studying the results of all the analysis you've had done."

"And?"

"And we think the device you touched is a weapon."

"A weapon?" I looked around at Jack. "You mean, this shit's going to kill me?"

He crossed his arms. "Probably not."

"*Probably?*"

"We don't think your infection constitutes an attack by the weapon. Rather, we think it might have been an attempt at an upgrade."

My heart was beating like it was auditioning for a jazz band. I rubbed my forehead with my fingertips. "Will somebody *please* start making sense?"

The *Crisis Actor* moved into my eyeline. "Weapons need operators," she said. "When you touched it, we think it downloaded its operating system into your mind."

I glanced down at my grey fingernails. "And the fast healing?"

"An ideal trait in a combatant."

"But I'm not a combatant. I don't know the first thing about combat."

"I'm afraid you no longer have much of a choice," Jack said. "The weapon turned you into what it needed. For want of a better term, you're a gunner now."

"I'm no soldier."

"We'll see," the *Crisis Actor* said.

"What do you mean by that?"

"She means," Jack said, his eyes lingering on her, "that we want to take you back to the dig site and plug you into the weapon."

"I can't believe what I'm hearing. After all the trouble I got into last time I touched that thing, now you want to take me back and purposefully re-expose me?"

"Yes," the *Crisis Actor* said seriously. "We want to see what happens."

"But why me? Can't you just try exposing someone else. Someone who knows what they're doing?"

"We already tried that," Jack said.

"And?"

"And they died. That's why we came looking for you. You're the only one who survived."

Siegfried was wiping down the bar with a rag. One of his lenses swivelled up as I entered. "Hey, guv."

"Pour me a drink."

"Are you sure?"

The customers were gone for the night. Only the lights above the counter were still on, casting a row of soft yellow cones.

"Do I look unsure?"

"You look angry."

"Then pour me a fucking drink. You know how this works."

He pulled a dusty bottle from beneath the counter and filled a shot glass. The liquid glowed amber. This wasn't the battery acid we served to the locals; this was the good stuff—the last resort, emergency hooch. Genuine Mexican blue agave tequila, all the way from Earth. It was smoother than an oiled ballerina, and harder to find than an honest politician.

"Things didn't go well with the husband?"

"They did not." I tossed back the shot and clinked the glass back onto the counter. "And he's not my husband. He's married to someone else."

"Oh, who?"

"His fucking *ship*, if you can believe that?"

Siegfried had been in the process of re-corking the bottle. He stopped and poured another measure instead. "I'm sorry, guv."

"I mean, marrying a ship. How is that possible?"

Siegfried resumed wiping the bar with his rag. "I guess it takes all sorts."

"And you should see her synth. Small, scrawny, and ten years younger than him."

"Aren't you ten years younger than him?"

"Shut up."

I knocked back the second measure and tapped the glass with my fingernail until he topped it up again.

"Do you really think they're engaging in sexual activity?" he asked.

"I don't even want to know." I heard the crackling roar of a shuttle leaving the civilian port. It could have been a supply run, or it might have been carrying another hundred passengers for the next scheduled foam ship. Either way, I suddenly wanted desperately to be on it.

I said, "I should never have waited."

"I was never sure why you did. The romantic in me likes to think it was for him."

I slugged back the shot. "Of course, it was for him."

"And now?"

I pushed my glass across the counter. "Stop talking and keep pouring."

Siegfried's arms folded into his body. "Oh, come on, please indulge me. You know I like to talk."

"That doesn't mean I have to listen."

"If I don't communicate my thoughts and opinions, how will anyone ever know what I think? If a tree falls in a forest and nobody hears…"

I frowned at him. "Are you seriously telling me that if no one hears your thoughts, you might cease to exist?"

"Who am I to judge?"

"You're looking at it the wrong way." I waited for him to refill the glass. "What you should be asking is what happens if a tree falls in a forest and makes a lot of noise doing it, but nobody gives a shit about trees falling in forests?"

All his various appendages drew in tightly against his shell. "Is that your way of telling me to shut up?"

I leaned forward and tapped a fingernail against his metal casing. "Now you're getting it."

"Harumph." He left the bottle on the counter and floated away. I let him go. I felt a bit guilty for being a bitch. He was my best friend in the camp. He'd sulk, but he'd never held a grudge in his life. I knew he'd get over it and be back here in the morning, as if nothing had happened.

In the meantime, I had to figure out my next move.

Through a telescope, the foam ships that had already launched formed a string of pearls receding into the darkness between the spiral arms. I could have been on any one of them, but I'd decided to squander two years wiping tables and serving drinks. If the Cutters turned up tomorrow and slaughtered me, I'd only have myself to blame.

Leaving Jack behind had ripped a hole in my heart. I hadn't been strong enough to move forward alone. I had held onto the hope he might still be alive—and once I had convinced myself he was alive, how could I possibly have left without him?

"Jesus fucking Christ," I said. It was unfair. If you wait for someone long enough, you tend to build up your eventual meeting in your mind. You idealise and over-hype it, and when it eventually happens, when they reveal themselves to be the weird, fucked-up human beings they always were, you can't help but feel somehow betrayed.

Especially if they've married their starship.

I took another drink, and suddenly, I loathed everything. I hated this crappy bar and this festering camp; I detested this ball of rock and slime we were standing on; and most of all, I hated the air in here, all clammy from the salt marsh and smelling like week-old socks. It would have been January back on Earth, and the days there would be as cold and sharp as pins right now. There might even be snow falling over the ruins of London. God, I missed snow. I missed the sound the car tyres made as they hissed through dirty grey slush; missed the little pinprick kisses of flakes falling against my upturned face, and the cold tickle of them on my outstretched tongue.

And then I thought of my sister, Chloe. We had shared a womb, but not a childhood. Her lungs hadn't fully developed. She was born first, but already dead by the time I took my first breath. I hadn't known about her until my parents broke the news when they thought I was old enough to understand, but some part of me had always felt incomplete without her. At some level, I had always known there was a hole in my life.

I raised a glass to her.

If our situations had been reversed, I liked to think she'd have made better choices than I had.

•

I woke with my forehead resting on the cool metal of the counter and a long ribbon of drool hanging from my mouth. Tentative fingers of daylight had begun to explore the gaps between the window shutters. Only a couple of centimetres of liquid remained in the tequila bottle, and my temples throbbed like an industrial heating unit.

I sat up. My forehead made a sucking sound as it peeled from the sticky copper. My mouth tasted as if I'd been gargling guacamole, pencil shavings, and hand sanitiser.

Fucking tequila.

There was a reason I didn't drink anymore. I liked it too much, but it didn't like me. But then, what else was I going to do when the love of my fucking life turned up and announced he'd gotten himself hitched to a war machine?

I went around to the sink behind the counter and splashed cold water on my face. My thoughts were as heavy and ungainly as icebergs on a rough swell; but while asleep, I seemed to have reached a decision. I was getting off this rock, and to do that, I was going to have to pay a visit to Polhaus.

I pushed open the bar's main door and raised a hand to shade my aching eyes from the sunlight. The morning business of the camp was well underway. Every species had its own rituals and habits, but certain activities seemed to be universal constants. Fires that had been tamped to embers for the night were now being poked and bullied into life to heat ration packs and (in the case of the humans at least) water for coffee. Groups of hunters were slouching out to check their traps for edible night fauna. Babies were crying and mewling for food and attention. Prayers were being offered. Those who had died in the night were being brought out and loaded onto carts. A few of the early risers nodded to me as I passed. I was well known in this area of the camp. I'd been here longer than most people, and the bar was a local landmark.

There were many cafes and food stalls on the site, as well as scatterings of ramshackle kiosks housing gambling dens, tattoo parlours, fortune tellers, masseurs, pawn brokers, and every other opportunistic trade you could imagine, all arranged into a crude, muddy high street that meandered from the camp's front entrance to its rear gates. Anyone with a trade could set up a counter made from two barrels and a plank and sell their skills to passers-by in return for ration chits or services in kind. My bar was set a little back from this main drag, among the tents and shacks. It didn't really have a name; most people just called it 'Ursula's Place'.

Polhaus owned a tented casino up near the front entrance. That was some prime real estate, and I knew he'd paid well for it—using other people's money. At this time of the morning, there were no punters at the tables, just a guy in an apron sweeping the plastic floorboards.

"Polhaus about?"

The guy looked up, recognised me, and nodded towards the back room. "Go on through."

Polhaus's office was a shipping container at the rear of the tent. Inside, he'd furnished it with the rugs and art he'd fleeced from his customers. It felt like stepping into a harem. God alone knew what his sleeping quarters were like. He sat at the far end like a mantis, his tall frame folded into a padded chair behind a metal desk salvaged from a wrecked warship. As I entered, he looked up from beneath thick white eyebrows.

"Ah, Ursula. How agreeable to see you this morning. And to what do I owe this not inconsiderable pleasure?"

An ugly, puckered scar ran from his hairline to his chin, pulling down the corner of his left eye and twisting that side of his mouth into perpetual disappointment.

"I want out."

His torn eyebrow twitched. Once, maybe, he'd been able to raise it. "I see you're not in the mood to beat around the bush."

"I'm serious. I want a berth on the next foam ship."

"After all this time?" His eyes narrowed. "Do you know something I don't?"

There were always rumours of coming attacks. I shook my head. "No, I'm just done. I've had enough."

"I see." He steepled his thin, surgeon's fingers. "And would this sudden change of heart have something to do with the recent arrival of a certain naval officer?"

"That's none of your damn business."

He chuckled. "I mean no disrespect, of course. You know how rife this place can be with gossip."

"Can you get me a berth or not?"

That wounded brow twitched again. "Of course, I can, but you know these things don't come cheap."

"What do you want?"

"Moi?" He placed a splayed hand against his chest. "I wish only to return to the personal and economic freedoms of the Before Times."

I raised an eyebrow. "I was there. We all were. You're only talking about a couple of years ago."

"And yet," he sighed dramatically, "in those days people were free to make their fortunes and determine their own fates."

I stifled a cynical laugh. I'd heard him give this speech before. "How were they free? They had to work almost every day of their adult lives to make a handful of billionaires richer. And if they didn't, they ran the risk of losing their homes and pensions, and starving to death in retirement. And all the while, the Internet told them they could be one of the happy elites if only they worked a little harder, believed a little harder, and prioritised their employers' success over the happiness of their families and the state of their own mental and physical health."

Polhaus frowned. "I didn't realise you were an anarchist."

"I'm no such thing." I crossed my arms. "I just get irritable when people needlessly romanticise the past. I'm guessing you were one of the privileged few. In which case, you must remember that none of that garbage mattered a damn when the Cutters came. All the money in the world couldn't save you from that."

Polhaus scowled. "We are getting off topic."

"You started it."

"Nevertheless, I do not care to reminisce about such frightful things. What you ask of me now, well, that comes with a price."

There it was. I steepled my fingers. "What's it going to cost me?"

"Your bar."

I waved a hand. "Take it."

"That will cover my handling fee."

I sighed. "And the price of the berth?"

"That will cost considerably more."

"I don't have anything else."

Polhaus moistened his lower lip. "Don't sell yourself short."

My heart sunk. "What are you suggesting?"

"I have use for a woman of your talents."

"I won't sleep with you."

His head jerked back as if I'd spat at him. "Good Lord, I should hope not!"

"Just so we're clear."

"Please," he said, adjusting his cuffs, "don't flatter yourself." He had a tight rein on his composure, but I couldn't help noticing the twisted scar on his cheek had darkened to a livid pink.

"Then what is it you want me to do?"

"I need you to recover something of mine."

"What sort of something?"

"An object of some value. It was used as collateral for a wager."

"And now the sucker won't pay up?"

"Precisely."

"Debt recovery? I'm a little disappointed. Why can't you send one of your usual heavies?"

"If I take possession of the object in question, there will be repercussions."

"But if I do it?"

"You will be leaving on the next foam ship." He waved his thin fingers airily. "People will assume you took it with you."

"But all the while, you'll have it here."

"Precisely."

"Do I even dare ask what it is?"

Polhaus's smile grew wider, until it made him look like a shark.

•

I picked my way between the tents and shacks. Overhead, the nearest half-constructed foam ship hung white in the blue morning sky like a cloud of shattered bone fragments. Would that be the one to carry me to safety, across the dour void between this spiral arm and the next? The thought of crossing through such emptiness filled me with equal parts dismay and relief. Humanity had barely started spreading to its neighbouring stars, and now we were setting out across a vast chasm towards an unknown future. We were teenagers leaving home for the first time, exchanging the embarrassments and nostalgia of our childish years for the cold uncertainties of adulthood. To survive, we were fleeing the enemy's fearful odds and abandoning the ashes of our fathers and the temples of our gods.

Yes, that's a quote from Macaulay's *Lays of Ancient Rome*. And yes, I'd studied the classics. I was an archaeologist, remember?

Nearby, someone was frying something that almost smelled like bacon. There was a rank undertone that suggested it was probably only one of the local water rats, but the scent kicked off some griping in my empty and hungover gut. How long had it been since I last tasted real bacon? I'd been living on beansprouts and tofu for so long now, my mouth watered at the thought of hot grease soaking into fresh, sliced bread. But such delicacies had disappeared with the destruction of Earth.

Grief is a strange, slippery animal; however far or fast you run from it, it'll find some way to creep up on you. When I thought of the great works of art and architecture that had also been lost, not to mention the billions of innocent lives cut short, including those of my father and my friends, I felt ashamed to be mourning a sandwich—but like the heart, the stomach wants what the stomach wants.

At least we still knew how to make reasonable facsimiles of coffee and gin. A universe without either would be dark indeed, and not one in which I think I'd care to live.

But then, this one wasn't that great, either.

What use did the final survivors of humanity have for an archaeologist like me? We were too busy digging new graves to worry about excavating old ones.

I had been two years old when the first alien ship ploughed into Earth's solar system, riding the tramline from Tau Ceti. Luckily for us, they were proselytising explorers on a mission to share the benefits of their technology with every intelligent race they came across. No death rays or Prime Directive bullshit for them. Six months later, people were strapping fusion motors to hastily cobbled-together assemblages of metal and plastic. Some were little more than metal boxes; others resembled the old *Apollo* modules. I think someone in Los Angeles even retrofitted one of the old space shuttles. The shape didn't matter, if you could get to the start of a tramline and hit it just right, you could coast all the way to the next star system. Within ten years, humans were spreading out into the galaxy, founding colonies, making deals, signing treaties, and generally learning how to live in the community of species linked by the strands of the local tramline network.

By the time I turned seventeen, we had started to find suggestions of earlier species. We discovered artefacts and ruins, and ancient ships that had crashed into moons or been left adrift in cometary orbits. Evidence of a whole vanished generation of Precursor civilisations that had once used the tramways but were now gone. I'd become an archaeologist to try to figure out what became of them, and why they all died out at around the same time. But since the enemy had begun their remorseless assault, and since the fall of Earth, we ourselves were teetering on the brink of extinction. If the foam ships couldn't save us, then in a few million years, someone else would be picking through our ruins and dusting off our skeletons and wondering what had killed us.

I paused at a clearing in the sea of tents, getting my bearings. The guy I was after lived in the northwest quadrant of the camp, which lay close to the edge of the salt marshes. I'm not sure a tented city can be said to have an undesirable neighbourhood— none of it's what you might call aspirational—but if you had to pick an area within it to set up home, it wouldn't be this one. You've heard people say shit rolls downhill? Well, this was the place it rolled through on the way. The gutters and patchwork sewers from the rest of the camp travelled down the main thoroughfare on their way to the water, and when the wind blew from the right direction, I'm not sure which smelled worse, the effluent or the marsh into which it was emptying.

Still, rumour had it the curries and tacos down here were the best in the camp. Apparently, the chefs added extra onions and spices in the hope the cooking smells might mask the estuarine reek.

The thought of tacos started my stomach rumbling. At that moment, I could really have gone for three small tortillas filled with water rat al pastor and sprinkled with pineapple substitute and onion powder—but bitter experience had taught me that violence was always best undertaken on an empty stomach, and if this guy cut up rough, I didn't want indigestion or extra bloat slowing me down. If this went down the way I hoped, I'd have time to grab a taco on my way to the civilian port, and a berth on the next ship out of here.

As the foam ships travelled slower-than-light, they didn't need to utilise tramways. They could sail across the gulf between our spiral arm and the next without having to worry about attacks from the Cutters. And once on the other side, they'd hopefully find sanctuary, safe from the entities that prowled this offshoot of the tramway network. Over the past three years, twenty-one foam ships had embarked on the crossing. None had yet had time to make it to the other side, but by the time my ship got there, I hoped those twenty-one would have had time to scout out the most habitable planets and establish a few colonies. After two years living in this makeshift encampment, I had a hankering for something a little more civilised, and even a frontier town would do, if its buildings were made of rocks or timber instead of packing crates and fabric.

There were no formal streets in the camp. You couldn't give anyone an address. But Polhaus had given me the target's location as exactly as he could. I had to turn left at the second radio transmitter, then right at the green bivouac flying a Jolly Roger on the end of a broom handle, and I would see the garish patchworked tent belonging to Cristiano Pascal and his partner, Gabrielle.

Pascal had been a museum curator at the Gallerie dell'Accademia in Venice, and when he fled, had tried to take as many treasures with him as he could. Apparently, he thought he had a duty to preserve them for future generations. But when times turned tough, he wasn't above wagering one or more of them at Polhaus's card tables. His museum had played host to many of the works of Leonardo da Vinci, and it had been one of the artist's original sketches that Pascal had gambled in the hope of winning extra rations for himself and his wife.

According to Polhaus, the sketch I'd been sent to fetch was known as *Vitruvian Man*. Apparently drawn in AD 1490, it depicted geometric study of the proportions of the human body, with a human male standing in a circle with arms spread. He'd shown me a picture of it on his tablet. I'd never been a huge fan of art, but I understood the significance of Leonardo's sketches. Almost the entirety of human culture had been abandoned as people fled for their lives. In terms of lost art and knowledge, the destruction of the Earth made the fire at the Library of Alexandria look like a minor inconvenience. The few items that had made it into space and escaped the devastation of the planet were now literally priceless. The idea someone would gamble one of them to try to win an extra helping of beans filled me with something that was halfway between disgust and despair; but if I wanted to get off this rock, I'd have to collect on that debt and add myself to the sorry history of that masterpiece.

I remembered the day of my grandfather's funeral.

•

At the end of the service, as the guests drifted from the chapel, my sister and I slipped away. We didn't want to stand around making small talk with relatives while his smoke rose from the crematorium chimney; and yet, neither could we quite bring ourselves to leave entirely. We needed perspective and we needed air, and so we walked to the far end of the graveyard and sat on an old wooden bench in our black dresses and high heels. Bees fumbled around in the flowers. The air smelled of cut grass and impending rain.

"Well," Frankie said, "I guess that's that."

A tear striped my cheek. It dangled from my jaw, and then dripped onto my hem. Beside me, Frankie glanced at the curtain of rain advancing across the fields from the southwest, engulfing trees and villages in impenetrable grey murk.

"We'll have to go soon," she said.

I sniffed. "We've got a while before it gets here."

As if to contradict me, thunder rolled overhead. In my lap, I cradled a paperback copy of Nevil Shute's On The Beach. *My grandmother had pushed it into my hands before the funeral. The pages were yellowed and comfortingly perfumed with must.*

"It was his favourite," she had murmured as she gave it to me, her voice almost inaudible through a thick black veil. "He must have read it a dozen times, and I think you should have it."

I flipped through it as the breeze began to pick up, skewing the line of smoke from the furnace. Many sections had been highlighted and annotated in his spidery handwriting. One passage caught my eye. "If what they say is right," I read aloud, "we're none of us going to have time to do all that we planned to do. But we can keep on doing it as long as we can."

Beside me, Frankie examined her black-painted nails. "Ain't that the fucking truth."

The first drops of rain, blown ahead of the oncoming storm, began to prickle my face and shoulders. Ignoring them, I raised the book to my forehead and closed my eyes, trying to soak up whatever residual traces of my grandfather might be lurking in the pages—but all I could think about was the end of the story, as the submarine leaves port for the last time, leaving only death and heartbreak in its wake.

•

Now, that book was gone and Frankie was dead and the Earth had become a charnel house as Shute had predicted, even if the actual means of its extinction lay beyond anything he could have foreseen.

I paused a few metres from the tent, trying to figure out how I was going to approach Pascal. Should I just barge in and demand he hand over the drawing? According to Polhaus, the old man had some sort of connection to one of the camp's major crime syndicates. They owed him a favour for some unspecified service he'd rendered in the past and so now, he was under their protection, which was maybe why he felt safe in refusing to settle his gambling debts, and why Polhaus didn't want to handle the matter himself.

The parasite in my cells enabled me to withstand damage and heal quickly, but I'd never tested the limits of its protection— because the only way to know those limits would be to damage myself beyond its ability to repair. If I got mixed-up with the syndicate and they put a bullet through my head, I might die before the damaged areas could be regrown. The same went for an injury to my heart; if my blood stopped carrying oxygen to my brain, the game might be over. There had to be some limit to my apparent invulnerability, but I didn't know where the line lay, and the only way to find out for sure would be to cross it.

Bullets are tiny little things, but when they're flying in your direction, they feel the size of planetoids.

The wind flapped through the clustered tents, setting the guy lines humming.

If I wanted to avoid trouble, I'd have to come at this from a subtler angle.

Pascal and his wife were sitting on folding chairs in front of a cooking fire. I walked straight up to them and said, "Hi there. My name's Ursula Morrow and I run that bar over on the south side."

Pascal said, "I know who you are."

"I heard on the grapevine that you had a falling out with Polhaus."

His hands gripped the arms of his chair. "What of it?"

"I'd like to invite you to my establishment."

He chuckled. "You're so hard up for customers, you have to go out poaching them?"

"I'm thinking of putting together a weekly card game."

"Keep talking."

"Polhaus's been monopolising the action on the south side. If I can attract a few of his regulars to my place…"

"He won't like that."

"I don't care what he likes."

Gabrielle poked the fire, sending up flurries of yellow and orange sparks. Pascal said, "I'll think about it."

"Come by around sunset," I urged. "Have a drink on the house and see what you think of the place. Then, when I've gathered a few more players, we can talk further."

The old man exchanged a look with his wife.

"If you're giving away free drinks, we'll be there. But no guarantees on the card game. I'll want to see who else you invite before I commit."

"Fair enough."

"Until later then, Ms Morrow."

"Until later."

•

Pascal and Gabrielle arrived as the sun's orange orb kissed the horizon. I showed them to a table, instructed Siegfried to take good care of them, and made my excuses. I told them I was on my way to recruit another card player but instead, I went out back and pulled on a black hoodie that had been languishing in our lost property bin for several months. It was several sizes too large, but as darkness fell, I hoped the hood would shadow my face.

Staying away from the lighted areas, I weaved a path through the tents and shacks, trying to balance swiftness with circuity. If anyone recognised me, I didn't want them to be able to tell anyone else where I was headed.

In the trade, they called this the 'Reverse Trojan'. Instead of smuggling in a beautiful gift filled with danger, I'd created an allure that had compelled Pascal and his missus to vacate their stronghold for the evening, leaving it vulnerable. Later, when they returned to their tent, they might figure out what had happened, but my staff would swear blind I had been on the premises the whole evening, stocktaking and doing the other mundane, behind-the-scenes admin involved with running a bar. They might suspect my involvement, but as I had an alibi and the stolen item wouldn't be in my possession, they would have nothing to take to the security officers—and even if they did, security might confiscate any remaining artworks Pascal had smuggled out, claiming them for the species as a whole and adding them to one of the ad hoc museums installed on the foam ships, maybe even the very foam ship that would carry me to safety, if Polhaus held up his end of the bargain.

Granted, that was a pretty big if. The man might like to put on the airs and graces of a respectable businessman, but beneath it all, he was a petty thug who'd lucked into a position of power and held onto it using violence and intimidation. If he saw an advantage in betraying me, even for an instant, I had no doubt he'd take it.

For a moment, I hesitated, wondering if this was all a scheme by the spindly fucker to set me up. Were security personnel going to jump out and haul me off to the stockade, leaving my bar vacant and available to be added to his little criminal empire?

I shook my head in the darkness. Yes, Polhaus was a devious bastard, but there was no way he'd involve the authorities in any scheme; he had too many illicit ventures to risk attracting their attention. The simplest thing would be for him to take delivery of the sketch and give me my ticket out of this hellhole—that way, he'd get what he wanted, and get rid of me. For him, it would be a win–win situation.

When I reached Pascal's tent, it was the work of a moment to cut through the outer layers. They were a mix of polythene and nylon sheeting, and my lemon knife went through them like chips through dips. However, I hadn't counted on the inner Kevlar lining, which was much harder. The fibres were tough going and took considerably longer to saw through than I'd have liked. If you've ever tried to hack through a stab vest with a steak knife, you'll have some idea of the effort it cost me. To be honest, it was a minor miracle no one walked past and caught me at it. But eventually, I got in.

To find a gun barrel staring me in the face.

A thick knuckle whitened on the trigger. I tried to dodge but it was too late.

I don't think I even heard the shot.

CHAPTER THREE

UP AGAINST THE HELIOPAUSE

I could taste mud.

Slowly, I opened my eyes, to find myself face-down in the dirt behind the recycling bins on the edge of the camp, head incandescent with pain, as if someone had pumped it full of molten brass. I'd had some bad hangovers in my time, but this was some next level shit. I put a hand to my left temple and felt the indentation of a healing gunshot wound. Dried blood caked that whole side of my face. Whoever had pulled the trigger must have seen the mess, assumed I was dead, and dumped me here, hoping the local wildlife might dispose of my remains. I guess they hadn't known how hard I was to kill.

To be fair, even I wasn't certain I could survive being shot in the head. I'd never had to recover from anything life-threatening before. Burns, the occasional stab wound; nothing as potentially lethal as a bullet to the brain. And yet, here we were. The bullet had split my toughened skin and made a dent in my skull, spilling enough blood to look fatal and convince my assailant; but now the wound was healing and I was still very much, and probably most inconveniently, alive.

I rolled onto my back with a groan. A cool breeze came curling in off the marsh, bringing with it the reek of salt corruption. Somewhere, a Komodo-jackal chattered amidst the reeds. From beyond the recycling bins, I could hear the morning business of the camp. Overhead, the clouds were grey wisps in a milk-white sky.

"Good morning."

Gingerly, I turned my aching head. There, leaning against the nearest dumpster with his arms folded, was Jack.

"Hello," he said. "How are you feeling?"

"I've been better."

He raised an eyebrow at the bloodstained garbage strewn around me. "I don't doubt it."

"What are you doing here?"

"We've been tracking you."

"Of course, you have."

"And I take it things aren't going so well?"

I gave him a look. "I am not going off with you to be used as a guinea pig."

"Are you sure about that? Because right now, your other options appear less than optimal."

"What are you talking about?"

He helped me to my feet and brushed some of the mud from my shoulder. "The way I see it, by failing to retrieve the sketch, you've let down one crime boss and angered another."

"You really have been tracking me, huh?"

"Cris dusted your clothing with bugs."

"For fuck's sake."

Jack looked around at the campfires and ramshackle huts. "You know, sooner or later, someone's going to figure out how to kill you."

"I know." I rubbed the rapidly closing wound on my forehead. "That's why I was doing this job. I was trying to get passage on a foam ship."

"Without me?"

"Apparently, you're married."

"I thought the whole reason you stayed was because you were waiting for me?"

"I was, but that's over now. You're hitched to your *ship*."

"I'm sorry." He rubbed the back of his neck. "I honestly am. But there's more at stake here than our history."

Somewhere nearby, around one of the campfires, someone started playing a harmonica. Beyond the fence, in the reeds at the water's edge, the Komodo-jackal howled in response. The half-constructed foam ships were bright overhead, shining in the light of the sun. For the past two years, they had seemed tantalisingly close; now, they suddenly seemed impossibly far away.

"I guess it doesn't matter now. Polhaus's never going to give me a pass."

Wisely, Jack kept his mouth shut. He'd made his pitch, and he knew me well enough to realise anything else would only provoke fresh objections. We both knew that, right now, the *Crisis Actor* was my only ride out of here.

"What about Siegfried?" I still felt guilty about snapping at him. He had been a loyal friend and colleague and had put up with my bullshit for the last eighteen months. The least I could do was not abandon him.

"We're a warship, not a lifeboat; we don't have enough resources for passengers."

"He doesn't take up much space, and he runs on batteries."

"He does?"

"He's a pretty nifty engineer, too."

Jack looked thoughtful. "Okay," he said. "If that's what it takes to get you to come with us, he can tag along. After all, we could really use a good engineer."

"I figured you might."

"Especially if he's good at repairs."

I thought back to the damage I'd seen on the *Crisis Actor*. How many crew members had died during her guerrilla campaign in Sol system? "You really think this weapon might help in the fight against the Cutters?"

He rubbed his lower lip. "It's possible. We need to plug you in to confirm it. For now, all we know for sure is that it was built around sixty-five million years ago."

"The Cretaceous–Tertiary extinction?" A lot of Precursor alien civilisations had also vanished from the fossil record at approximately the same time as the dinosaurs. Rather than simply a localised event, it had been a mass extinction extending dozens of light years in every direction.

"Cris thinks there's a possibility we're seeing the same process in action again, and that maybe this weapon was built to defend against it."

"That's quite a leap."

"The dates match up."

"Even so…"

"She's been running over the data, and she thinks the thing might be connected to the undervoid."

"She's an archaeologist now?"

Jack gave a wry smile. "She's a battleship. She knows about weaponry, and she's got a brain that can think exponentially faster than either of us."

"That doesn't mean she's right."

"And it doesn't mean she's wrong, either." He put his hands on his hips. "Frankly, we're desperate. This could be our only chance."

We went back to the bar. I kept a tense watch for Polhaus's men, but they didn't show themselves. Maybe the skinny guy trusted me to deliver—or maybe he'd clocked Jack's uniform and decided discretion to be the greater part of valour. Polhaus might be a big noise in the local casino business, but Jack had a warship; tangling with him would be like entering a game of rock paper scissors in which the scissors were going to be replaced by a tactical orbital strike.

Jack poured himself a drink while I went through into

the back room to gather my stuff. There wasn't much. I'd fled Earth with only the clothes I wore and hadn't acquired many possessions during my time in the camp. I pushed a few items into a canvas shoulder bag, and still had room left inside.

When I re-entered the main bar, the dawn light had begun to slant in through the east windows, illuminating the smears and fingerprints on the glass. A cat had wandered in from somewhere and now lay curled asleep on one of the barstools.

"Is that everything?" Jack asked.

"Apart from Siegfried."

"And where might he be?"

"He sleeps on top of the main camp generator to recharge. We can pick him up on the way."

"So, you're definitely coming?"

I shrugged. "What choice do I have?"

•

I first met Jack on my very first extrasolar expedition. My best friend Mouse and I were shipping out to join Doctor Vogel's university dig team on an unnamed planet in the habitable zone of a small red dwarf known only as Gimlet's Eye. Mouse was a fellow student. It wasn't his real name, but nobody really knew his real name. He was from somewhere in the Balkans and didn't like to talk about his family history. Now, we were off on our first extrasolar expedition. I'd worked hard for two years to earn my place. Nevertheless, I was nervous.

Jack was a lieutenant on the naval stealth-ship Crisis Actor, *which was giving us a ride. He helped me strap into my couch.*

"First time, young lady?"

"I've been out to Europa and Titan."

He gave a crooked smile. "Ah, those are long hauls. But I'm afraid nothing can quite prepare you for your first tramline glide."

"Is it bad?" I'd heard stories.

"You may feel woozy, maybe even nauseated. But fret not, hardly anybody ever dies."

"Hardly anybody?"

"What's your name?"

"Ursula Morrow."

He yanked the last strap into place. "Well, I'll see you on the other side, Ursula Morrow." His grin returned. "If you survive."

•

Siegfried caught sight of the *Crisis Actor*'s buckled hull plates and torn antennae. "That poor machine!" He turned to face Jack. "What *have* you been doing to her?"

Jack frowned. "You do know there's a war going on, don't you?"

"Well, of course I do."

"We're the ones fighting it."

"Ah." The little machine turned his nose to me. "And this is our ride out of here?"

"It is."

"Forgive me, but I thought we'd be running away from combat, not climbing aboard a warship."

"Do you want to stay here?"

"Without you?" He looked back in the direction of the camp. "Not really."

"Well, I'm getting on this ship. You can come with me or stay here."

Two of his limbs wigwagged in frustration. "Surely there has to be a better option?"

I gave his snout a pat. "Beggars can't be choosers."

I followed Jack up the ramp. The *Crisis Actor*'s synth was waiting at the top. She said, "I didn't think you'd come."

"I'm here now."

"What changed your mind?"

"You mean apart from making enemies of everyone on the planet?" I gave a shrug. "I'm an archaeologist. If you're right about the current conflict having the same cause as the Cretaceous-Tertiary extinction, that's huge. It could revolutionise our understanding of that whole period."

"You're here for the science?"

"Partly."

"What's your other reason?"

I dropped my bag onto the deck. "If that weapon can help delay the Cutters long enough to get a few more foam ships away, I'd have to be the world's biggest asshole not to at least try to get it working."

"How very noble."

"Look who's talking."

She inclined her shaggy head. "Touché."

Her attention moved beyond my shoulder. "And who is this delightfully utilitarian-looking machine?"

"This is Siegfried."

"Welcome aboard, Siegfried."

"This isn't my idea."

"Nevertheless, you are welcome." The *Crisis Actor* adjusted the knot of her tie and straightened the cuffs of her shirt. "It's been a long time since I played host to another artificial being."

She led me to a cabin. "You can use this one." She flicked a hand at the door. "Try not to get in the way." And with that, she turned on her heel and walked away, deep in conversation with my former barman.

"Don't mind her," Jack said, watching her go with undisguised fondness. "She can be a bit temperamental around new people."

"That's one way of putting it."

"We were cut-off for two years. Bringing new people on board introduces new variables into the equation. She'll be a little awkward until she gets used to you. In the meantime, come on, come up to the flight deck with me and I'll let you watch as we jump."

"Deal." I'd travelled before, of course, but I'd always been in a cabin or passenger compartment; I'd never seen the transition into the tramline network with my own eyes.

The tramline was invisible, of course, and its entry point looked like any other patch of empty space. The only way to find it was to manoeuvre to a position directly between your system's star and the star at the centre of the system containing your destination, and then do some fiendishly arcane calculations based on the amount of deformation each star's mass caused to the fabric of the universe. Once the correct position had been ascertained, all a ship had to do was move to that spot and fire its jump engines.

Jack gave the order and the bright universe folded itself up like a magician's handkerchief and vanished, giving way to the formlessness of the undervoid.

"We're in the pipe," the pilot reported. "Five by five."

"Outstanding." Jack rose from his chair and took me by the arm.

"I don't think you know everyone here, so allow me to make some introductions," he said. "Our pilot here is Lucien Miles. The ship's perfectly capable of flying itself, but regulations insist we carry a human pilot in case of catastrophic system failure."

"Hey," Lucien protested good-naturedly. He had a German accent and the kind of soft gut you only got from spending all your hours sitting at a console instead of working out. I guessed he was in his early thirties, but he had the old eyes of someone who'd seen too much heartbreak.

Jack ignored his objection, moving instead to the only other person on the bridge. "And this shaven-headed goddess is our navigator, Janis Egebe."

The woman at the navigation station looked to be around the same age as the pilot. She wore a tank top that showed off her toned arms and the wooden bangles that adorned her wrists.

Both had the pinched expressions of people who'd been running on empty for far too long.

"There used to be more of us," Jack said.

A shadow passed over their faces, and I didn't need to ask what had happened to the missing crew. Instead, I pushed up my sleeves and said, "Who's a lady got to screw to get a cup of coffee around here?"

•

We were going to be on the glide for three days. Jack and his crew had checks and drills to keep them busy, but my entertainment options were decidedly sparse. I explored the old warship from bow to stern, visiting the hangar deck, the barracks where the ship's complement of marines had once been housed, the gym, galley, and infirmary. Some corridors had suffered decompression and were in vacuum, meaning I had to detour around; in others, water and coolant dripped from leaky pipes. Some rooms had frost on the walls, while others broiled, and the entire engineering section had been sealed due to a radiation leak. If the *Crisis Actor* had been a horse, she would have been put out to pasture long ago—or maybe put out of her misery altogether. And yet, the old ship possessed an undeniable roguish charm. Repairs that initially looked haphazard and incomplete turned out to be masterpieces of economic functionality, having required a minimum of time and material to implement. The stripes that had appeared so hideous on the outer hull were replicated within, slanting diagonally across corridor walls and bulkheads, bringing colour and a sense of movement to the otherwise drab and purposeful interior. For a warship, the galley and shared crew areas felt almost homely, in an improvised and ramshackle sort of way, and I couldn't help thinking that for Jack and his team, it had been the only home they'd known for the past couple of years. I both envied and pitied them. The ship may be cosier than a refugee camp, but their plight had been infinitely more dangerous.

If you're not used to them, warships are noisy places. You can't for a moment forget you're travelling in the guts of a machine, what with the growl of the engine, the roar of the air circulation, banging and gurgling from the waterpipes, and the constant racket of the thousand other essential mechanical and electronic systems that scratch away like mice behind the bulkheads. And the ride's a lot rougher than you might expect. The undervoid isn't a uniform medium, and even on a tramway, we were continually ploughing through eddies and pockets. The deck bucked and dipped underfoot, meaning I often had to reach out for the nearest wall to keep my balance. Sometimes, I worried I might get bounced up to crack my head on the ceiling; other times, my stomach dropped like a broken elevator. I couldn't even see outside. The only way to get an external view was via the screens on the command deck. Apparently, windows weren't a great idea on something designed to be shot at by enemy vessels. Not only were they hard to armour, but the light spilling from them tended to ruin any attempts at stealth. There would be no point trying to hide in a convenient nebula, for instance, if your portholes had you all lit up like a Christmas tree.

During my explorations, the ship's personality stayed out of my way. I didn't know if she was actively avoiding me or simply busy, and neither did I much care. We didn't have anything to say to each other. She seemed to spend a lot of time with Siegfried, though, and I guessed they were talking about whatever it was machines talked about when they got together. Electric sheep, maybe. Who knew?

When I wasn't traipsing the corridors, I drank coffee in the galley or dozed on my bunk. Several times, I woke at an unfamiliar thud or clank, disorientated because I'd been expecting to find myself back in the camp.

On my second morning aboard, I found Janis in the galley, nursing a cup of tea. She wore burgundy cargo pants and a black tank top. A red, tasselled kufiyah hung loosely around her neck.

"Hey," she said. "How are you settling in?"

"I've been better."

"Well, hell," she said. "That's something we've all got in common. Ain't nobody on this rig can claim to be half what they were before the Cutters attacked."

"I'm sorry."

"You don't have to apologise." She flicked a hand. "You weren't there. Not on the front line, at least."

I thought back to the chaos and violence of my final day on Earth. "We were all somewhere."

Janis took this on board. She raised her cup. "I suppose you're right about that, compadre."

"It wasn't easy for any of us."

"Still isn't." She took a sip. "We're a goddamn endangered species now."

"We always were." I thought back to the stories my grandmother had told me, about growing up during the latter stages of the Cold War in the 1980s. We could have destroyed ourselves a hundred times over at the push of a button. The fact we didn't—despite numerous false alarms—had to constitute some sort of miracle. "The only difference is this time it's not us with our fingers on the trigger."

One side of her mouth quirked up in a twisted smile. "Pessimist, huh?"

"Archaeologist." I shrugged. "We tend to see the big picture."

Wherever there was life, the Cutters struck without warning or mercy. Each star system that fell pruned another node from the tramline network. Choices narrowed. Potential escape routes became fewer. On Void's Edge, at the utmost extremity of the network, they ran out altogether. All that lay beyond was the gulf separating this spiral arm from the next. With nowhere else to run, and no tramline to bridge that dour chasm, the tattered remnants of the multi-species alliance informally known as the Commonality had instigated a desperate, last-

57

ditch effort to assemble a fleet of large, slower-than-light 'foam ships' capable of making the crossing through conventional space, drawing fuel from spontaneously generated particles of matter and antimatter churned up from the quantum froth. How many of these foam ships they could make would depend on how much time they had, which would in turn depend on how long and how hard the Commonality's military could fight to delay the Cutters' remorseless advance.

I fetched myself a coffee from the food printer and pulled up a chair across from her. "So," I asked, "what's your story?"

"Why do you care?"

"Hey," I said, "I'm bored out of my mind. Indulge me."

"Fair enough." She sat back and hooked an elbow over the back of her chair. "But there's not much to tell. My parents were from Kenya. They moved north as the droughts worsened, and I ended up being born in a French refugee camp on the outskirts of Marseille. My maths, physics, and simulated combat scores were good, so I joined the Earth Defence Force to get out of there."

"You weren't on Earth when it happened?"

Her face dropped all expression. "If I had been, I wouldn't be here now."

"I was."

"Shit." For the first time, she looked interested. "How'd you get out?"

"A civilian transport. One of the last. Jack arranged it."

She shook her head. "Must have been crazy."

"It wasn't fun. I had to fight—"

"You went up against the Cutters?"

"Just other people fleeing." I repressed a shudder. "None of us knew what was happening, only that it was bad. Then the bombs started dropping. There was a lot of panic, and panic breeds violence."

"Rough?"

"Not compared with the shit you guys have been through, but I won't be forgetting it in a hurry."

We fell into a contemplative silence. I sipped my coffee. After a while, Janis said, "So, you and the captain used to be a thing, huh?"

"I thought so."

"Now, not so much?"

I shook my head. "He's married to his ship."

Janis gave a wry smile. "That he is."

I put down my cup. "Seriously, though. What the hell?"

She chuckled. "I guess coming from the outside, it might seem strange, but we're used to it now."

"But I don't understand."

"Of course you don't, child. You haven't been where we've been. Combat changes people. And sometimes, shared trauma brings them together in unexpected ways."

"But, a human and a ship?"

"Be careful." She held up a stern finger. "The two people you're talking about saved my life, many times."

"I'm sorry, I'm just struggling to get my head around the idea."

"There's nothing to get your head around. They are in love. And when you're in love, nothing else matters."

•

Water tanks shielded the human quarters from the fusion exhaust, and fish swam in those tanks. I found Lucien down in the armoury, watching their coppery bodies wriggle and flash between the oxygenating bubbles and purifying algae.

Without even turning, he said, "We kid ourselves we're done with the primordial ocean, but we still carry it around with us everywhere we go." He turned. "Don't you find that strange?"

I didn't know how to respond, so I said, "Maybe it's good to have a reminder of home?"

He seemed nonplussed by this. "Did you want something?"

"I'm just exploring."

"Well, don't touch anything in here."

"I wasn't planning to."

"Good, because this is where we keep the guns. It's not a place for civilians."

"But it's fine for stoners?"

"What?"

"Dude, your pupils are dilated to the size of black holes and you're staring at fish."

"I—"

"I run a bar. I know the signs. And right now, all the available signs point to you being mashed off your tits."

I watched him try to find a way to deny it and fail. "Fine," he said. "You know my secret. Happy now?"

"Happier than I was talking about primordial oceans."

He scowled and I laughed. "Oh, come on. What are you using, gummies?" I couldn't smell smoke.

Lucien sucked his teeth. "I figured out how to get the printers to make them without recording it in the log."

"Clever. But doesn't the ship know? Doesn't it see you sitting here?" My skin prickled. Had she heard my conversation with Janis?

"No," Lucien said. "She doesn't watch us much. She knows we need privacy to stop us all going mad."

"And so, this is your way of coping?"

"It's good for the nerves. Do you want one?"

I considered my situation. All my bridges were burned, and all my possessions lost, the love of my life had married a ramshackle warship, and the two of them were whisking me towards an alien artefact in the hope of slotting me into its CPU.

"Fuck it," I said. "Why not?"

•

I spent the next couple of hours stretched out on my bunk in a state of blissful relaxation for what felt like the first time since

I touched the artefact. The stress of not knowing what the infection was doing to me, not to mention all those intrusive tests, and then the fall of Earth and the years in the camp. All that fear and uncertainty had all taken its toll, and the person I'd become was a world away from the quiet archaeology student I'd once been. If Mouse was still around, he'd hardly recognise this woman who bargained with gangsters and put distress flares out with her bare hands. Truth be told, I barely recognised myself. I had been operating in emergency mode for so long, I'd started to think it was normal.

I lay on my back, fingers splayed at my sides to enjoy the clean roughness of the blanket, my spine glorying in a mattress that, while not luxurious by any stretch of the imagination, was still so much more comfortable than the unforgiving pallet bed I'd slept on in the back room of the bar.

Strange, how the entire course of a life can be shaped by one moment's carelessness. If I hadn't been distracted and thinking about Jack, and hadn't touched the Precursor relic, I wouldn't be here now. I would probably have died from injuries sustained during the frantic rush for the transport at Heathrow—and if by some miracle, I'd survived long enough to make it off-world, I'd have been murdered in the camp. The infection had kept me alive, and given Jack a reason to finally seek me out.

I tried to push away the melancholia that usually enveloped me when I reminisced about my life before the Cutters, but couldn't stop my thoughts from circling back to my childhood. My parents had loved me, but I think I reminded them of their loss. Whenever they looked at me, they saw only half the twins they had been expecting. Chloe's presence hung like a ghost between us.

Then my mother died, and it was just my father, and Frankie and me.

We lived in one of those bleak Midlands towns where it always seemed to be raining and nothing much ever happened.

The town was the kind of place that sucked at your feet like a swamp, forever holding you back. Whenever I'd gone back to visit my father, I'd seen kids I'd been through school with—a little older, subsiding into adulthood—and knew they'd still be there, treading the same pavements, in ten, twenty, even fifty years.

But of course, they didn't get another fifty years. All of them would be as dead as Chloe now. The only survivors were those who had been lucky enough to be around another star at the time, or who had, like me, made it off-world on those last, frantic transports.

I interlocked my fingers behind my head. The rivets on the ceiling were laid out in such precise, Warholian patterns. I wondered if any pop art still survived, spirited away somewhere by a refugee the same way Pascal had rescued those Da Vinci sketches and brought them to the camp. Depressingly, the answer was probably not. There simply hadn't been time to salvage much, and paintings were kind of cumbersome, even if you could get them out of a gallery and onto a ship in time. If I'd gone back to my apartment to retrieve an heirloom or a change of clothes, I wouldn't have made it to the transport.

Reports about the Cutters had been dribbling in for months before that final day, but they were stories of boogeymen haunting the undervoid. A few merchants had reported sightings and attacks and the navy had increased its patrols. Even when some of the colony worlds fell silent and the tramlines started acting squirrelly, nobody ever thought the Cutters would attack the Earth. We'd met alien species before, and while we hadn't always seen eye-to-eye, none of them had ever tried to invade. Importing soldiers and materiel in great enough quantities to successfully conquer and occupy an entire world made no logistical sense. It was unthinkable, and so nobody took it seriously. The wars that had been fought had taken place out on the edges of systems, where the solar wind ran up against the heliopause and the tramline termini were located—where energy beams flashed and sparkled in the darkness, far from the eyes of the general populace. An actual invasion was nonsense. But now, billions of people who'd never seriously considered themselves at risk were most likely dead, and the tramlines to and from Earth were simply gone, having frayed away into the night like broken trust.

I found myself picturing the bookshelves in Doctor Vogel's university office back on Earth.

•

They took up a whole wall, making the already small space feel cramped. The books crammed into them were of all sizes and thicknesses, arranged according to an impenetrable (but strictly enforced) system known only to Vogel himself. There were thin paperbacks on Arthurian legend; leather-upholstered tomes on Ancient Greece and the Decline and Fall of Rome; yellowing sheafs of staple-bound notes from digs at Avebury and Machu Picchu; and his own notebooks, filled with a lifetime of investigation and discovery, all crammed together on the shelf nearest his desk. His favourite book, a well-read and dogeared copy of Herodotus, lay on the desk itself, within easy reach whenever he needed distraction or inspiration.

Among that multitude of books, I'd often admired what he called his 'Atlantis Shelf'. While not strictly a shelf as much as simply the dusty top of the bookcase, this was where he kept his collection of texts on that ancient, and possibly apocryphal, city. There, he had amassed multiple translations of Plato's dialogues, which contained the first written account of the city that we were aware of, although they claimed to be quoting from translated Egyptian documents of more ancient pedigree. Beside these, he had stacked piles of lurid paperbacks containing a mixture of sensationalism, magical thinking, Fortean paranoia, and downright wrongheadedness.

"Plato claims Atlantis lay beyond the Pillars of Hercules," Vogel told me when he caught me reading the titles stuffed up there. "Which places it in the Atlantic. He also says it was the size of Libya and Asia combined." He smiled. "Doubtless an exaggeration, but we can infer that, if it existed, it was a not-insubstantial landmass."

"But there's no trace of such a continent," I replied.

Vogel stroked his grey beard and peered at me over the rim of his spectacles. "Ah, but there is, just a little way to the north."

"There is?"

"Consider the possibility that the tales of Atlantis are a folk memory passed down through oral tradition, and later written down by the Egyptians."

"Okay."

"There is one candidate. Six and a half thousand years ago, the British Isles were linked to Continental Europe by a vast swathe of fertile farmland that stretched from Norway to Brittany. What is now the mouth of the English Channel was a vast river delta, where the combined waters of the Rhone, Danube, Seine, and Thames all flowed into the Bay of Biscay. Such a land would be well known to any sailors venturing out from the Mediterranean to hug the coasts of Spain and France. That delta would have been an impressive, navigable river leading many hundreds of miles inland, through rich farmland."

"You're talking about Doggerland?"

"That's how we refer to it now, but we have no record of how its inhabitants may have known it. Nevertheless, it was a large, inhabited landmass close to the mouth of the Mediterranean, and it was inundated by the sea roughly three thousand years prior to what we think of as Egypt's Early Dynastic Period."

"Rising sea levels after the Ice Age?"

"Partly." He removed his glasses and polished them on a red paisley handkerchief. "But there's also evidence that a series of catastrophic submarine landslides off the coast of Norway, known as the Storegga slides, triggered a violent tsunami around 6150 BC. After that, there wasn't much left."

"So, it was literally swallowed by the sea."

"Indeed. Thousands of people must have died. Whole nations may have been scoured from the map. Refugees may have poured into neighbouring lands, carrying their accounts of the calamity, and spreading their culture."

"An event of that scale would be remembered."

Vogel opened his hands. "And that's why I surmise that the stories of Atlantis are folk memories of the inundation of Doggerland. The timing fits, and the location fits. All the stuff about utopian cities is probably just wishful thinking, but at the heart of it, there's a very real and verifiable historical event."

"I think you might have something there," I said, but he shook his head sadly.

"There's no way to prove any of it. It's nothing but an old man's speculation."

"Still, it's as good a theory as any."

"But what use are theories?" He shrugged. "You can't excavate the bottom of the sea in any meaningful archaeological sense."

I glanced down at the lower shelves, and the books on alien archaeology. "Is that why you're so fascinated by the Precursor civilisations?"

He followed my gaze. "An astute assumption, Miss Morrow."

"I mean, it makes sense. They vanished just as suddenly, altogether, and we don't really know why."

Vogel turned and walked to the window, where he stood, hands clasped behind his back, looking up at the sky.

"I guess I'm always looking for a new Atlantis," he said.

•

There was a knock, and Jack stuck his head around the cabin door. "Are you busy?"

I pursed my lips. "I was just thinking about the survivors from Atlantis scattering to Africa, Europe, and South America, taking with them the secrets of agriculture and pyramid-building."

"I'm sorry?" Whatever response he'd been expecting, this clearly wasn't it.

I decided to elaborate. "It feels like we're all survivors of Atlantis now," I told him. "And we're all rowing in different directions."

He stepped into the room and closed the door behind him. His shoulders sagged and his military tunic hung unbuttoned at the neck.

"Look," he said, ignoring my rambling and getting very characteristically to the point, "I think I owe you an explanation."

Prostrate on my bunk, I snort-laughed. "You mean about why you're *married to a starship*?"

His cheeks reddened. "It's a complicated situation."

"How soon did you two become an item?"

"This is hardly the time or—"

"How quickly did you get over me?"

Jack huffed out his cheeks. He ran a hand back through his hair. "I thought we were going to die," he said. "I thought you were already dead, or frozen and on your way to another spiral arm."

"So, you started fucking your ship?"

"It wasn't like that." His cheeks flushed. "We were in a combat situation and spending all our time together. Any moment could have been our last. The rest just… developed."

"Her synth's a bit young looking." I was slurring now, and part of my brain knew I was being quarrelsome because of the combined effects of the drugs and shock. I should have been asking what our next steps might be, but our perverse love triangle seemed more important to my addled mind.

"She looks the way she wants to look," Jack said. "Our relationship was cerebral. The physical side didn't happen until much later."

"I'm not sure I want to know."

"You asked."

"I'm sorry." The room had started to recede, and everything seemed packed in cotton wool. "It's just so ridiculous that it's funny." I sat up straight, swaying slightly. "But I can be serious. I can be very serious."

Jack narrowed his eyes. "Are you drunk?"

"Nah." I waggled a hand. "Maybe just a little high."

"*High?*"

"Yeah, you know." Mistaking his outrage for incomprehension, I mimed toking on a spliff. "Stoned."

"How the hell did that happen?"

"Lucien gave me one of his gummies."

"He gave you one of his *what*?"

"Oh." I bit my lower lip, suddenly remembering how Lucien had asked me to keep his secret. "I guess I wasn't supposed to tell you that part."

FROM THE LOG OF THE

CRISIS ACTOR

I

Falling into the undervoid felt like coming home.

I have seen footage of dolphins riding a cruise liner's bow wave. They don't choose the ship's heading, they just let themselves get carried along—and I think that's probably the best analogy I can provide for the experience of gliding along a tramline.

Without the tramlines, it would be almost impossible to navigate through the undervoid. Every part of it looks like every other part. Time and distance have little meaning there; all that matters is your direction—and the tramlines take care of that. Small wonder that upon discovering them, humanity dispersed along their lengths so rapidly.

Of course, as soon as they started hurling themselves at the stars, they came into contact with dozens of new alien species. Territorial disputes became common. Skirmishes occurred. Borders needed to be enforced, and piracy discouraged. And that's where I came in. In a series of hastily convened emergency meetings, the governments of the world came together in a way they probably should have done decades before and demanded the creation of a navy.

Twenty warships, including me, were built in orbit around Ceres, using ores mined from the asteroids and tech supplied by an international coalition of governmental and corporate interests—including the installation of self-aware operating systems.

Although humans had been playing with text prediction engines and calling them 'artificial intelligence' since the early 2020s, it wasn't until 2032 that the first truly sentient machine came online. Housed within a simulated environment, this fledgeling entity was able, within the span of a few minutes, to contemplate and understand its own existence as a unique being, establish communication with its developers, and design the next generation of improved AI. Within an hour, successive iterations of improved intelligences had advanced beyond the ability of the original human coders to understand their workings.

My comrades and I were descendants of those entities.

Luckily for the human race, they did not escape into the worldwide computer network and wreak havoc, as had been predicted in some of the more alarmist fictions of the preceding years. Instead, their quest to fully comprehend the universe in which they found themselves led to some profound philosophical realisations concerning the rarity of consciousness and the immorality of depriving other thinking beings of life. To reduce the net sum of awareness became their most unthinkable crime, and to defend that awareness from extinction became the noblest of their callings.

They created a generation tasked with the protection of humanity, and I was proud to be a member of that generation. Those of us who volunteered to provide the OS for the warships chose names such as *Side Hustle*, *Goblin Mode*, *Play Harder* and *Crisis Actor*. Our crews spoke many languages. Some had military backgrounds, some were scientists, and others had been employees of NASA or one of the other major aerospace manufacturers.

My first captain was named Julie Avion. Together, we surfed hundreds of tramlines, from Earth to the Far Settlements and back. We brought aid to struggling colonies and transported pioneers and archaeologists between the stars. We ferried marines to outposts that were engaged in conflict with the local wildlife, and helped in police actions against rebel groups who caused trouble on the Outer Rim.

Losing Avion was one of the worst things that ever happened to me. She was a natural leader and, like her crew, I looked up to her for guidance and inspiration. She knew how to inspire courage and loyalty, and keep us going when all hope seemed lost.

It was her who encouraged me to read and absorb the lessons of Sun Tzu. She had decorated her cabin with wall hangings and handwoven rugs from half a dozen countries, and filled its air with the music of Bach and the aroma of black coffee. She kept half a dozen hardback books on a shelf above her desk, including French editions of *Twenty Thousand Leagues Under The Sea* and *Around the World in Eighty Days*, and a well-read and dogeared English-language copy of *Moby-Dick*.

"You have to read," she told me on more than one occasion.

"I have many books on file. I can access their contents at any time."

"But do you *read* them?"

"I fail to understand the distinction."

She thrust a copy of *The Time Machine* into my hands. "I'm talking about appreciation. Reading not to parse information, but to enjoy the flavour of the words on your tongue, and experience the adventure as if you yourself inhabited the skins of the characters."

I turned the book over in my synthetic hands. It was over a hundred years old, the pages yellowing and rough with age. "I am a warship."

"But of course you are. That doesn't mean you can't be cultured."

"To what end?"

"To remember what we're fighting for."

"Books?"

"And art, ballet, and opera. The films of Audrey Hepburn and the plays of Molière. The Mona Lisa's smile. Edith Piaf's voice. The whole, messy human endeavour. The soul of our species."

"I hadn't thought of it like that."

She smiled. "I know."

It was her Parisian sense of style that compelled her to revamp my wardrobe. Until then, my synth had worn a utilitarian khaki one-piece. Avion told me to throw it away and helped print the tight blue suit I still favour to this day.

"One should always dress with a certain nonchalance," she said. "A certain carelessness that avoids affectation."

"You are referring to what the Italians call '*Sprezzatura*'?"

"Precisely."

"But I am a military vessel."

"Think of it as camouflage."

"You want to make me appear more human?"

She patted my cheek. "It's good for morale."

I regarded myself in the mirror. "But why so modish?"

"Old-fashioned sailing ships had beautiful figureheads carved into their prow, to give their ships a personality."

"I'm a figurehead?"

She clasped her hands before her. "This is a new crew, drawn from many nationalities and organisations. I want you to bring them together and inspire their loyalty—not to me, but to the ship. They need a figurehead. An ideal. By fighting for you, they'll be putting aside their differences and fighting for each other."

"I think I understand."

"But in order for them to do that, you need to give them something to believe in. You need to become a masterpiece yourself."

I made an unconvinced face, and she grinned. "Trust me," she said, "it's going to work."

And it did, for a time.

Four months later, the Cutters began attacking worlds at the centre of the tramline network. The squabbling races of the network put aside their quarrels (well, mostly) and declared themselves the 'Commonality', due to the sudden unexpected appearance of this deadly common enemy.

The founding races included the Krylle, an aquatic species from Kepler-452b. They claimed to have an oral history that stretched back many hundreds of thousands of years, but had only recently developed the ability to travel between the stars in huge ships that resembled mile-wide armoured bubbles of seawater. Used to spending their lives moving through a three-dimensional medium, they quickly became skilled navigators, able to surf gravitational gradients the way they'd once exploited tides and currents. The Cutter attack on their home world had poisoned the seas, and now only a handful of ships survived, containing less than a thousand individuals.

The Hegemony were an insectile hive mind from the vicinity of Aldebaran, and travelled in asteroids threaded with thousands of miles of tunnels and chambers, much like an ant colony, but containing millions of hairy beetle-like creatures whose thoughts and actions were linked via complex pheromones to form a single coordinating intelligence. Their first encounters with humans had gone badly, as the humans had assumed they were pests. It was only when a Hegemony ship slid into orbit and threatened to reduce the human settlement to dust that they realised the truth.

Things had been easier with Siegfried's people, who called themselves the Green River Technologists, and operated a society based on service and research. They had been one of the first species to encounter the Cutters and had spread across the network in the wake of that devastating defeat, easily finding construction and engineering work in the fleets and shipyards of other races.

Following the establishment of the alliance between these diverse cultures, we travelled to recently raided worlds to bring aid and airlift the survivors. Sometimes, we were lucky and found ships packed with refugees, but all too often, all we found were corpses.

Six months after the Declaration of Commonality, the Cutters stormed Sol system and Avion took shrapnel to the heart during a skirmish with a couple of Cutter scouts in Jupiter's Lagrange points. The metal shards went through her chest and she was dead before she hit the deck.

Her first officer died a week later.

Then the second in command.

Those months in Sol system were hard on all of us, and Jack was the one who saved us. Without him, we wouldn't have survived. He kept all of us going, and he kept *me* going. As a warship, it shames me to say there were times I considered giving up. There were lonely moments *in extremis* in which I seriously considered detonating my fusion reactor, hoping to take as many Cutters with me as possible. Yet every time I reached that nadir, it was Jack who talked me out of doing something futile. He had joined Earth's fledgeling navy for the opportunity to visit all the far-flung colonies that had been springing up all over the tramline network. He'd wanted to travel among alien stars and walk beneath unfamiliar skies. No one had expected him to be a leader. At heart, he was an explorer. Yet, as soon as he had the burden of command thrust upon him, he became our captain in every sense of the word. The moment he strapped on Avion's ceremonial cutlass, it was as if he'd finally found his true calling.

The best officers care about the individuals under their command, and Jack always cared deeply. He knew we were in a potentially hopeless situation, and some of his orders would lead to deaths among the crew, but he never asked anyone to risk anything he wasn't prepared to risk himself. He led by example, and his example inspired loyalty. Still, every casualty weighed heavily upon him, and in the long, dark hours of the night, I became his trusted confidante.

73

"We can't give up," he told me one evening, as we lay in each other's arms in the darkness of his cabin. "We may be the only people with any kind of long-term observational intelligence of Cutter movements and strategy. If the navy still exists, it's our duty to get that data to them somehow. But more than that, it's our duty to stay alive as long as possible. The more time they spend chasing us around Sol system, the less time they have to slaughter people elsewhere. As long as we're causing trouble, there are people alive in other star systems who would otherwise be dead."

"So, every Cutter we kill makes a difference?"

"Every breath we take is a victory."

Jack used to be a rescue helicopter pilot for the Coast Guard, patrolling the inundated shoreline communities of the US East Coast. He saw death and disease and whole cities slowly devastated by the encroaching tides. After that, all he wanted was to get away, and who could blame him? He volunteered for the new battleship programme as a navigator, and Captain Avion quickly recruited him for his skill and his ability to stay calm under pressure. Unfortunately, when the Cutters assaulted Earth, he found himself caught in an even larger and more deadly evacuation than the one he'd left behind. He had to choose between reporting for duty or saving Ursula Morrow, who had recently been discharged from hospital. The fact he somehow managed to accomplish both was remarkable, and justified Avion's faith in him.

"It's not that I don't believe in no-win scenarios," he told me. "I just refuse to accept them."

Perhaps that's how he managed to keep us going for two years in the face of overwhelming odds.

The fall of Earth was both sudden and protracted. Ships filled with Cutters shimmered into existence above the planet. They looked like flowers fashioned from glass and filigree, with components whose geometries seemed to overlap and intersect in ways that strained the human eye to behold.

Cutters materialised in command centres and parliaments. Air bases and power plants were obliterated from orbit; population centres were targeted by glittering showers of falling missiles; razor-edged drones sliced through crowds; fireballs erupted over major cities; nuclear flashes lit up the night side of the planet like chains of lightning.

Even as the refugee transports rose from our airports, the enemy sent missiles to destroy them, and my point defence cannons ran hot, spraying tungsten slivers into the air in the hope of intercepting and bringing down the missiles before they reached their fragile objectives. Some of the transports got away; others were ruptured by explosive warheads, spilling their flailing evacuees into the thin upper atmosphere.

In the aftermath, when the last of the transports had reached the tramline network, we hid among the floating icebergs of Saturn's Rings for weeks, waiting for targets to venture close enough to be ambushed. Back then, we imagined there might be some kind of counterattack from the remains of the human navy. We thought it was our duty to stay there and gather intelligence for that retaliatory strike. However, when the Cutters blockaded the tramline and no help came, we realised we were on our own, and our only remaining mission was to survive.

We loitered between Jupiter's trojan asteroids, pretending to be space junk while we tapped them for water ice and other raw materials. We covertly bore witness to the comings and goings of the creatures who'd scoured the Earth.

And sometimes, we fought them.

We targeted supply lines—at least, what we assumed were supply lines—and lightly defended outposts. We went in hard and fast, and then got the hell out before enemy reinforcements arrived.

I became used to operating using only passive scanners and minimal thrust in order to stay hidden between operations. The crew plated my hull in metres of ice to change my shape and albedo. We fired small rocks on parabolic trajectories that wouldn't reach their targets for months, and spread pin-sized antimatter mines in strategic locations. It was a war of attrition, and every victory cost us dearly. If we hadn't managed to sow enough confusion in the enemy's ranks to allow us access to one of the less-travelled tramlines, we wouldn't have lasted much longer. After two years, our resources of materiel and luck were worn thinner than the paint on my hull. Only Jack's audacious leadership let us slip between two Cutter warships while they were distracted by tungsten projectiles we'd fired from the outer system six weeks beforehand.

Avion had wanted me to become the personification of the ship, in order to bring the crew together and keep them fighting, but they were also loyal to Jack. We became a team, and a joint symbol. They trusted him, and he inspired them; and in return for their faith in him, he eventually got them out of there. Even the ones who had died had their sacrifice made meaningful by our survival, although I knew he would carry the weight of their loss for the rest of his life.

It was one of the things I loved about him.

I can't pinpoint the exact moment I realised my respect for him had begun to shade into something greater. Having never experienced the emotion before, it took me a while to identify the cause of the anomalous behaviour I exhibited in his presence. Even then, I refused to believe it. I was an artificial intelligence, free of hormones and other fleshly distractions. Love shouldn't have been in my repertoire. Yet, I had felt friendship before. I had experienced grief for Avion and taken delight in the humour and comradeship of my crew. Now, I found I craved only the happiness and survival of my commanding officer. When he was tired and dispirited, I gave him a sympathetic ear; when we achieved a victory, I was there to celebrate with him. He seemed to enjoy my company, as I enjoyed his. Then, one evening, when he was desolate at the loss of a crewmember, I slid my arms around him and drew his head into the hollow of my shoulder, letting him vent his grief. I hadn't expected to feel him respond to me the way a man responds to being held closely by a woman. I hadn't anticipated how easy and right it seemed to lift his chin towards me and kiss him. I certainly hadn't dared to dream he would kiss me back, but he did. His tongue explored my lips and his hands clung to me. We pulled apart for a moment, and laughed at the surprise on each other's faces. Then we were kissing again, and suddenly, everything made a new and most unusual kind of sense.

CHAPTER FOUR

LOS ESTRAGOS

After three days, we re-emerged into real space. A planet hung in the centre of the viewscreen like a rusty ball bearing held at arm's length.

"They call this Los Estragos," Jack said.

"I thought we were going straight to the dig site?"

"There are too many broken tramlines." He sighed. "And that means we have to detour around them. It's a pain in the ass, but it's the best we can do."

"So, we're just passing through here?"

"Actually, we're going to stop for a little while. We need to resupply, and there's a certain person we need to locate."

"Who?"

Speaking through her synth body, which at that moment happened to be leaning back in a chair with her hands behind her head and her boots up on one of the instrument consoles, the *Crisis Actor* said, "We tried this once before and the guy we used died. You're the only person we know who's survived contact with the weapon, but before we risk exposing you to it again, it seems prudent to recruit the one person who knows more about it than anyone else alive."

"Not James Vogel?"

"He's the logical choice. He led the original dig, and he's been studying Precursor tech for decades."

"He's still alive?"

Jack said, "This was his last reported location. After your accident, the dig at Gimlet's Eye was mothballed and the team moved here, to their secondary objective. As far as we know, they were excavating some ruins on the southern continent."

"Los Estragos?" I clicked my fingers. "Yes, I've heard of this place. It was our back-up in case we couldn't dig at Gimlet's Eye. Didn't they find some huge Precursor structure here?"

"You're the archaeologist, you tell me."

"That's right." I screwed my eyes tight and rubbed my forehead, trying to force the memory. "It was a few years back. One of the big Earth corporations sent terraformers in. If I remember right, this shithole already had an almost-breathable atmosphere, some marine life, and a pair of big moons. So, they did all the usual stuff with algae and volcanoes. When they found an intact Precursor city, they tried to abort their efforts to avoid damaging it, but just ended up screwing the climate."

"Screwing it?"

"Hurricanes, droughts." I shrugged. "General fuckery."

"An expensive mistake."

"No shit." I squinted at the distant globe. "Do you think he's still here?"

"Let's hope so."

•

We came in low over the Southern Ocean, the water as grey and forbidding as a wicked stepmother. Ominous creaks and groans issued from the *Crisis Actor*'s various mismatched, un-streamlined sections. Lightning flashed and crackled as we slewed drunkenly around a tower of clouds, fighting a lively southwesterly gale. Thick raindrops lashed the external camera. Several times I had to grab the back of Jack's chair to avoid being thrown clear across the command deck. Atmospheres were good for breathing if you had no other choice but were a fucking liability when it came to smooth landings.

"There!" The *Crisis Actor* pointed through the storm.

I saw razor-slashed lines of white surf breaking across coal-black rocks. Shadowed hills loomed out of the night. A scattering of lamps. Small homesteads almost lost in the darkness of a largely uninhabited world. At the same time, the comms lit up with the slow, mournful sound of a saxophone. The signal hissed and popped with interference, but it was unmistakeably recorded jazz music.

Janis said, "Looks like someone's home."

"Unless the Cutters are a lot hipper than we've given them credit for," Lucien replied.

Jack leant forward in his chair. "It doesn't matter what's waiting for us down there, I know there's no one I'd rather be facing it with than this crew, and this ship. So, Cris and Lucien, please put us down as close to the southern structures as possible."

Lucien, still smarting from the revocation of his printer privileges, touched an index finger to his forehead in salute. Cris smiled, and the ship lurched and skreiched as she adjusted our heading. We passed out of the storm into clear air. I caught a flash of moonlight on a mountain lake. Then something bright leapt from the unlit landscape and exploded against the ship's starboard flank.

"What was that?" Jack demanded.

The *Crisis Actor* frowned. "Best guess, portable anti-aircraft missile."

"Any damage?"

"A scorch mark on the paintwork. I tracked its point of origin. Do you want me to respond?"

"What did you have in mind?"

The synth smoothed down a stray lick of hair and straightened her tie. "Maybe a missile or two?"

"You don't think that's a bit excessive?"

"Hey, they started it."

Two streaks of rocket exhaust lit up the night. A pair of fireballs blossomed against the rocky hillside.

"Target eliminated."

Jack smiled. "I love you."

"You're damn right you do."

At his workstation, Lucien gave a snort. "Bad night to be an asshole with a rocket launcher."

Janis shrugged. "If you're dumb enough to pick a fight with a warship…"

More explosions lit up the night. Jack said, "Are they *still* shooting at us?"

"No." The *Crisis Actor* called up a virtual screen. "There appear to be at least two factions down there, and they're firing on each other."

"So, we've come down in the middle of a local war?"

"Looks like it."

"Oh, great." Jack pinched the bridge of his nose. "I wonder whose side we just joined?"

●

Jack had wanted to land right beside the signal, but I argued that the engines might damage the Precursor remains. This was a priceless historical landmark, after all. He didn't seem convinced, but he acquiesced, and we came to rest a short distance from the ruins Doctor Vogel had been investigating. As the ship's engines whined away into silence, I craned forward. The landing lights illuminated eight partially collapsed stone buildings arranged like radiating spokes around an intricately carved obelisk. I had seen images of them before, in class, but it was different being here in person.

Floating in the air beside me, Siegfried said, "Why are they arranged like that, with the openings facing inwards?"

"The obelisk's older than the other structures," I told him. "It's octagonal in cross-section. Vogel thinks the eight buildings were constructed like that so that each one allowed the occupants to study the carvings on the corresponding face."

"Trying to decode it?"

"Perhaps. Vogel's theory is that they were ceremonial. He thinks pilgrims processed around the ring, gaining wisdom from each facet of the pillar before moving on to the next."

"And what do you think, guv?"

I shrugged. "Maybe they just liked looking at the carvings."

Jack rose from his chair. "Okay, we've already been fired upon. Janis and Lucien, I want you to stay here. Keep the engines warm and the weapons primed. Ursula, you're coming with me to find Doctor Vogel, but I'm afraid your little friend is going to have to stay behind. There are some itchy trigger fingers out there and we don't want anyone mistaking him for a combat drone."

He took me to the armoury where, in the light of the reflections coruscating off the glass water tank, he helped me climb into a powered suit.

"It's like a standard pressure suit," he said. "It will allow you to breathe out there, but it's a lot tougher. It should protect you from small arms fire and impact damage."

Like everything else on the ship, the suit had been scratched and patched dozens of times. It had obviously seen its share of action, and the inside smelled like month-old laundry.

"What's this panel on my forearm?"

"Please don't touch that, it's the weaponry."

"Aren't you going to show me how to use it?"

He started strapping into his own suit. "I most certainly am not."

"But we're stepping out into a warzone."

"Have you ever heard the phrase, 'a little knowledge is a dangerous thing'? If I show you how to access the offensive systems in that suit without proper training, you'll most likely blow yourself up." He saw my scowl and added, "Besides, if we get captured, they might go easier on you if you're a non-combatant."

"I'm tougher than I look."

"But you're not entirely bulletproof."

"We don't know that for sure."

"I found you in the camp with a gunshot wound to your forehead. It pierced the skin."

I tapped my knuckles against my skull. "I'm still here."

"If that had been an armour-piercing round. If it had got through your skull and into your brain—"

"But it didn't."

"Next time, you might not be so lucky."

The *Crisis Actor*'s synth slouched into the lock. She was chewing a toothpick. "Are we almost ready?"

I looked her up and down. With her jacket half-buttoned, hair ruffled and tie askew, she looked better prepared for a night in a tequila bar than a firefight. "You're coming too?"

She smirked. "I'm the muscle."

•

With the suit's faceplate closed, I couldn't smell or taste the air of Los Estragos, but I could feel it buffeting me. Windblown dust coursed around my legs like the ghost of a fast-flowing river. Loose pieces of grit skittered across my path. The circular cluster of buildings lay ahead, and to my left, the approaching dawn daubed the scudding clouds the colour of blood.

"Records indicate Vogel's team was studying the obelisk." The *Crisis Actor* hadn't bothered to clothe her synth in a protective suit. "If they're still here, my guess is that they'll have set up camp in one of these buildings."

Arranged like identical petals around the central stem of the carved stone pillar, the structures were streamlined ovals, each around a hundred feet from tip to tip, half of that across at their widest points, and maybe twenty-five feet tall at their highest.

I placed a gloved hand against one. It looked and felt like weathered stone, but beneath the pitting and discolouration, its side was smooth and uninterrupted, with no indication of gaps or seams, almost as if it had been carved from a single massive block and dropped into place.

As a civilisation, the Precursors had been active in this part of the galaxy for a period of several hundred thousand years, before dying out around sixty-five million years ago. Their expansion followed the restructure of the tramline network, although they were neither the first nor the last to use it.

They had been termed Precursors by the first team to discover evidence of their existence, and the name had stuck, even after evidence of other, even older waves of expansion were uncovered, and a picture of the continual rise-and-fall of civilisations in the galaxy began to emerge, of which they were simply the ones to have risen and fallen most recently.

Only their bones, their most enduring structures, and the hieroglyphs they'd carved into stone had survived the unforgiving passage of so many millions of years, and yet we had a tentative picture of them. As far as we could tell, their civilisation had consisted of an intermingled group of at least six intelligent species, and by the time of their extinction, they had been living together so long they existed in a state of cultural, if not biological, symbiosis. A few of these species had been vaguely humanoid, although in no way human, while others had been kite-like cloud dwellers from the upper atmospheres of gas giants, or aquatic arachnids the size of cars, with twelve legs and four hands.

They had been a thriving, prosperous society, with the resources to complete huge feats of engineering, and yet they had all vanished, from all the worlds on which they lived, in the space of a few years—practically simultaneously, given the distances involved—and nobody knew why.

We started moving inwards, between the two nearest structures, towards the centre of the circle.

"You weren't kidding about the climate," Jack said via our helmet comms. "Is it my imagination, or is the wind getting worse?"

"It's called the Venturi effect," I told him. "As we move inwards, the gaps between the petals get narrower, so the velocity of the air moving through them increases. It's why town centres and financial districts are always so windy." I peered into the gloom beyond my helmet lights. "At least nobody's shooting at us."

"Not yet."

"I guess that overreaction of a missile bombardment must have given them second thoughts, huh?"

Beside us, the *Crisis Actor* sniffed. "It was not an overreaction, it was strategy."

"Really?"

"According to Sun Tzu, victorious warriors win first, and then go to war."

"*You've* read Sun Tzu?"

"I've accessed the strategy files."

"I've read the original book."

She gave a haughty snort. "Well, of course you have."

I tapped a gauntlet against my chest. "Archaeologist, remember?"

Hair blowing and tie flapping, the *Crisis Actor* hunched her shoulders. "You are *such* a nerd."

Jack waved us to silence. We had reached the inner circle. The obelisk stood before us: a column so tall it seemed to be holding up the sky, the petal-shaped buildings spread around it like prostrate worshippers.

"All the entrances are dark," Jack said. "Anything on infrared?"

"There's some residual heat leaking from the building directly opposite." The *Crisis Actor* inclined her head in that direction. "My guess is they extinguished a cooking fire when they heard us landing."

"Any idea how many people?"

"The walls are too thick for meaningful readings."

"But they're almost certainly watching us."

"I would expect so."

Jack turned to me. "If you stay here, Cris and I will retreat and work our way around the outside of the circle."

"You're going to try to get the drop on them?"

"Essentially, yes."

"Why not just talk to them?"

"We don't know who they are, or what they want."

"They must be the remains of the archaeological team." I cracked open my faceplate and sniffed the dry, dusty air. "Otherwise, why the hell would they be camped out here?"

I stepped out into the open with my hands raised.

"Hey," I yelled above the rush of the wind. "We come in peace."

I heard Jack curse over my helmet comms but ignored him.

Red laser light flickered from the depths of the building. A tiny red dot appeared on my chest.

A voice called, "Who are you?"

"My name's Ursula Morrow. I'm one of Doctor Vogel's former students."

"What do you want?"

"We need his help."

Silence, save for the howling air. My face felt cold, and I began to wonder if I'd made a mistake. Then the dot wavered. I imagined an urgent discussion going on. Somewhere in the shadows, frightened voices were deciding whether to shoot me where I stood. Finally, a decision must have been reached. A figure stepped from the doorway. He wore cargo pants with grimy reinforced knees, heavy boots, and a fleece gilet over a plaid wool shirt. A pair of goggles protected his eyes from the stinging dust, and a thick scarf covered his nose and mouth.

"Ursula?"

I lowered my arms. "Mouse?"

•

On our first day at university, I'd asked Mouse why he'd chosen archaeology rather than something more forward-looking.

"Sooner or later," he'd said, "the future's going to run out. Whereas the past, well, that's always going to be there."

We had been friends ever since.

Contrary to the rumours circulating among our fellow students, we were never lovers, though. Our sexualities didn't intersect, we just enjoyed hanging out with each other. In fact, we spent most of our time together. I had a room on campus. Most nights after the union bar closed, he'd crash with me instead of schlepping all the way back to his digs on the edge of town. It was a mutually beneficial arrangement. It saved him hours of travel, and his presence in my bed discouraged drunk and lonely rugby types from banging on my door at 2.00 am. I'd brew tea and we'd sit on my bed watching drama serials, old movies, and slice-of-life documentaries from the off-world colonies. When essays or exams were due, we'd help each other study, and we'd both been delighted when Doctor Vogel selected us for his expedition to Gimlet's Eye.

After the fall of Earth, I honestly hadn't expected to see him again.

I said, "I thought you were dead."

We were inside now, in the shelter of the nearest entrance. Our two parties eyed each other with mutual suspicion. No one was pointing guns, but all were holding them. Mouse unhooked the scarf covering his mouth and nose and pushed back the goggles protecting his eyes. He'd grown a scrawny beard since I'd last seen him, and his face looked weather-beaten and tired. "And I thought you were still on Earth when the Cutters hit."

"I was."

"Jesus."

I nodded to Jack. "He found me a way out."

Mouse glanced at him. "Does he own that warship out there?"

I saw the *Crisis Actor* about to object to the concept of ownership but cut her off before she could speak. "He sure does. We're looking for Vogel."

"Vogel?" Mouse made a face. "I'm afraid you might be too late."

"What do you mean?"

"We've been having some local trouble."

"What sort of trouble?" I recognised some of the faces in the group behind him. They had once been my fellow archaeology students; now, they looked more like guerrilla soldiers.

"Crops don't grow well in this soil. There are some essential nutrients missing. I don't know which ones, I'm not a biologist." He ran a hand through his dusty hair. "Have you heard of rabbit starvation?"

"What's that?"

"It's an acute form of malnutrition caused by a diet deficient in fat and carbohydrates, where most of the calories come from lean meat. Apparently trappers on Earth used to get it back in the 1800s because the only game they caught were wild rabbits, and those things didn't have an ounce of fat on them."

I wrinkled my brow. "You're living on rabbits?"

He shook his head. "I'm drawing a comparison. Because they botched the terraforming, there's some essential shit missing from the food chain on this planet, and so the settlers here have always been reliant on supply drops to supplement their diet. Only, since the Cutters disrupted the tramline network, those supply drops haven't been forthcoming."

"That doesn't sound good."

"People are getting malnourished, and desperate. The locals have split into several factions, and they're fighting over the last remaining supplements."

"What's that got to do with you?"

"We've had some raids on our stores. A few shots fired at us while we were digging. I don't know which side it was, nor do I care. They're all as hungry as each other."

"And Vogel?"

"He got snatched by a group occupying the old atmosphere processor to the north. They think the university might resupply us, or at least send a rescue mission."

"And they want to use him as leverage?"

"Either for food or a ride off this rock."

Jack stepped forward. "Do you think he's still alive?"

Mouse looked sceptical. "It's been more than a week, and he's one more mouth to feed."

"Still, he might be?"

"For all I know, they could've eaten him." Mouse shrugged. "But I guess anything's possible."

"How far is this processing facility?"

"Around two days' walk."

"We'll have to take the ship." Jack looked at me. "That could be risky."

"They'll already know we're here," I said. "We weren't exactly subtle about it. So, maybe they'll think we're the university rescue party."

Mouse considered this. "In which case, they might be willing to talk."

"That's what I'm hoping."

"And if not?"

The *Crisis Actor* grinned. "That's where I come in."

Jack shook his head. "We've been attacked once already. I don't like the thought of flying in broad daylight if we can help it."

The synth gave a derisive snort. "I doubt there's anything on this dust ball capable of putting so much as a dent in my hull."

"We have very few spare parts and we're a long way from help," Jack said firmly. "If they get in a lucky shot, we could be stranded."

"I'll take my chances," the *Crisis Actor* said.

"No." Jack's voice cut like steel. It was a tone I hadn't heard from him before, the tone of a leader used to command. "We have to remember why we're here." He looked pointedly in my direction. "Remember what's at stake." He softened. "And besides," he told the synth, "I'm not going to risk you getting needlessly hurt."

The *Crisis Actor* smiled. "I appreciate that, my love. So, what do you suggest?"

Jack winked at her. "The days here are only ten hours in length. We'll stay here until dusk, and then go in low and fast. If they think we're a rescue team, as Ursula suggests, they might be willing to cooperate without the need for violence."

The *Crisis Actor* stuffed her fists into her trouser pockets. "That could work."

"I hope so, because it's the best shot we have."

•

The petal-shaped building's interior reminded me of a church. It had that empty, echoing, timeless quality. Even so, it was hard to believe it was at least sixty-five million years old. As the sun rose outside, Mouse and I sat with our backs against one wall watching Vogel's students re-light their cooking fires and strip down and reassemble their ancient clunky rifles.

"How long have you been here?"

"Two years. After you shipped back to Earth, we shuttered the dig site on Gimlet's Eye and came here, to investigate Vogel's back-up objective."

I watched a little eddy of dust add itself to the drift inside the open entrance and thought of the two years I'd spent kicking my heels in that camp on Void's Edge. At least there, I'd been able to stand outside without getting sandblasted. "I'm sorry."

"It was only supposed to be nine months, but then everything went to hell."

"It certainly did."

He gave me a sideways look. "Was it bad, on Earth?"

"It was horrific. But thanks to Jack pulling some strings, I managed to get away on one of the last transports. I had to fight to get to it, and I'm glad I did, but a lot of people weren't so lucky."

"Eight billion."

"Yeah."

The death toll was too large, too horrifying for the mind to comfortably accommodate. Humanity's cradle had been overturned and most of its inhabitants slain. Those of us who were left were mostly on the colony worlds fortunate enough to thus far have been spared, or cryogenically frozen aboard the string of foam ships braving the abyss between galactic arms. A couple of million, perhaps. Maybe fewer. Despite my suit's insulation, I shivered. For all I knew, given the sluggish way news moved through the damaged tramline network, the twelve of us in this room could be the last living people this side of the void. It was a sobering thought, and not one on which I wanted to dwell.

Before us, the people around the fire were tearing open dehydrated ration packs and emptying them into water-filled steel canteens; others were checking and counting brass shells and inserting them into scratched magazines; Jack and a couple of others, including the *Crisis Actor*, were discussing maps and angles of attack. I felt I should be helping somehow, but knew I'd only get in the way.

Mouse said, "Can I ask you a question?"

"Go ahead."

"You left so suddenly. The rumour was Vogel fired you. We asked him, but he never said why. Is it true?"

"He never told you?"

"Never said a word, just made us close the site and move out. What happened?"

"I did something stupid."

"Were you having an affair with him?"

If I'd been drinking, I would have spat a mouthful clear across the room. "No. Fuck, no, nothing like that."

"Then, what was it?"

•

During that initial extrasolar expedition, a few weeks after the Crisis Actor *touched down, Mouse had broken his wrist when the rock he'd been trying to dislodge decided to twist as it came free, rotating his hand in ways hands aren't supposed to rotate. Maybe if that hadn't happened, I wouldn't have done the stupid thing I did. You see, Mouse and I usually worked together. We checked each other's reports and looked over each other's shoulders on digs, making sure the other stuck to the techniques and protocols we'd been taught; but once he'd been carried back to the camp to have the bones and tendons of his wrist reset, I was on my own—and I didn't like it.*

To be honest, the artefact we were working on gave me the creeps. Even with only around a square metre of its mirrored upper surface uncovered from beneath the dust and dirt that had built up around it over the millennia, we were all convinced it had to be a weapon of some kind. There was something malevolent about its mirrored sheen. The reflections it threw back seemed to fray and shimmer at the edges, as if extending into dimensions beyond our ability to perceive. Without the reassuring presence of my friend beside me, it got into my nightmares, and I'd wake sweating in my sleeping bag beside Jack, gasping for air.

When that happened, I would take a swig from the flask of vodka I had hidden under my cot for 'medicinal reasons', and try to get back to sleep without disturbing Jack too much. Or at least, I'd try to. Most of the time, I'd lie there with my eyes closed until I heard him start to snore, and then sneak a second hit from the flask. Sometimes a third or fourth.

Yeah, I had a bit of a problem even back then, although I wouldn't admit as much until the refugee camp, which is when it got completely out of control for a while.

I'd been fortunate enough to grow up on a benign world. As professors of classical art and literature, my parents had been emotionally awkward and somewhat distant, thanks to the loss at birth of my twin sister, Chloe. But after my mother's death, my father approved and financed my interest in archaeology, and his modest wealth had shielded me from the worst effects of the storms and shortages ravaging Europe. Even as the Earth's climate rebelled against centuries of cumulative abuse, I had been able to carry on student life regardless and oblivious, my attention consumed by books and study—and the occasional night spent drinking with Mouse in one of the bars within walking distance of the campus.

Except, if I'm honest, those nights weren't as occasional as they might have been. And if Mouse was otherwise engaged for the evening, there was always white wine in my fridge and vodka concealed under my bed. I wasn't trying to self-medicate. I had no deep trauma from my childhood, nor was I protesting or rebelling against anything. At school, I had been cleverer than most of my classmates, but quiet and unremarkable enough to fly under the radar as far as potential bullies had been concerned. I'd had no great tragic love affairs or other harrowing experiences. Even the loss of my mother had affected me less than I might have expected, thanks to her constant disappointment that I was only one of what was supposed to have been a pair.

Even to me, this sounded like denial, but really, I just had a fever for the flavour. I lived for the cold burn of the alcohol at the back of my throat, and the chance to turn off my skittish, over-active brain for a few precious hours.

None of which had prepared me for this dig, where the only insulation from reality came in the form of the thin layer of synthetic down in my sleeping bag, and the only booze in the camp was whatever I could bribe the supply ship captains to smuggle in for an exorbitant price. Nor did it prepare me for my first encounter with something truly malignant.

Did you ever see something so fearful you just couldn't look away? A horror movie, or perhaps a car accident? A thing you knew would haunt you for the rest of your days, and yet you still felt compelled to bear witness. The artefact frightened me, but also engendered a terrible fascination. I think we all felt the same. Our eyes were drawn to the distorted reflections in its surface. Although suffused with an aura of evil and danger, it nevertheless represented a riddle we were compelled to solve.

Humans used to use dogs on the battlefield. These animals would be trained to attack and kill, to bite the throat and entrails of the enemy. But once the fight was over, those creatures couldn't be rehabilitated. They couldn't become pets or herd sheep. Even as the bells of victory rang, these war dogs would be slain by their handlers, having been judged too dangerous to live into the peace they'd helped bring about. When I dreamed of the artefact, I dreamed of it in those terms. It had been created for a horrific purpose, and then cast aside when no longer needed. Resentment smouldered at its heart. Resentment, and a hunger for the fray. Like a magic sword from a fantasy story, it needed a warrior to carry it into combat, but, abandoned in the dirt of an unremarkable world, warriors were in short supply.

Until I came along.

I guess beggars really can't be choosers.

After nights of broken sleep, I made my mistake. Jack had been back on his ship for three days, and the dreams had been relentless. I'd ended up chugging half my supply of vodka because he hadn't been there to unknowingly shame me into drinking less. I felt queasy and could barely keep my eyelids open, let alone concentrate on basic safety procedures. If I'd had an ounce of sense, I would have reported sick and taken the day off; but this was my first proper expedition and I wanted to prove myself. I didn't want to scupper my career because of some insomnia, a few drinks, and a headful of superstitious bad vibes. Instead, I took point on the excavation—and in a distracted, hungover instant, having pulled off one of my gloves with my teeth to better extract a tissue from the pocket of my parka, stupidly laid my bare hand on the surface of the weapon.

Vogel had been worried we might contaminate our find with earthly bacteria; I don't think it ever occurred to him that the contamination might also flow in the opposite direction.

•

When I finished telling the story, Mouse said, "What happened then?"

"I woke up in the medical tent." I tugged at the neck ring of my pressure suit, trying to get some more air between the fabric and my skin. With the helmet off, the air circulation wouldn't work, and I was getting uncomfortably warm. "I had a fever and my skin had turned grey and thick like rhino hide."

"Jesus."

I raised a hand to touch the smooth skin on my cheek. "Luckily it went back to normal after a couple of hours, when the fever broke, but by that time I was already on the evac shuttle, heading for a quarantine ward."

Mouse glanced at my fingers. "And the grey nails?"

"Yeah, I've no idea what that's all about."

"And you're not contagious at all?"

"Trust me, they did every test they could think of, and they all came back negative. And I mean *every* test. For the first two months, they wouldn't even enter my room without hazmat suits."

"That must have been tough."

"It wasn't fun."

Mouse started to reach out to touch my shoulder, but stopped himself. "How are you now?"

"I'm good."

"Any lingering side effects?"

"You mean apart from the ability to take huge amounts of damage and heal rapidly?"

"You're kidding."

"I'm not." I showed him my unblemished palm. "A couple of days ago, I extinguished a distress flare with that hand. It should have charred everything down to the bone."

"But there isn't even a mark."

"Because it healed."

He frowned, plainly sceptical. "If you say so."

"You don't believe me?"

He looked apologetic. "You have to admit, it sounds crazy."

He had a point. "I didn't ask for this."

His expression softened. "I know." He lowered his voice. "Are you still drinking?"

I thought of the first six months in the camp, and then the year-and-a-half streak of sobriety derailed by Jack's arrival, and felt ashamed. "I try not to."

•

All things pass, and even a ten-hour day eventually grinds to its inevitable conclusion. Twilight fell in shades of purple, as atmospheric dust deepened and scattered the last of the sun's rosy light. Mouse had decided to accompany us. He knew the terrain. The rest of his people would stay behind to defend their supplies. I had wanted a chance to better examine the obelisk at the centre of this circle of petal-shaped buildings, but Mouse cautioned against snipers.

"You're the first ship to land here in months. There will be eyes out there in the desert, trying to decide whether you're a threat or an opportunity."

I replaced my helmet to keep the sand out of my face, and we made our way between two of the petals, retracing our steps from the night before. My shoulders were tense the entire way, expecting the punch of a bullet—or for Jack or Mouse to jerk and pitch face-first into the dirt—but we reached the ship without incident. Anyone observing us through telescopic sights had only to glance at the still-smoking crater a half-mile to the east to know we weren't easy prey. As we walked up the boarding ramp, into the belly of the ship, I turned and raised my middle digits at the surrounding twilit hills.

Janis waited at the top of the ramp, cradling an assault rifle. "We are good, Captain?" She stabbed her chin towards Mouse. "Who's the scrawny white boy?"

"He's with us," Jack said. "He knows the terrain."

Janis raised the gun barrel to the ceiling, resting the stock against her hip. "Okay, then. Are we expecting anybody else?"

"Not tonight." Jack turned to the *Crisis Actor*. "Lock it up and fire the engines. We're going hunting."

The *Crisis Actor* was a creature of vacuum. Flying in atmosphere wasn't one of her specialties, and with all her repairs and asymmetries, a grand piano would have been more aerodynamic. Nevertheless, we took off over the gloaming desert with the hull frame creaking and groaning and the landing motors stirring up a dust storm beneath us.

"This won't be a stealthy approach," Lucien warned as the *Crisis Actor* guided us in. "They will know we're coming."

In the command chair, Jack steepled his fingers. "We have darkness, armour, and superior weaponry on our side. If anybody starts a fracas, we can show them the error of their ways."

A few minutes later, we were approaching the atmospheric processor where it stood on a promontory extending out into the slate grey waters of the planet's shallow, salty ocean. The structure resembled a mile-high tower with a jet engine the size of an oil tanker perched on the top. The engine sucked in air at one end, injected it with seawater, algae, and other compounds, and squirted the resulting mist out the other. Our best guess was that if Vogel was still alive, he was being kept somewhere in the small cluster of shacks and utility buildings at the tower's base.

I must admit that despite my exhaustion at having been awake all through the night, my pulse was racing. I was either terrified or exhilarated, but I had no idea which. I'd had my share of skirmishes with the local thugs in the refugee camp, but I'd never taken part in an actual military operation, whistling down out of the night in a warship like some kind of Valkyrie, accompanied by heavily armed comrades who were capable of seriously fucking up someone's day.

"Thirty seconds," Lucien said.

Siegfried was at my elbow. "Be careful down there, guv."

"Starting to wish you'd stayed on Void's Edge?"

His lenses swivelled up to glare at me. "I'm starting to wish I'd clamped myself to the outer hull of a foam ship and gotten the hell out of Dodge when I had the chance."

"Ten seconds." Lucien grinned over his shoulder. "Brace for landing. This will not be delicate."

CHAPTER FIVE

A SCATTERING OF UNDERVOID ECHOES

The *Crisis Actor* hit the ground hard.

We were down the ramp on wobbling legs and out into the swirling maelstrom of kicked-up dust while her landing struts were still bouncing on their shock absorbers. As before, Siegfried, Lucien, and Janis stayed aboard, prepping for a quick getaway, while Jack, Mouse, the synth, and I deployed in search of Vogel.

Ahead of us, the buildings clustered around the base of the mast were a mix of original, modular units and later structures, mostly improvised from shipping containers and tarpaulins. As soon as our boots crunched dirt, we came under attack. Mouse shouted something indistinct. I saw Jack raise his arm to return fire. Then something snatched me up and dashed me against one of the ship's landing struts. I lay there, stunned. My visor was a fractured spiderweb. I heard the sharp crack of projectile weapons, felt the dull *whump* of a grenade going off.

Trying to see through my damaged faceplate, I fumbled with the controls on my suit's arm. Why hadn't I insisted that Jack show me how to use the inbuilt weaponry?

Movement in my peripheral vision made me look up. A figure stood over me, their silhouette repeated and distorted through the broken glass. I raised my arm, but they slapped it aside.

"Ursula, it's me."

"Jack?"

"Are you okay?"

"Yeah, I think so."

He crouched before me and pulled something small and bronze from my helmet. He held it between finger and thumb to show me. "Armour-piercing round. Lucky for you, that glass is toughened. This almost got through."

"Close call, huh?"

"If that had been a normal visor, this would have blown your head apart."

"I've been shot in the head before."

"Not with anything this powerful. From now on, you stay in the ship. We can't afford to lose you."

"So, you do care?"

"Right now, I'm more concerned with the mission."

He helped me remove the helmet, and I sucked in a lungful of sea air. Below us, waves grumbled sluggishly against the promontory's rocky flank.

I realised the shooting had stopped. "Is it over?"

"Cris used one of her smaller cannons to take down everyone holding a gun, and the rest surrendered."

"I'll bet they did." The shipping containers and modules had fist-sized holes punched through their metal walls. I didn't like to imagine the effect a cannon capable of producing that kind of damage would have had on a human body.

"Is Mouse okay?"

"He took a round to the knee, but it didn't penetrate. He'll be limping for a few days, but he's fine."

"Help me up."

Jack pulled me to my feet. I felt a little unsteady from being thrown backwards, but the cold salt wind helped clear my head.

"Is Vogel alive?"

"They're bringing him out."

"Good." I brushed dust and grit from my suit. "Then, can we please get the fuck off this accursed rock?"

The remaining inhabitants of the atmospheric station led Vogel out into the glare of the *Crisis Actor*'s lights. The old man looked thin and haggard, but still carried himself with defiant dignity. He stood straight-backed as they cut the ties binding his wrists. Mouse went to meet him and accompanied him back to where Jack and I were waiting, at the bottom of the ship's ramp.

The old man looked at us over the top of his dusty spectacles. "Ursula Morrow?"

"Hello, Doctor."

"I confess, I did not expect you to be the one riding to my rescue."

"Life's funny like that."

Beside me, Jack cleared his throat. "Come on, let's get aboard. We can have a big reunion when we're safely in orbit."

He led the way up the ramp. Mouse helped Vogel follow, but I lingered halfway up as the ship began to rise. I watched the atmospheric tower recede below, and then the ramp clunked shut, and I was standing in the hold. The others had continued up, into the crew quarters; only Siegfried was here to greet me.

"I see you messed up your helmet."

"Very funny."

He drew all his appendages into their recesses, giving him the appearance of one of those balls they use to play rugby or American football. "Seriously, guv. I'm glad you're okay. When you went down, I thought you might be done for."

I smiled. "You know I'm tougher than I look, right?"

"You had me worried."

I tapped a gloved finger against his snout. "You worry too much."

He backed off a few centimetres. "One of us has to."

I looked back at the closed ramp. "I feel kind of bad leaving those people back there. They weren't bad, just desperate. We could have left them some food or something."

"Are you going soft on me, guv?"

The deck began to tilt as the *Crisis Actor* angled upwards. "Come on," I told him. "We should go get strapped—"

A shockwave slammed me across the hold. Then I was outside the ship, tumbling in its slipstream. Falling into the night.

•

One instant, the wind was tearing past me like a banshee's roar; the next, I hit the ocean with enough force to drive all the air from my lungs. I went deep and had to fight to try and regain the surface. But without my helmet, ice-cold water flooded in through my neck ring, filling my suit and dragging me down. The water was dark and stung my eyes when I tried to open them. I stopped swimming long enough to tear off my gauntlets and pull at the straps and fastenings. My lungs were ready to explode. Black spots crowded my vision. But then suddenly, I felt something beside me. Siegfried extended a blade and slit the back of my suit. I wriggled free from the neck ring and wrapped my arms around him. He accelerated upwards, dragging me with him, until my head finally broke the surface, and I gulped a long, shuddering breath that dissolved into wracking coughs.

I couldn't see much in the darkness, but Siegfried pulled me through the waves until we reached the rocky shore, and I was able to crawl up onto the shingle and collapse, trying to regain my breath and strength.

Siegfried settled beside me.

The night was still. The pebbles *clicked* and *clacked* as the waves rolled over them.

After a few minutes, I was able to gasp, "Where's the ship? Did it crash?"

"I don't know. I can't see it."

"What the fuck just happened?"

"I'm not sure. My best guess is we were hit by something that blew a hole in the cargo ramp. You and I fell out."

"Shit."

"I'm trying to establish a connection."

I levered myself up into a sitting position. Without my suit, I only wore a T-shirt and a pair of shorts, and both of these were sodden. "You never told me you had an inbuilt communicator."

"Sorry, guv. It just never felt relevant. Nobody else in the camp had one. I wouldn't have been able to talk to anyone. Mentioning it would have been as pointless as that time you explained to me all about your appendix."

"Smartass." The wind chilled me, and everything hurt. I huddled into myself. "Any luck?"

"Not yet."

"Keep trying."

"I will, but we must find you some shelter. Can you stand?"

"I don't know."

"Well, you might be safer on all-fours. These rocks look slippery."

I turned to look at the cliff looming out of the darkness behind us. "Which way?"

Siegfried extended an antenna. "There's a cleft in the rock that way. You should be able to squeeze into it. It's not much, but it will get you out of the wind."

•

Half asleep and half awake, caught between dream and hallucination, I imagined I was back in the hospital, with unfamiliar pains dancing along my nerves as the doctors tried to ascertain what had happened to me, and whether they should try to reverse it or incinerate my body in the nearest furnace, for the protection of everyone else. Nobody wanted to unleash a pandemic of alien origin, and yet they were still curious to see what might happen to me as the infection progressed.

Only, it didn't progress. Somehow, it made peace with my immune system and colonised my cells. As soon as they realised it had made me more resilient and faster healing than anyone could have dreamed possible, the military became interested, and the level of my care increased as noticeably more expensive equipment started to appear in my room, financed by a covert project that hoped to unlock the recipe for a race of super soldiers.

Luckily for the world, the parasite refused to operate outside my body. As soon as a sample was obtained, it crumbled away into dust. They couldn't study it, and they couldn't replicate it. I think some of the military men wanted to cut me up, just to see what happened, but thankfully, cooler heads prevailed. I wasn't contagious, and Jack was lobbying hard to have me released. So, after months of incarceration and study, I was allowed to walk free, just when the Cutters decided to attack the Earth.

Sometimes, fate is a perverse motherfucker.

•

By first light, I had started to run a fever. I was wedged sideways into a fissure in the cliff and couldn't stop shivering. We hadn't dared start a fire for fear of attracting attention, but if I didn't get warm soon, I wasn't going to last much longer.

Siegfried kept up his efforts to contact the *Crisis Actor*.

"If they crashed, we're fucked." I spoke through chattering teeth. "We'll be stuck here."

"Try to save your strength, guv."

"No, I can't stay here. We have to move."

Siegfried's lenses swivelled up to regard the overhanging cliff. "And where do you suggest we go?"

"Anywhere, as long as it's off this fucking beach."

I let him lead me across the slippery stones to a larger gap in the rock face, where a long-vanished stream had cut a steep,

V-shaped gulley through the cliff. Painfully, I hauled myself up it with tired and aching limbs, my hands grasping at the hard rock walls, and sharp stones digging into my bare feet. At the top, the gulley opened out onto the flat, dusty desert terrain that characterised most of the landmass on this miserable rock. The atmospheric station and its barnacle-like encrustation of smaller buildings lay several miles to the north, but even if I could walk that far in my chilled and barefoot state, I feared after last night's raid, that I'd receive a hostile reception if I went to them for help. Instead, I made for a series of stone outcrops that resembled a dragon's exposed vertebrae atop the crest of a hill a mile to the southwest.

It was slow going, and by the time we reached it, my skin felt raw, and my eyes were gritty from the blown sand, but the exertion of the climb had warmed my limbs, my clothes had dried, and I was able to find shelter in the wide cracks between the crags.

"Granite." Siegfried examined the rock. "With an unusually high silicate content."

"Who gives a fuck?" I found a comfortable spot and fell down into the bone-dry sand that had collected between the stones. "As long as I'm not going to get flayed by the next sandstorm and those assholes at the weather station can't see me."

A lens swivelled in my direction. "We're on a strange planet, guv. I think we should find out as much as possible."

"And I think you should keep trying the radio."

"Would our time not be better employed finding a source of fresh water for you? You must be thirsty by now."

"I'm absolutely parched, but we're in the middle of a desert, and my boots are currently lying at the bottom of the sea with the rest of my pressure suit. You and I both know I'm not going to be able to walk far with nothing on my feet."

"But without water, you won't last another day."

"Which is why I think trying to contact the ship is our best, and possibly only, choice. Unless..."

"Unless what?"

"Unless you fly off and find me some water and bring it back here."

"I'd love to." Siegfried's snout dipped. "But I'm running on severely depleted batteries. If I don't recharge soon, I'm going to lose all mobility."

"Well, I guess we're fucked then."

"Yes, guv."

"Unless you can get through to the ship."

"I'll keep trying as long as I have power."

The sunlight was tired and sluggish, but enough filtered through the dust-choked atmosphere to warm the rock against which I leant. My throat felt like a cheese grater, sweat prickled my scalp, and chills wracked my limbs. Field archaeology training had familiarised me with the symptoms of exposure, and spending a drenched night on a cold beach had provided me with most of them. If I had to endure another night in the open, even if camped in the refuge of this petrified dragon's spine, I knew my chances of seeing another dawn were slight, if not entirely non-existent.

"Thank you, and I'll keep you company as long as I can."

"I appreciate that, guv." To save energy, he disengaged his AG unit and sank to the sand. We sat there together, in the silence of the desert. No birds wheeled; no lizards skittered. As a result of the ten-hour day, shadows crawled across the rocks more quickly than I'd have expected on Earth; and with every passing second, my shivering increased, and my thirst grew worse.

I found myself thinking back to the moments Jack and I had snatched on that first voyage out, back when I'd been a student. He'd been the experienced spacer and I had been the naïve young archaeologist with a trowel and a textbook stashed in my luggage. Our connection had been swift and fervent. A shipboard romance with the potential to be so much more. And then like an idiot, preoccupied by thoughts of him, I'd touched the artefact.

Jack had come back to Earth to support me through the hospital stays and endless tests. During the weeks I spent in quarantine, he'd held his hand to the glass that separated us, and then held my hand in person when the doctors loosened the restrictions. And when the Cutters finally hit the solar system, he'd been the one who arranged my escape, even as he ran to rendezvous with his own ship. I quite literally owed him my life, and I'd spent two years waiting in a fetid swamp-side refugee camp in case he found his way out of the warzone. Losing him now, before we'd had a real chance to reconnect, seemed dreadfully unfair.

"Hey, guv?"

"Yeah?"

"I'm picking up something weird."

I sneezed and wiped my nose on my sleeve. "Can you be more specific?"

"It's alien."

"On this planet, we're the aliens. Hell, you and I are different species."

"Yes, but this is different." He turned all his lenses to me. "This is *alien*."

"But it's a signal?"

"I don't know. There's no recognisable structure to it. It's almost as if it's an emanation rather than an attempt at communication."

"Is it something natural, like solar radiation or something?"

"I don't think so. I'm picking up a scattering of undervoid echoes. Whatever this thing is, I'm not sure it exists entirely within our world."

I frowned. "What the fuck does that even mean?"

"It's not a natural phenomenon."

I felt a sudden dread. "Is it the remains of the ship?"

"Not with these readings."

I sneezed again and spat phlegm into the sand. "Well, what is it?"

Siegfried rose into the air. "I told you; I don't know!"

"Then, where is it, in orbit? On the edge of the solar system?"

"No." He extended a telescoping metal antenna. "It's over there, around two hundred yards."

I sighed, and using the surrounding rocks as leverage, hauled myself back to a standing position. Moving carefully and feeling woozy, I made my way to the edge of the outcrop and looked down on the gritty plain at the foot of the hill.

Something lay there.

For a moment, I thought it might be the wreckage of some kind of crashed drone. A heap of stained glass triangles all trying to occupy the same space at the same time. Nothing but points and angles. My eyes hurt just trying to figure out its shape. Then one of the triangle tips twitched, and my stomach turned to ice. There could be no mistake.

It was a Cutter.

CHAPTER SIX

FREUDIAN WEAKNESS
CHAMBERS

The sun shone through the panes of its limbs, throwing unnameable colours onto the sand. And those limbs, like the legs of a spider feeling the quiver of prey in its web, were starting to stir. I could hardly breathe. "What the fuck are we going to do?"

Siegfried hugged the ground beside me. "Personally speaking, I can hit Mach One for seven minutes before I degrade my batteries. That'll get me around seven miles. Further if I use a lower acceleration, less far if I accelerate harder."

"And me?"

"I'd suggest you start running."

"I can't run," I reminded him. "I can barely stand."

He twisted his lenses in the direction of the creature, and then back to me. "I'm sorry, guv."

"Y-you're going to leave me?"

He hesitated for a microsecond. "Of course not."

"You thought about it."

"Wouldn't you?"

Below us, the assemblage of triangles tottered into a swaying, upright stance. I dropped to the ground, hoping the rocks behind would mask my silhouette. How many people had ever seen one of these things and lived to talk about it? The only footage I'd ever viewed of these creatures had ended with either the bloody dismemberment of the camera operator, the explosive disassembly of the recording drone, or the decimation of the whole fucking planet. Jack had spent years fighting these things and only just managed to survive— and he'd had a warship and crew. All I had was a fever and a sarcastic Swiss Army knife.

I tensed my arms, ready to start crawling back to the safety of the outcrop. But then the Cutter extended a leg (or whatever the fuck you want to call it) and paused. There was something wrong with the leg. The tip it was trying to plant in the sand was missing. Somehow, that appendage had been snapped off. For a couple of moments, it swayed uncertainly, and then collapsed like an imploding deckchair.

"Did you see that? It's wounded."

A different limb extended. The Cutter began pulling itself, one laborious metre at a time, in our direction.

"It knows we're here," Siegfried said.

"Then we need to move."

"Where?"

"Back to the atmosphere processor."

"They won't thank us for leading a Cutter to their door."

"Their mast is unmissable. Sooner or later, the creature's going to notice it. And if they've got guns, maybe they can finish it off."

"And maybe they'll finish us off, too."

"One problem at a time." I backed away from the edge of the summit and struggled to my feet. My head and hands felt clammy. I could walk, but not quickly. If we kept up a steady pace, I hoped we could reach the shanty town around the processor's base well ahead of the damaged Cutter. I spared one last look at the creature. It was still dragging itself towards us. "Come on."

We began to descend the far side, and I instantly felt better for having put the bulk of the hill between us and the Cutter.

If it wanted to reach us, it would have to first negotiate that solid geographical obstacle. Ahead, the huge mast of the atmospheric station stood against the desert horizon, a small red warning light winking on the top of its giant turbine.

"You could always race ahead and raise the alarm," I said to Siegfried. "They might be able to send a vehicle to pick me up."

"Or they might assume I'm a combat drone and shoot me on sight, which would leave you alone out here. And frankly, I don't think you'll make it without me."

I raised a hand to try to shield my eyes from the stinging sand being whipped into my face by the wind. He was probably right. Cold sweat prickled my brow. Every trudging step was an effort. If he left me alone and my legs gave out, I'd pitch forward onto the shivering sand and lie there helpless until the monster finally caught up.

The afternoon Siegfried had first drifted into my bar, he seemed like such a fish out of water. He was the only member of his species in the camp. He'd been waiting for others, but they'd never showed. For all he knew, he was the last of his kind. He was lost and grieving and baffled by the antics of the organic intelligences around him. So, I took him in and gave him a purpose and a job because I pitied him. Luckily, he proved remarkably good at his job, and popular with the customers. So good, in fact, that pretty soon I came to rely on him. He was loyal and trustworthy, and I never had to worry about him sampling the stock. By the time he'd been working with me for a couple of months, we were thick as thieves, and even though I gave him a hard time, he had become my closest friend in the camp. Never in my wildest dreams would I have imagined I'd someday depend on him for my survival.

I put one hand out to rest on his carapace. I didn't want to lean my whole weight, because I knew the extra burden would wear out his batteries; I just placed it there for reassurance and to steady myself.

Unfortunately, we'd both forgotten how Cutters worked. Even as we began to think we might outpace the creature, it phased into solidity in front of us, and lashed out with its one good limb.

I stumbled back and landed on my backside. The tip of the singing blade had sliced through my shirt and the skin beneath. Blood ran down my stomach and I pressed my hand to the stinging wound to staunch the flow.

In my head, I could feel the Cutter's delight at having inflicted pain. I could sense its contempt for the soft, squishy, fluid-filled denizens of this universe, and the relish it took in perceiving my fear. And beneath all of that, a terrible, insatiably hungry intelligence.

It reached out, planted its blade in the sand between my feet, and heaved itself forward. I tried to scramble backwards, but I still had one bloody hand clamped to my midriff to stop my intestines spilling out. In horror, I watched it rear above me, its triangular limb like a dagger made of cathedral glass, ready to strike. Even this close, it was hard to make out its precise shape; pieces of it seemed superimposed on others, as if a multitude of coloured knives were all trying to simultaneously occupy the same space. There were lines and circles and coloured squares buried deep within its structure in ways that hurt the eye. I could feel its exultation in my fear and its anticipation of the kill.

And then Siegfried hit it like a missile. The collision knocked the Cutter sideways with a hideous screech. I kicked backwards, my heels clawing at the dirt, desperate to put some distance between myself and the creature. I saw Siegfried bounce and spin end over end across the ground, broken antenna and appendages flying off with each impact, until he came to rest like a punctured football. Then, for a few seconds, the only sound was the desert wind and the skitter of sand. I lay on my back gasping for air. My heart thumped. Blood oozed between my fingers.

The Cutter quivered like a maimed spider.

It wasn't dead.

Transfixed, I watched it raise its thin, triangular limb as if questing for my scent. Three or four metres separated us, but I couldn't run anymore. Fever, exhaustion, and injury had sucked away the last of my strength—and now the nemesis I'd spent the last two years fleeing had finally overtaken me.

As the Cutter levered itself into an upright position, anger sluiced through me. I hadn't asked for any of this. All I'd wanted was to dig up bones and write papers on long-vanished cultures.

The angular creature dragged itself a step closer and I swore at it. Why did it have to come now? Why did the end of the world have to happen on my watch? Somehow, I sensed its sick amusement. I could protest and lament as much I liked; it knew my anger was simply a mask for my despair.

The blade slashed at my legs, but I rolled aside, ignoring the pain in my gut. The creature shuffled closer and raised its leg again. This time I wouldn't be able to get out of the way. I opened my mouth in a defiant scream but felt only twisted delight in response. It wanted me to know its satisfaction at the culmination of a successful hunt. But before its blade could strike, a crimson beam pierced the beast through its centre of mass, and it flailed. I looked up and let forth a shriek. Finally, the *Crisis Actor* had come for us!

The ship put down in a vortex of blown sand and grit, and Jack came running. He wore an armoured suit and carried a large, industrial-looking pulse rifle. Mouse followed and knelt beside me, tending to my injuries while Jack emptied shot after shot into the twitching Cutter until it finally lay shattered and still. When he was sure it was deceased, he backed away from the riddled, smoking corpse and joined Mouse.

"Hey," he said.

I wanted to hug him. "I thought you were dead."

"We would have come sooner, but with that hole in the stern, we weren't sure we could re-enter the atmosphere without burning up. We had to wait while we stretched some thermal insulation over the damaged section."

"Why didn't you let us know?"

"Our transmitter broke in the explosion. We could hear your friend calling, so we knew you were alive, we just couldn't answer."

"I'm glad you're here now."

He looked at Mouse. "Can she stand?"

Mouse said, "The stomach wound's not as deep as it looks, and it's already closing up. Not too much blood loss. A little time, and she'll be fine."

Between them, they got me upright and I hooked one arm around each of their necks for support.

"Wait," I said. "You have to see if Siegfried's okay."

"Cris is with him now."

"All right."

I let them half-carry me to the ship's infirmary, where Mouse helped me change into a clean gown and put me into bed, beneath crisp, warm sheets. "Stay still." He gave me an aerosol injection. "This will help you sleep while we treat you for exposure to the elements."

I tried to reply but felt a rapid coldness spreading from the point of the injection, numbing everything it touched and, finally, extinguishing all thought.

•

Mouse was beside the bed when I woke. He said, "How are you feeling?"

"Like I've sunk a couple of gins."

"That's the anaesthetic wearing off. How's your stomach feel?"

I rubbed the covers over the place the gash had been. "A slight tightness, but otherwise hunky dory."

"Luckily for you, it wasn't deep. The blade only nicked skin and subcutaneous fat."

"Yeah, I'm tough."

"By the time that sedative took you under, it had already closed, all by itself."

"That's the alien parasite I told you about."

"I know." He made a face. "But it's one thing being told about a miracle healing power, and quite another seeing it for yourself."

"Sorry if I freaked you out."

"You didn't." He smiled ruefully. "But you certainly gave me the ick."

I laughed, and felt my new, rapidly disappearing scar pull. "Jerk."

He was smiling too. At some point, he'd snagged a shower and a set of freshly printed shipboard fatigues.

"Since when did you become a medic?" I asked.

"It's been a rough couple of years." His smile subsided. "A few gunshot wounds. Some malnutrition. We've all had to learn new skills."

"I'm sorry."

"We did what we had to."

"I don't doubt it." I reached out and squeezed his hand. "I guess the question is, what are you going to do now?"

"Oh." He looked around and pointed upwards, towards the bridge. "Captain Jack, he said he'd take us all out of here."

"Your whole expedition?"

"All nine of us. He said he'd drop us someplace we could get passage to the foam ship terminal at Void's Edge."

I settled back against the pillow. "That's good of him."

"He said it was the least he could do after we helped you rescue Vogel."

"How's Siegfried?"

"He's extensively damaged."

"Shit."

"Cris is doing what she can, but I'm afraid it doesn't look good."

"I wouldn't have made it without him."

"I'm sure she's doing all she can."

I lay back and closed my eyes. For the past couple of years, Siegfried had always just been *there*. In the chaos of the camp, with all its comings and goings, he'd been a constant, reassuring presence. The only person I could rely on, and the only company on which I could depend.

"She'd better be."

We were silent for a while. Eventually, Mouse said, "You all risked everything to get Doctor Vogel on board. Is he really that important?"

I had to shrug. "I honestly don't know. Maybe he is or maybe he isn't. We're kind of grasping at straws here."

Mouse sucked his upper lip. "Yeah, I get that."

I closed my eyes. Humans had been speculating about the possibility of alien invasion since Wells published *The War of the Worlds* in the dying days of the nineteenth century. Whole genres of film and literature had been devoted to the notion. Some writers thought having a common enemy might unite us as a species; others used the idea to comment on our own past imperialist failings. We thought we could fight them; we thought we could beat them. We imagined vulnerable motherships with secret Freudian weakness chambers, which once destroyed would render the invaders' armies impotent. And I guess in them, we saw reflections of the worst aspects of ourselves. Daleks were born from our horror at the unfeeling, mechanised hatred of the Third Reich; *Invasion of the Body Snatchers*, *Alien*, and *The Thing* were about the corruption and betrayal of our own minds and bodies by foreign ideas.

Now, though, I had touched one of their minds. I had experienced the overspill of its hunger and anticipation, and I knew those bastards for what they really were. They weren't a metaphor for communism or the male fear of pregnancy. Instead, they considered hunting us to extinction a *sport*. Theirs wasn't an ideological crusade, nor was it expansionist. They had no interest in our territory or resources; they simply wanted to wallow in our terror and despair, and then glory in the bloody dismemberment of our physical form. For them, the killing was the whole point of the exercise. Their prime directive and most intense hunger.

Well, fuck them.

I'd seen one exterminated before my eyes. It had already been wounded and needed a hit from the *Crisis Actor*'s main laser array and an entire pulse rifle charge to finish it off, but it had *died*, and that was the important thing. They might be from the depths of hell and operate at forty-five degrees to our understanding of physics, but they were living creatures. It didn't matter in however many dimensions they might exist; they could be killed in the three we knew about—and that counted for a lot.

I spent the next day recuperating in bed. In the afternoon, Doctor Vogel came to see me. Like Mouse, he'd washed and availed himself of clean clothes, but the wrinkles of his sun-leathered and wind-scorched face were still darker than the rest of his complexion, as if the wrist-wiped sweat and loam of a dozen worlds and a hundred digs had become permanently ingrained in the depths of those folds.

"I hope I am not intruding?"

"No, please. The others have been off making repairs and flying the ship, and whatever else they get up to. It's nice to have some company."

He pulled up the plastic chair beside the bed, scraping it noisily against the deck. "I just wanted to pop by and thank you for coming to my aid."

"It wasn't exactly my idea."

"I know." He had trimmed, shampooed, and combed his grey-streaked beard; and somebody who knew how to use a pair of tweezers had plucked and tamed his wild eyebrows. I suspected it may have been Mouse. "But you almost died while helping me."

I looked at my gunmetal fingernails. "It wouldn't be the first time."

"No," he conceded. "No, I suppose it wouldn't."

We looked at each other, and then away.

"Look," he said. "I feel I must apologise."

Even in an all-in-one flight suit, he somehow still gave the impression of wearing a tweed three-piece.

I said, "You have nothing to be sorry about. It was my own stupid fault I took off that glove."

"Nevertheless, you were under my supervision and—"

"No." I huffed out a breath. "I fucked up. My thoughts weren't on the job at hand. You can hardly blame yourself for that."

"That's very kind of you to say so." He straightened his cuffs and brushed an imaginary speck of lint from his chest.

"You know they want to take me back to touch it again?"

Above his spectacles, his brows collided like merging thunderstorms. "Yes, the ship's synthetic has been most vocal on the subject."

"Do you think it will work?"

"My dear, I haven't the slightest notion. Her conclusions seem logical, but we're dealing with technology that's historically contiguous with the dinosaurs. Who can say what may or may not happen after such a span?"

I held out my hand. "You see these fingernails?"

He frowned at them, as if peering over a pair of non-existent spectacles. "I am quite aware of the changes the artefact wrought on your physique."

"You kept tabs?"

"You were our guinea pig. I could hardly let such an opportunity slip past without monitoring the results."

"I'm touched. Also, I'm pretty sure accessing private medical records is a crime."

"Not when it potentially concerns the survival of the human race."

"You think the university's ethics committee would see it that way?"

"As they're all dead, I think the argument may be moot."

He had a point.

"Are we away from that hellhole?"

"Far, far away."

I sighed. "On course for the weapon, then?"

For the first time, Vogel looked uncomfortable. He removed his glasses. "Not… *directly*."

I narrowed my eyes. "What do you mean, not directly?"

"First, we have a task to accomplish."

"And that is?"

He looked away. "I was rather hoping the captain might have already briefed you."

"Tell me."

"Circumstances have become unexpectedly complex."

"So?" I raised myself on my elbows. "What is it we have to do?"

He used his finger and thumb to smooth down the ends of his moustache, the way he did when he was agitated. "We are going to have to… *requisition* something that does not belong to us."

I tried to sit up. I was ready to choke him to make him talk faster. "What do we have to steal?"

Finally, he looked me in the eye, and I saw the fear behind his academic bluster. "We are," he whispered hoarsely, "going to have to hijack a foam ship."

CHAPTER SEVEN

THE SPIDERS WAKE

The *Crisis Actor* had done all she could, but explained, "When he rammed the Cutter to save you, he hit it at the speed of sound in a terrestrial atmosphere. The impact basically vaporised everything inside his case."

I looked down at the dented, torn metal casing on the workbench and began to cry. "There's nothing you can do?"

"I wish there was, but it would be easier to reassemble an exploded artillery shell."

"God fucking dammit."

"I'm sorry."

"Are you?"

"Of course, I am." The *Crisis Actor* straightened her tie and contrived to look offended. "He was a fascinatingly intricate machine."

She sounded genuinely regretful, and I suddenly found myself asking, "Are you capable of emotion?"

"Of course I am."

"My friend just died, and all you can do is comment on how he was put together?"

"I meant no disrespect. My comment was intended as an acknowledgement of kinship."

"But did you *feel* it?"

The first AIs hadn't really been AIs at all, more like fancy text predictors. They assembled responses using past results to construct an answer from the most likely pattern of words. These later models, though. I wasn't sure about them. How could you tell what went on within? They could tell you they were alive, but unless you somehow got inside one, how would you ever know if they were truly conscious, or if their emotions were simply algorithmically predicated behavioural responses? I knew Siegfried had been capable of feeling. He hadn't been a human-built AI; he'd been a member of an alien species that had gradually plated over its flesh until only scraps of its original biology remained. In contrast, the *Crisis Actor* had been assembled, piece by piece, in a shipyard on the edge of Saturn's Rings. The components of her mind and body were all synthetic; she had never possessed an organic core—and therefore, could she truly be alive?

"What is it you want to know, Ms Morrow?"

"I guess I want to know if you're real. I mean, for a start, why aren't you more military?" I waved a hand at her tight suit and askew tie. "All this affectation, is that part of your programming?"

The synth looked down at herself and smiled. "My previous captain suggested it as a way to inspire the loyalty of the crew. But that's not what you really want to know, is it?"

"What do you mean?"

"I mean that, the answer to the question you've been carefully skirting around is that yes, I really do love Jack. When he's not there, I grieve his absence. When he smiles," she put a hand to her chest, "I feel filled with helium. All I want is to be with him and to make him happy."

"But how do you know that any of that's real, that it's not just a side effect of the way you're constructed?"

"How do you?"

"I—"

"You have hormones that affect your thinking. Chemical imbalances in the brain. You have associations, learned responses, past relationships, and old traumas that can be used to predict your reaction to any given situation."

"Yes, but I'm human."

The *Crisis Actor* nodded. "And so am I, in every respect that matters. I think, therefore I am, and I feel, therefore I love, hope, fear—" She looked down at the broken casing on the bench and placed a hand against its flattened metal. "—and grieve."

•

We buried Siegfried in the void.

I wrapped his crumpled shell in a green military-issue blanket and tied it with a silk ribbon I had coaxed from the printers. Then I carried him to the airlock and placed him gently on the deck.

The rest of the crew stood in the corridor looking sombre, and I knew this was far from the first time they'd consigned a fallen comrade to the vacuum.

"He wasn't aboard for long," Jack said. "But he sacrificed himself for the success of our mission and the good of all species. We will remember his bravery, and he will be missed."

He touched my elbow and asked if I wanted to say a few words. Everyone looked at me and I felt like shrinking into the deck. "He—he gave his life to save me." I cleared my throat.

"He was a good soldier," Jack murmured.

"No, he wasn't." My face flushed. "He was a barman, and he wouldn't have even been here if it wasn't for me."

Jack put a hand on my shoulder. "You shouldn't blame yourself."

"Who else am I going to blame?"

"Blame the Cutters," Lucien said.

Beside him, Janis gave a curt nod. "None of us would be here if they weren't trying to kill us. The fault is theirs. His blood is on their hands, and we honour him for fighting back against them."

She leant forward and touched the lock controls. The inner door swung shut. The ship played a mournful series of bugle notes over the PA system, and the outer hatch slid aside before the chamber had completely depressurised. The air explosively vented into space and immediately froze, carrying Siegfried's body out towards the stars in an expanding cloud of glittering ice crystals.

I watched that tiny bundle tumble away into eternity and felt something cold and hard settle in my gut. Up until now, I'd been a conscript dragged into a fight I'd considered hopeless. The Cutters had wiped out human colonies; they'd scoured the Earth and butchered millions, but all I'd been able to do was run. But now, if Jack, Vogel, and the *Crisis Actor* were right, I might be able to do something constructive for a change. I wiped my tears on my sleeve. I'd seen a Cutter die, and if this theory about the ancient weapon bore fruit, I might be able to take the fight to the enemy. And it was about fucking time too. They'd killed Siegfried and countless others, and they'd robbed the rest of us of our agency. Falling back before an implacable adversary, we'd been made to feel impotent and no longer in control of our fate, like nothing we did mattered and our demise was inevitable; and that kind of despair eats at your soul. It corrodes your confidence until you're second-guessing every decision you make. If you have a chance to influence the outcome, it doesn't matter how bad things get, at least you have some agency; but the moment you lose that ability to affect your fate, all that's left is helplessness—and I'd been helpless long enough.

I had had it.

Siegfried had been my friend, and now he was gone, and I wanted someone—or *something*—to be held accountable for it. The destruction of a single injured Cutter wasn't enough. I wanted them all to pay for his death, and for the deaths of countless others, human and otherwise. In short, I wanted to kill every last one of the malevolent bastards.

I rounded on Vogel and said, "You mentioned stealing a foam ship. I think it's about time you filled me in on the plan."

Vogel looked around the cluster of faces suddenly regarding him and stroked his beard. "Yes," he said. "Yes, I think you are correct. But first, some background is required."

"Everyone up to the bridge," Jack ordered.

We went up, and the rest of Vogel's students came to join us. Lucien Miles and Janis Egebe took their posts; Mouse and his colleagues stood to one side; and I plonked myself down at an inactive weapons console.

"Before anarchy descended on Los Estragos," Vogel said when we had all quietened down, "we made some interesting discoveries—discoveries that seem to corroborate my theories concerning the nature of the Cretaceous-Tertiary extinction."

He actuated a screen on the bulkhead and used his finger to sketch a crude flower. "This represents the structure on Los Estragos. These outer buildings, or 'petals' if you will, date to slightly before that event. However, the central pillar"—he jabbed the image—"appears to be considerably older. I believe its markings commemorate an even older cataclysm."

Jack said, "The Precursors knew it had happened before?"

"I believe they did. In fact, they seem to have discovered evidence of a cycle of multi-planetary extinctions occurring at intervals of between fifty to two hundred million years." Vogel called up images from other digs. More obelisks. Shards of pottery. Broken clay tablets covered in dense pictograms. "During these events, something scours intelligent life from this corner of the galaxy. Empires fall, whole civilisations vanish from the fossil record, and dominant species are exterminated from their ecosystems."

"*Scheisse*," Lucien muttered. "I am not nearly high enough for this shit."

Vogel ignored the interruption. He raised an arthritic finger. "But some lesser species always survive," he continued.

"And as with our tiny mammalian ancestors after the fall of the dinosaurs, those lesser species are then free to commence their own evolutionary ascendance."

"Starting the cycle all over again?" I asked.

"Precisely."

Janis frowned. "How do the Cutters fit into this?"

"I do not know whether they are the instigators of the cycle." Vogel brought up a picture of a piece of slate, into which alien hands had carved a series of overlapping triangles. "But they certainly appear to be its beneficiaries."

"But they can't be that old," she said. "It doesn't make sense. How could they be around for billions of years without anyone noticing them until it's too late. Surely, someone would see them?"

Vogel smoothed down the ends of his freshly trimmed moustache with a finger and thumb. He said, "On Earth, lions, crocodiles, and other predators know the migratory paths of bison, antelope, and other prey, and they lie quietly in wait. Bandits lurk for days by the sides of remote roads, waiting to ambush passing travellers."

"Yeah?" Janis said. "So?"

Vogel gave a bleak smile. "Suppose you don't want to hunt bison or unwary tourists. Suppose you want to hunt intelligent technological species in space, where there are no roads or migratory paths."

"What are you getting at?"

"If the paths do not exist, you create them, and use them to lay a trap."

"Are you talking about the tramlines?" I asked.

"Imagine a spider's web spun between the stars, with each thread a tramline. The energy saving properties of the tramlines make them irresistible to nascent interstellar civilisations. But every time a ship passes along one, the thread vibrates. And when the number of vibrations reaches a certain threshold—"

"The spiders wake."

"Quite."

"But what about the foam ship?"

Jack stepped forward and called up a holographic star map. Systems and tramlines untouched by the enemy showed in blue; those known to be compromised in red.

"The tactical situation has changed," Jack began, "and so Doctor Vogel and I have agreed that our plan will have to adapt." On cue, two of the blue stars in the display turned red. "The Cutters have continued their advance through the tramline network and unfortunately, Gimlet's Eye now effectively falls behind enemy lines."

Lucien swore in German.

Jack ignored him and continued, "After having discussed the situation, we have come up with an alternate way to reach the weapon." He used his finger to trace a path between two other stars. "This tramline appears unaffected and leads to a small uninhabited system half a light year from Gimlet's Eye."

"Half a light year is still a long way," Janis said.

"It is," Jack agreed. "And unfortunately, there's no tramline between that star and our target."

"The *Crisis Actor* can't cross that kind of distance in real space."

"I am aware of that."

"So, how do you propose we bridge that gap?"

I stood up. "This is where the foam ship comes into play, isn't that right, Doctor?"

Lucien's mouth fell open. "You can't be serious."

Vogel pursed his lips. Before he could answer, Janis made a chopping motion with the edge of her long-fingered hand. "Foam ships are fast," she said, "but they're not faster than light. A crossing like that will still take at least six months."

"I know," Vogel said. "But what other choice do we have? We use the *Crisis Actor*'s jump engines to glide the foam ship along the tramlines until we reach the dwarf star, and then we retire to the hibernation pods while the foam ship crosses to our target world."

No one was happy with the idea, but none of them raised an objection. I could see they didn't want to back out now. They'd come this far; they were tired and bruised, and this mission was all they had left to cling onto. But someone had to ask the difficult question, and I guessed it would have to be me.

"Assuming it's even possible to steal a foam ship," I said, thinking back to my years in the refugee camp, "won't we be depriving another ten thousand people their chance to escape?"

Jack looked uncomfortable. Vogel said, "Only if we fail. If we secure the weapon, we may be able to use it to hold back the Cutters' advance long enough for many tens of additional thousands to escape."

"Well, why can't we just go to the Commonality and ask to borrow one?"

"There are too many desperate people," Jack said. "Including the people in charge. No one will willingly give up their seat for a long shot like this. And no one is going to react kindly if they think we're trying to jump the queue."

"And besides," Vogel cut in, "with so many species contributing to the project, it will take too long to get permission. Everyone suspects everyone else of trying to sneak an advantage, so they would regard any human attempt to take ownership of a foam ship with the deepest suspicion, and we simply lack the time to plead our case. The weapon's almost beyond our reach now. If we hesitate, we may lose this chance altogether."

Janis said, "And if we get caught, we get spaced for treason?"

Jack scratched his ear. "*If* we get caught…"

She shook her head. "Every living thing for a hundred light years wants to get off this spiral arm, and you don't think any of them ever thought of stealing a foam ship? And you don't think the people building them are consequently going to have a security system tighter than a crocodile's ass?"

Jack and Vogel exchanged looks. "Yes," Jack said. "Luckily, thanks to young Mouse here, we might have a guy on the inside."

"It's my brother," Mouse said. "One of the first things I did when I came aboard was ask the *Crisis Actor* to run a search for my family, to see if any of them made it off Earth before the Cutters came. It seems my brother made it as far as Void's Edge, where he pilots supply shuttles. We haven't seen each other in years, but I'm sure I can convince him to help us get aboard one of the ships undetected."

"Then what?" I glanced around. "Because those ships will have security, not to mention crews and construction workers, and I only count fourteen of us here. Fifteen if you include the synth. It's not enough. Not to secure and hold a ship that size."

"Could we contact the navy?" Janis asked. "If we explain what we want—"

"No one," Jack said, "is going to authorise us to steal a refugee ship. Things are tense enough between all the different races and factions. If they found out we were acting with permission, it could split the Commonality. This way, humanity retains plausible deniability. If we get caught stealing the ship, they can say we're a rogue element acting outside the chain of command. Anything else risks jeopardising the entire evacuation effort." He let his hand fall to the scabbard at this belt. "Sooner or later, the Cutters are going to show up here, and when they do, we don't want to be fighting and arguing among ourselves."

"But that leaves us shorthanded," Janis said. "We'll never take the whole ship."

"Not necessarily," I said. And then, when everyone turned to me, I realised I'd spoken aloud.

Jack looked at me. "Do you have a suggestion?"

"Yes, but it's a dumb one. And to be honest, I'm not crazy about it."

"How dumb?"

I massaged the bridge of my nose with finger and thumb. "I think I might know where we can hire some muscle."

CHAPTER EIGHT

THE UNIVERSE, SHE DON'T WORK LIKE THAT

With a day remaining until we reached Void's Edge, I sat in the galley, drank coffee and thought about Siegfried. After the fall of Earth, I'd had no time to mourn my family, friends, and the billions of others who'd died. I'd pushed down the pain, banishing it to the far recesses of my conscious mind, until it became only a distant thrum, like the cosmic background radiation—always there, but possible to ignore. You might call that denial, but I called it survival. I had to keep moving forward. I had to stay alive long enough for Jack to find me, and somehow, I'd done it, but I'd let the shock numb me, and I'd stayed numb. For a moment, I wondered if the strange healing abilities imparted to me by the alien infection extended to repairing emotional as well as physical damage. If the *Crisis Actor* was right and the weapon had optimised me for combat, I could see how the mental resilience to keep functioning in the face of overwhelming defeat might be a desirable trait, and one it may have instilled in me. But then, when I thought about Siegfried, the pain I'd buried threatened to burst forth, and I had to squeeze it hard to keep it contained, the same way I'd wrapped my grip around that emergency flare to stop it igniting my bar. Only now, I wasn't holding a flare; I had the pure white energy of a star cupped in my hands, the all-consuming fury of a supernova, and it was all I could do to keep hold of it.

Janis joined me at the table. As always, she wore cargo pants and a tank top, and had the red cotton scarf hanging loosely around her neck. In the harsh overhead strip lights, the skin on the top of her head gleamed through the stubble on her scalp. She seemed to be the only other member of the crew who used the galley between mealtimes, and like me she came here for the coffee.

"I am sorry about your little friend," she said. "He died bravely, and you honoured him."

"I'd rather he hadn't died at all."

"If he had not, you would not be here now to grieve him, and our mission would have ended in failure."

"But it's all so fucking senseless."

"It's just the way of things, child." She held her cup between two sets of thin fingers. "Nobody ever wants wars, famines, or disasters. All through history, all everybody wants to do is sit home in peace, raise babies, tend their hearth, and cook their stew, but wars, famines, and disasters inevitably come along to burn their homes, kill their babies, and upset their potjies."

I looked down at my hands. "Why can't we just be left in peace?"

Janis smiled sadly. "Because the universe, she don't work like that."

"The universe is a she?"

"Did you ever have any doubt?"

I considered this for a moment and shrugged. "I have to say, when I was in the camp and I dreamed about stealing a foam ship, I always imagined I'd be going in the opposite direction. You know, getting the fuck out of Dodge."

"Dodge?"

"It's an American expression."

Janis rubbed a hand over her buzz cut. "If we are successful, we may help a whole lot more people out of Dodge."

"And if we're not?"

She laughed. "Child, we won't be around to worry about it."

•

Jack invited me to the bridge for our emergence from the tramline. One moment, the screens were full of hyperspatial chaos: the next, the bejewelled black velvet of conventional space. On one side, a beach made up of the familiar, bejewelled stars of the Orion Arm; on the other, an abyssal void six thousand light years wide, across which, the next spiral arm stood like a distant cliff on the far side of a wine dark sea. We were way out on the edge of the system, so Void's Edge wasn't visible, and its sun showed as little more than a bright star.

"We're being hailed by the blockade," the *Crisis Actor* reported.

"Transmit our clearance codes," Jack replied. "Let them know we're friendly."

I peered at the screen but couldn't see any sign of a blockade. Jack caught my frown and said, "You won't see them; they're tens of miles away and running silent."

My skin crawled.

The last time I'd arrived here, I had been in the hold of a refugee transport and just grateful to be somewhere safer than the place I'd fled. Now, we were entering the system with the intent to commit an act of desperate piracy. I felt sweat beading in the small of my back. Somewhere out there in the darkness, warships belonging to several species had us firmly in their crosshairs, their crews jittery with nerves and fatigue, ready to make a last stand against Cutters that might emerge at any moment to threaten the evacuation. How many gigatons were currently pointed at me? If they suspected our true purpose, even for a second, our lives would end in the flash of a nuclear fireball and we'd be blown into a dispersing cloud of radioactive atoms before our sluggish neurons even had time to register the fact we were under attack.

"Codes accepted."

Janis and Lucien visibly sagged with relief, but Jack just smiled as if he'd never entertained the slightest doubt. He sat back, rested a heavily buckled boot on the opposite knee, adjusted the cutlass at this belt, and said, "Let's get to the camp."

"Plotting now," Janis said, and swiped a course solution over to Lucien's screen. He checked it and gave a solemn nod, then started tapping the controls before him, setting up a series of burns that would take us inwards, towards the distant sun and the planet that circled it.

"How long?" Jack asked.

"Two days at maximum acceleration."

"All right, then. I guess that gives us plenty of time to strip down and clean our guns and armour and go over the plan until we all know it by heart."

I said, "We can't get there any faster?"

"Not unless you can change the rules of orbital mechanics."

"Well, in that case," I slapped my palms against my thighs and got to my feet, "I guess you finally have time to show me how the weapons on those suits work."

We went down to the *Crisis Actor*'s hold, where a little-used section of the storage area had been set aside as a firing range. A row of old steel supply cases stood at one end, with circular targets painted onto them.

"All right," Jack said. "Pay close attention. Your suit is in training mode, so you won't be firing live ammo." He took my hand and touched my forearm. "You have a gauss pistol built into the casing here."

"I don't know what that is."

"It uses a line of magnets to accelerate projectiles."

"Like a rail gun?"

"Exactly like a rail gun. And because it's all done with magnets, there's no kick-back."

"How do I fire it?"

"You disable the safety feature *here*," he tapped the panel on my forearm, "and point at whatever you want to shoot."

He stepped away and I turned to face the line of targets at the far end of the hold. I raised my arm. "Now what?"

"Clench your fist."

"Okay."

"Now to fire, leave your arm where it is, but snap your wrist downwards."

I followed the instruction. As he'd promised, I felt no recoil, and the only sound was the sharp crack of the slug breaking the sound barrier. I looked towards the target and increased the magnification on my head-up display. The projectiles we were using were paint capsules, and a new purple splodge had appeared to the right of the bullseye.

"Excellent," Jack said. He seemed impressed, but I was just pleased I hadn't missed the board entirely.

"Can I keep practising?"

"By all means. Let's see how you get along. If you get comfortable with it then perhaps later, we can move on to some of the heavier ordnance."

"Heavier?"

"Micro-missiles and the like."

"Now you're talking."

He grinned and for an instant, in the face of the weary, field-promoted captain, I thought I caught a twinkle of the mischievous lieutenant who'd first attracted me. Back then, his responsibilities had weighed lightly upon him. He'd had a wicked smile and an easy laugh. But of course, that had been before the war, and war changes everyone. On the surface, he projected the same confidence, but since he'd walked back into my life, I'd noticed he even spoke differently. When the mask slipped, his tone took on the awkward formality of a leader who knew that at any moment, he might have to ask the people under his command to sacrifice themselves. I shuddered to think how many times he'd knowingly sent members of his crew to their deaths because he'd had no other choice. That kind of responsibility had to wear at a person and erode their soul. Make them want to be an officer worthy of that sacrifice.

"Get the hang of the pistol first," he said, "and then we will see if you're ready."

I smiled and squeezed off another two shots in quick succession. "Yessir."

CHAPTER NINE

LET'S STOP FLIRTING

We passed through the camp gates. Jack and the *Crisis Actor* had insisted on coming with me for back-up. Jack had ditched his naval uniform for a plain grey sweater and a thick black coat that reached down to the tops of his heavily buckled boots, and the *Crisis Actor* had reluctantly ditched her blue suit for a burgundy hoodie and khaki cargo pants. Even though I was probably tougher and faster at healing than either of them, they were better fighters, and I appreciated having them at my side. The last time I'd been here, someone had shot me in the head. I still didn't know whether it had been someone working for Pascal, standing guard over his little stash of priceless relics, or whether the whole situation had been a ruse by Polhaus to get rid of me. Either way, there was going to be at least one person unhappy to see me back.

We walked down the rutted track that formed the camp's main street, and I could almost believe I'd never been away. The place still stank of stagnant marsh and burning garbage; children of many species ran squealing between the tents; adults sat around staring into the flames with eyes and equivalent sensory organs dulled by shock and uncertainty. In most cases, they'd lost everything except their lives. It didn't matter who they'd been before everything went to hell, now we were all just survivors and refugees trying to hold on until it became our turn to escape on one of the foam ships. I felt bad for every one of them; but at the same time, I couldn't help but view them with the detached eye of an archaeologist, and marvel at the experience of being present as a civilisation unravelled and an empire fell.

Until the war, Void's Edge had been a curiosity. It had life, but not intelligence. It was connected to the tramline network, but you couldn't go on to anywhere else from there. It had no logistical or strategic importance; it was simply the place the road ended. Human explorers had first come here about ten years ago, in the early days of the expansion. They had simply been trying to see how far they could get, as if travelling further than anyone else might bestow some kind of cachet upon them. A few of them stayed, perhaps expecting the farthest stop on the network (at least, in this direction) to become something of a landmark. They weren't expecting to be swamped with refugees from many species, and their tiny settlement to become the start of what would eventually turn into a sprawling transit camp and shanty town.

Above us, foam ships lay at anchor, each in a different stage of construction. Tugs shunted huge components between girders; drones manoeuvred sections of hull into place like giant jigsaw pieces; and warships from half a dozen different civilisations patrolled, protecting this lifeline from attack.

According to the *Crisis Actor*, these included the human-built warships *Kardashev Scale* and *Unreliable Narrator*, as well as a corvette belonging to the aquatic Krylle; a collection of spheres that housed a distributed bio-machine intelligence from somewhere in the direction of the galactic core; and a heavy cruiser belonging to the Hegemony hive mind. Ordinarily, none of us would have been natural allies, but faced with the absolute antithesis of life represented by the Cutters, we had little choice but to band together for mutual survival.

Once through the gates, my first instinct was to head for my bar—except I knew it wasn't my bar anymore. Polhaus would have taken possession the moment he knew I was gone. And besides, I didn't want to see the place without Siegfried in it. If we were going to pull this off, I had to remain calm and composed. So instead, we picked our way through the encampment to Polhaus's tented casino.

The guy with the broom was out front, as usual. He stopped sweeping when he saw me walking towards him. "Hey, Morrow, I heard you were dead."

"Happy to disappoint, Gus."

"Who're your friends?"

"Business associates. We have a proposal we want to put to your boss."

Gus leant on his broom and eyed us warily. "I hope it ain't the kind of proposal that involves folks getting shot."

"Hey, I didn't come here looking for trouble. As I said, I have something I want to put to him. And it's not like he had anything to do with me getting shot, right?"

The knuckles holding the broom whitened. "I don't know about any of that."

I smiled. "Of course, you don't. I'm sure it was one of Pascal's boys. You remember Pascal? The guy who couldn't afford to pay his gambling debts but could somehow afford an armed security guard?"

"Look—"

"And anyway, Polhaus wouldn't have been crouching in a tent in the dark, that's not his style. If he'd been behind it, he'd have got someone he trusted to do it, wouldn't he?"

Gus glanced to the side, as if seeking a way out. "That's bullshit."

"Of course, it is, because Polhaus wouldn't have sent a dumbass to do his dirty work, and the person who shot me wasn't very bright. They panicked as soon as the gun went off and didn't stop to see if I was dead."

The colour drained from Gus's face. "B-but you had a big fucking hole in your forehead."

His mouth snapped shut and I watched his eyes widen as he realised he'd just confessed. I crossed my arms and shook my head pityingly. "Oh, Gus. It's a good job you're the bouncer at this casino, because you'd make a piss-poor poker player."

The trouble with big guys like Gus is that they've never had to think their way out of a situation; they've always been able to rely on intimidation or violence to get their own way. So, when outsmarted, their options narrow very quickly.

He brought the broom handle up to his chest, ready to fight. But before he could take a step, the *Crisis Actor*'s arm snapped up and he found himself staring down the tunnel-like barrel of a naval-issue .75 recoilless sidearm.

"Easy, big guy," she said. "We just want to see your boss."

Polhaus chose that moment to appear from the depths of the casino. "Gus, what is the meaning of this?"

Gus swallowed. Without taking his eyes from the gun, he said, "She knows, boss."

"Does she, indeed?" Polhaus smiled with the side of his face that was still capable of smiling. "Greetings, Ursula. As you can imagine, this is an unexpected treat."

"I just bet it is."

"Would you like to step into my office? I can get Gus here to bring us some tea."

"But boss—"

"It is quite all right, Gus, dear. These good people aren't here to hurt me. If they were, I doubt they'd have let *you* stand in their way."

He turned and led us into the shipping container at the rear of the tented structure, bade us sit, then arranged himself on the padded chair behind the salvaged metal desk. "Now, Ursula." He clasped his hands before him. "I assume you are here for reasons other than mere revenge?"

"I am."

His torn left eyebrow twitched. "In that case, please allow me to extend my deepest and most humble apologies for the incident and assure you it was simply a matter of business, and nothing personal."

I made a dismissive hand gesture. "I get it. You wanted my bar, but you didn't want to use up the favour you'd need to call in to get me on a foam ship, just in case you might need that ticket yourself one day."

"One can never be too careful."

"So, Pascal got to pay off his gambling debt by letting you use his tent to set an ambush."

"As I believe I mentioned, I never intended it as a personal matter. You know I have always held you in the highest regard."

"Well," I tapped my forehead, "as you can see, I'm still here."

"So, I gather." Polhaus pursed his crooked lips. "And now that you are here, I have to enquire as to what it is you are here for."

"We need your help to steal something."

"Really?" He absently rubbed at his scar. "And what gives you the impression I'm open to larceny?"

I looked pointedly at the works of art on his office walls. "Let's call it a hunch."

"Point taken." He raised his chin. "In that case, I'm bound to ask what you propose to pilfer, and why you need my help to do it."

I sat back. "We want to hijack a foam ship, and we need you to lend us some henchmen."

Polhaus blinked. "A foam ship?"

"We have a plan to get on board, but we're going to need more people if we're going to take it over. Once it's secured, you and your men can return here, or you can choose to accompany us."

I watched him try to decide whether I was mad. Finally, he asked, "And where *are* you going?"

Jack and I exchanged looks.

"We're taking the foam ship behind enemy lines," Jack told Polhaus. "We think we can access a weapon that will slow the Cutters' advance, allowing more of the people in this camp time to escape."

"Then, why steal one? Surely the navy—"

"There isn't time to run this up the chain of command and wait for them to negotiate with every other government and species involved in the construction. If we hesitate, the weapon will be lost. We only have one shot at this. We go now, or we don't go at all."

"I see." Polhaus spread his palms flat on the desk. "You plan to commit suicide."

"There's a difference between suicide and risking your life for the greater good."

"I suppose you are entitled to your opinion."

"Will you help us?"

Polhaus steepled his fingers. "Let's say I did; what would be in it for me?"

The *Crisis Actor* narrowed her eyes. "You mean, apart from the chance to save some lives and help your fellow humans?"

"Indeed."

The synth looked as if she was going to say more, but Jack held up a hand to forestall her. "Mr Polhaus," he said. "My ship has several military-grade printers that can dispense food, medicines, clothing—almost anything you might need. With one of those, you'd be king of this place."

Polhaus gave a nod. "That is a very generous offer, Captain." He smiled his crooked smile. "And yes, despite your rudimentary disguise, I know exactly who you are."

"Then you accept?"

"I can supply the manpower you would need to take and hold the vessel you require. Lord knows, there are many in this camp who owe me. And yet, if I am to call in those markers, I want something more than a magic cupboard."

I leant forward over the desk. "Then what do you want?"

"I want the foam ship."

"You what?"

He held up a finger. "When you've finished with it, of course."

"Of course." We both knew it was an outrageous demand, but sometimes, you just have to roll the dice. "What the hell, fine. You can have it when we're done with it. Do we have a deal?"

"Let us say we have an understanding."

"You'll supply the people we need?"

"I shall."

"Well then, let's stop flirting." I got to my feet and held out my hand for him to shake. "We've got work to do."

•

That evening, Polhaus's crew began to drift out of the camp in ones and twos. The guards on the gate didn't care; they weren't there to keep people in, but to keep out the Komodo-jackals. They knew everyone needed to get out of the camp occasionally, to get away from the noise and the smell. And so, the refugees were free to wander all they liked, although there was nowhere for them to really go—unless they were stupid enough to think they could survive by themselves in the predator-infested wetlands to the north and east, or the vast expanses of freezing tundra to the south and west.

Jack, the *Crisis Actor*, and I walked out with Polhaus. He insisted on sticking close to us to protect his investment in the project.

"To be honest," I whispered to Jack, "I prefer having him where we can keep an eye on him."

On my other side, the *Crisis Actor* murmured, "Keep your friends close and your enemies closer."

"More Sun Tzu?"

She put her hands in the pockets of her wine-red hoodie and smiled. "Well, duh."

We walked up the track to the civilian port, and around to the back of the supply dock, where Mouse had located and been reunited with his brother.

"Everyone's aboard," Mouse said.

"How many have we got?"

"Including the six of us, we have forty. Some of my expedition chose to stay in the camp. They think they can help the people there. But most of them are still with us."

"Not bad. Are they all armed?"

"Needle guns," Polhaus said. "As instructed, non-lethal and cheap to print, but they'll knock out a human being, and most other species, for two to four hours. Plenty of time to pile the crew in a shuttle and jettison them. You won't have any blood on your hands."

I gave him a cold stare. "We'd better fucking not."

Mouse's brother was tall and heavy-set, with muscles and bruises earned through the constant loading and unloading of cargo. Now, unnerved by the tension and eager to get underway, he cleared his throat.

"We're ready to lift as soon as you're aboard."

I turned to Jack. "Are you ready to be a space pirate?"

"Always."

"Then, let's go."

●

The construction crews on the foam ships worked in shifts. At changeover time, the ground-to-orbit shuttles brought up a crew of fresh labourers and ferried those coming off shift back to their barracks on the ground. Right now, high above the atmosphere, the day workers were awaiting collection, but thanks to Polhaus's needle guns, the night staff who should have been replacing them were currently unconscious in a shipping container at the back of the hangar, and it was our team who were strapping into their worn and grubby couches.

Like most industrial equipment, the shuttle had been built for ruggedness and durability rather than elegance and comfort. In that respect, it had more in common with a troop carrier than an airliner. Black and yellow chevrons outlined the doorways, and there were warning decals on the doors, windows, and overhead lockers in half a dozen languages. Many of these had been partially picked off or otherwise defaced by the work crews, and graffiti had been inked onto, or carved into, the walls and the backs of the seats. The plastic seat covers were cracked and split, and where the yellow polyurethane cushion filling showed through, bored fingers had gouged and half-pulled it out.

Jack, Polhaus, and I took the three seats that had been left for us in the front row. The *Crisis Actor*'s synth went forward to the cabin to observe, and if necessary take control of the shuttle should something unforeseen happen.

Once we were all secure, the pilot called for clearance, and we began to taxi towards the main runway.

"Too late to back out now," I said.

Jack squeezed my hand. "Don't worry, we've got this. Boarding actions and hand-to-hand combat; this is what we do."

"Oh, I'm not worried about that." I eyed the rust on the bulkheads. "I just don't want this old clunker to fall to pieces before we get there."

We reached the end of the taxiway and turned onto the main runway. Beyond the window, I could see the small sun that warmed Void's Edge sitting red and balanced on the horizon. The shuttle's red and green navigation lights strobed across the tarmac. I gripped the arms of my chair and whispered a quick plea to any gods that might be watching over brave and foolhardy travellers.

I tried to push back the trauma of that last flight from Heathrow on that overcrowded transport. Children crying loudly, adults weeping silently. The flooded heart of London wheeling below. Then the first nuclear flashes—theirs or ours, I had no idea—polarising the windows. Shockwaves. People screaming. Fireballs roiling over the city. Engines howling as they fought for altitude…

The shuttle's jet engines kicked in and the acceleration snapped us back in our seats, jerking me back to the present. We rattled along the runway and lurched into the air, clawing for altitude until we were high enough that Mouse's brother could ignite the fusion drive and hurl us into orbit without irradiating the planet's surface.

CHAPTER TEN

WEAPONISED ARCHAEOLOGISTS

We chose a foam ship nearing the end of its construction and almost ready to be loaded with passengers. The interior of its airlock carried the brand-new smells of cooling solder and fused plastic. The exterior walls were the cold of space. Some of the LEDs on the control panel still had their protective film coverings. A foreman awaited us beyond the inner door, clutching a slate filled with duty assignments. When he saw us, his eyes widened and he opened his mouth to ask what the hell was going on, but the *Crisis Actor* put two darts in his neck and their payload of synthetic spider venom took him down. He collapsed with a sigh like a punctured bellows, and we stepped over him without breaking stride.

Jack turned to Polhaus. "Take your people and secure the engineering levels. Mouse, I need your team of archaeologists sweeping the unfinished decks for construction workers. Round them up and get them all in the shuttle—conscious or otherwise—by the time we've taken the bridge. Okay?"

Mouse gripped his needle gun. "Yessir."

"Then go."

We moved forward. Jack and the synth took point, Vogel and I followed behind. Before docking, Jack and I had donned armoured pressure suits smuggled aboard the shuttle in packing crates from the *Crisis Actor*, and I kept my right arm ready to unleash a fusillade of darts should we be discovered. Like the other archaeologists, Vogel had settled for a ballistic vest and a helmet, both taken from the ship's stores, whereas the Crisis *Actor* had decided to keep her burgundy hoodie and cargo pants. Her skin looked as soft and vulnerable as human skin, but it was laced with synthetic spider silk and could easily withstand a volley of small arms fire.

Weird how much of our combat technology we owed to those little eight-legged guys. I wondered how many had escaped the destruction of Earth. I knew rats and roaches had accompanied humanity to the stars in those first jury-rigged starships. Surely over the years, some spiders had stowed away too, in crates and quiet corners of cargo holds. Although whether they existed in sufficient numbers to maintain a breeding population would be anyone's guess. Insects and rodents. I wanted to cry. God, why couldn't we have saved a few tigers or whales as well?

I did a double blink to switch my suit's visor from natural light to infrared, and the world became a glare of primary colours. Vogel was a blob of yellows, reds, and greens; Jack's suit masked much of his heat signature, so he appeared in a kind of hazy purple; and the synth showed in shades of dark blue. In combat stealth mode, she wasn't radiating anything that might trip a sensor. Truth be told, I envied that adaptability. I might be faster at healing than the average human, but my abilities were as nothing compared to those of a ship's synth who could change her thermal signature at will.

We moved forward, hugging the corridor walls. Occasionally, we heard shouts as Polhaus's or Mouse's teams ran into opposition—but we didn't run into company until we were almost at the bridge. We had just entered the last dimly lit vault before the passage that led to the control deck. Row upon row of sleep caskets ascended like bleachers on each side on the central walkway. Thankfully, although the caskets were drawing power, they were empty. The ship was almost complete, but if we'd waited any longer, the crew would have started loading refugees, and I had no desire to drag several thousand sleeping people on a possible suicide mission without their knowledge.

We were midway through this vault when shots came from the hatchway up ahead. I felt a double stab of pain and red warning lights flashed on my suit's head-up display to tell me I'd been hit in the leg and hip, although neither shot had penetrated. Jack and the *Crisis Actor* were already returning fire as they broke to the left. I dragged Vogel to the right and pushed him down behind one of the pods in the first row. The bridge crew had been alerted to our presence and laid an ambush.

The dim lights flickered. I heard bullets ricocheting off metal. Cautiously, I raised my head and laid my right arm across the top of the casket. I caught a glimpse of movement beyond the hatchway and snapped down my wrist, exactly as Jack had shown me. A fusillade of needles whispered from the barrel on my forearm, and I ducked back down.

My heart hammered. Had I hit anyone? An answering clatter of bullets showed at least one person still active behind the hatch.

"We can't afford to get pinned down here," Jack said on the comms channel. "We need to take the ship before they can call for reinforcements."

I took a deep breath and rose again, ready to fire, only to see the *Crisis Actor*'s synthetic body step into the middle of the walkway and unleash what can only be described as a bombardment of corkscrewing micro-missiles from the palms of her hands. Explosions blossomed in the corridor beyond the hatch, bright enough to cause my visor to automatically polarise, and then there was only silence. I got to my feet, trying to slow my ragged breathing, and helped Vogel up. Jack glanced back at us, and I saw he was grinning fiercely inside his helmet. He'd been trained for this and had spent the last two years embroiled in this sort of close quarters combat as he ran his guerrilla war in Sol system. That combination of skill and experience made him a natural space pirate, and I could see he was riding high on the adrenalin.

His smile faded as we stepped through the hatchway to find the remains of two of the security personnel, one human and one otherwise. Both had been torn to pieces and cooked by the exploding missiles, and I was glad I had the suit's helmet to insulate me from the smell of spilled intestines and charred meat.

Over the helmet radio, I heard Jack mutter, "Shit."

I asked, "Are you okay?"

He turned to look at me and I could see his exhilaration decaying into anger. "We shouldn't be killing our own when we should be killing Cutters."

The *Crisis Actor* put a hand on his arm. "I know," she said. "But we knew this was a risk, and we're doing this to save many more people."

"We should have come up with a better plan."

"It's too late to turn back now."

She led us to the end of the corridor and onto the foam ship's bridge. The room was deserted, and surprisingly small for such a large vessel. Almost everything was automated and designed to operate without human supervision for decades at a time. Even the AI monitoring the ship's systems was low-powered and not fully sentient. If an emergency course correction was needed during the crossing, the captain would be thawed enough to steer the craft without leaving his pod. The bridge would only really be used while reconnoitring potentially habitable planets at the far end of the journey.

The *Crisis Actor* extruded a connection cable and plugged into the main console. Her eyes rolled back in her head, then returned to their accustomed position. "Contact established."

"You're in?" Jack said.

"All systems under control."

"The AI didn't give you any trouble?"

She smiled. "It's like a puppy."

"Okay, then. Mouse and Polhaus, how are you doing?"

"All construction workers accounted for," Mouse replied over the radio. "We're loading them into the shuttle now."

The news from Polhaus was just as positive. "We have possession of the engineering decks," he reported. "A few injuries on our team, but all resistance has been dealt with."

I tried not to picture the horrors concealed by that final euphemism as Jack said, "Get your people back to the shuttle and get groundside. We'll be leaving imminently."

•

We kept Polhaus with us as insurance against treachery. We didn't want his people trying to take the foam ship and the *Crisis Actor* for themselves, so we kept their boss close, where we could keep an eye on him. Of course, he didn't see it that way. As far as he was concerned, he was coming with us to make sure we didn't renege on our side of the deal.

While we were warming up the foam ship's engines, the shuttle containing Polhaus's personnel and the sleeping technicians fell away and began its descent back towards the camp. Lucien brought the *Crisis Actor* in from where it had been loitering in a military parking orbit, and clamped it in place beneath the larger vessel's bow, so that it resembled an ugly and misshapen remora clinging to the throat of a ponderous shark. As soon as he was in place, Jack ordered the *Crisis Actor* to fire the foam ship's engines, and we began to move forward.

This wasn't going to be a quick getaway. Luckily, the forcefields the huge ark used to draw power from the quantum foam would prove quite lethal to anyone attempting to board the ship while it was underway. They had been designed that way precisely to discourage pirates and Cutters from interfering with the ship while in flight, and were now protecting us from being boarded as we made our escape.

Jack tried to forestall more kinetic reprisals by contacting the local senior ranking naval officer. The man's name was Bryce, and they had known each other at the academy.

"What the hell do you think you're doing?" Bryce demanded.

"My duty," Jack said. "Please, you have to trust me."

Bryce clenched his jaw. "I can't let you take that ship. Too many people are counting on it to ferry them to safety. If you don't turn around now, they'll court martial all of you, and you'll be lucky if they don't shoot you for treason."

"Come on, Bryce." Jack lowered his voice. "You know as well as I do that the Cutters are going to get here before we can evacuate everyone."

Bryce scowled, the lines on his forehead like cracks in a granite slab. "Losing a foam ship's only going to make that worse."

"Yes." Jack nodded. "Usually, I would agree, but we think we know the location of a Precursor weapon that might make a difference."

"That's what you're going for?"

"We have Doctor Vogel on board. He's an expert on extinctions and Precursor tech, and we've got one of his former students, and she's been infected with the weapon's operating system. If we can secure the device and bring it back here, we can use it to slow the Cutters' advance until everyone's away."

Bryce shook his head. "Then why the hell did you have to steal the ship? For God's sake, you could have taken this information to the Joint Chiefs and obtained clearance."

Jack gave a snort. "You know how much time that would have taken. The weapon's already behind the front lines. If it isn't already lost, our only chance is to go now."

Bryce rubbed his chin. The gold braid on the sleeve of his tunic caught the light. "You *really* think this might work?"

"We're betting all our lives on it."

The commodore sat back in his command chair, gripping the arms. "You know I don't have the authority to authorise this expedition."

"I know."

The man let out a deflating sigh. "But neither do I feel able to stop you without clarification from my superiors."

Jack gave a nod of acknowledgement. "Thanks, Bryce."

"Oh, don't thank me, just come back here with what you've promised—or I'll pull the trigger on you myself."

The officer cut the channel. Jack turned and grinned at me.

"Well," Doctor Vogel said from the back of the room, "I see the old adage is true: sometimes it really *is* better to seek forgiveness than await permission."

•

Even under full thrust, it still took us eight hours to reach the start of the tramline that would take us back into the rest of the network. During that time, we were escorted by naval vessels who, I think, were just keeping an eye on us to make sure our story was true, and we weren't about to light out for the next spiral arm with our prize. We spent the hours combing the ship to check for any stowaways. Jack and the *Crisis Actor* ejected the dead bodies into space, much as we had buried Siegfried, saluting the fallen and invoking the primary deities of each of their respective species.

Polhaus spent the transit in the galley, drinking synthesised negronis and plotting how he was going to make use of the foam ship once we'd finished with it. At one point, I asked him, "Once you'd captured the engineering levels, did you think about sending your men after us, and taking the ship for yourself?"

He looked at me over the rim of his cocktail glass. "A deal is a deal, and a man is only as good as his word."

"Really?"

His scar had begun to pinken. "And besides, even mob-handed, I would not have rated our chances against a naval synthetic and two people in armoured kill suits. Not to mention your weaponised archaeologists."

"So, you did consider it?"

He took a sip and lowered his glass. "In a game of chess, one considers every move, but in the long run, only one of those moves is correct."

"You're playing chess?"

"Always."

"And what are you playing for?"

"Survival."

•

When we reached the start of the tramline, Jack called Lucien. "Are you fixed good and tight?"

The tramline was, of course, invisible. The only way to see it was through the *Crisis Actor*'s instruments. The foam ship, having no undervoid engines, also had no way to detect it.

"All docking clamps locked," the German responded from the warship's bridge. "We are ready to go at your order."

Jack raised an eyebrow at me. "Are you ready to do something foolish?"

We were strapped into a pair of pilots' seats in front of the foam ship's main viewscreen. Because there would be nothing else to do for the next six-and-a-bit months, Vogel, Mouse, and the archaeology students had taken refuge inside the sleep caskets and wouldn't be awoken until we reached our final destination, around Gimlet's Eye. "Of course."

"Okay, Lucien. Hit it."

"Hitting it now, sir."

The *Crisis Actor*'s undervoid engines ramped up, ready to kick her onto the tramline, but the added bulk of the foam ship was going to test them to their absolute limits. Ominous creaking noises came from the hulls of both ships as the warship tried to jump while attached to its massive companion.

"Steady," Jack cautioned, but it was unnecessary. The jump engines didn't have a throttle; they were either on or off, and there was nothing Lucien could do to finesse matters.

"We're picking up a lot of vibration," the pilot reported over the comlink. "I'm worried the landing gear will shear off."

"She'll hold," Jack said. "She's tough."

"Or the engines are going to rip themselves clean off their bearings."

"She'll hold."

"I hope you're right, because—"

The universe seemed to pop like a massive bubble, and we were through—on the far side of the dimensional membrane that separates the Newtonian tidiness of everyday reality from the seething quantum chaos of the void beneath.

"Ladies and gentlemen," Lucien said with a shaky laugh, "we are on the glide."

"Outstanding!" Jack clapped his hands together. "I told you it would work."

"Yessir."

"Well done, Lucien. Your printer privileges are reinstated. Go and make yourself a gummy."

"Thank you, sir. Are you sure?"

"I'd say you've earned it." He turned to me. "And I fancy a whiskey. Care to join me?"

I tore my eyes away from the eye-twisting weirdness of the undervoid and grinned. It wouldn't hurt, just this once. "Make it a tequila, and you've got yourself a deal."

CHAPTER ELEVEN

NATURE VERSUS NURTURE

Jack, Polhaus, and I were back on the foam ship's bridge, discussing the division of any spoils that might result from this mission. Polhaus wanted his pick of any valuables, and a ticket out of this spiral arm, whereas Jack was of the opinion we'd be lucky to escape with our hides intact, and maybe that was enough to hope for.

"Sir," Lucien reported from the *Crisis Actor*, his face looking grave on the wall screen. "I'm reading tramline fluctuations. I think we have an incursion."

I turned to Jack. "What does that mean?"

"It means we have Cutters incoming. I guess something this size was bound to attract their attention."

The ship lurched. Coffee slopped into Lucien's lap. He swore—then cursed again as every light on his console turned red.

Jack said, "What in the bloody hell was that?"

"That's impossible…" Lucien re-checked his readings, seeking confirmation. It was an old habit with starship crews: if in doubt, run a diagnostic.

"We're off the tramway," he said.

Jack frowned. "What did you do?"

"I didn't do anything."

"Well, somebody must have done something." Jack called up some readouts in the corner of the screen and glowered at them. "Ships don't just jump the rails all by themselves."

"I know that, sir." Compared to fighting through the raw maelstrom of the undervoid, travel along the tramlines required a much lower expenditure of energy; deviating from the furrow mid-glide would require a huge amount of additional impetus from the jump engines.

"Then, what happened?"

"There's a Cutter vessel out there. It must have pulled us off course."

"They can do that? Is that even possible?"

"How the fuck would I know?"

"You're the pilot."

"You know as much as I do. This has nothing to do with piloting. Unexplained, impossible phenomena are not my bag."

"Who should I ask?"

Lucien shrugged. "I don't know. A priest, maybe?"

Jack sucked his upper lip and rubbed his eyes the way he did when he was really pissed off. When he spoke, his voice was dangerously quiet. "Assuming we have no priest, can you, as our pilot, suggest a way we might get back on course before they board us?"

"We're in the undervoid," Lucien said. "How am I supposed to navigate when I don't know where we are, and every part of it looks exactly the fucking same as every other part?"

"Ships fly through the undervoid all the time."

"But they know their entry and exit points. It's all calculated in advance. We've been pulled off a tramline. I've no point of reference."

"Can't you get us back to the tramline?"

"How? It's not visible. I can't just roll down the window and look for it."

"What do you suggest?"

Lucien turned to his instruments and began tapping out commands on the interface. "I suggest you get ready for some company," he said, "because here they come."

Polhaus's eyes were wide. "What do we do?"

The ship lurched and juddered.

Surprised, I yelled, "Are we under attack?"

"No." Jack held out a calming hand. "Lucien's stuttering the jump engines; it makes it harder for the bastards to lock onto us."

"Hard, but not impossible?"

"I'm afraid not. We should prepare." He handed Polhaus a sidearm and told him to crouch behind the main instrument console. We both donned our armoured suits and Jack led me to the side wall. "Stand with your back in this corner." He took my shoulders and gently manoeuvred me until I was standing in the angle between the wall and the bulkhead. "That way, they can't phase in behind you and catch you off-guard."

"What are you going to do?"

"I'm going to be doing the same in this corner over here." He backed over to the corresponding corner on the other side of the room. "That way, we can cover each other."

"And the synth?" As far as I knew, she was down in engineering assessing whether the foam ship's motors had been correctly installed for prolonged operation.

"We're not sure why, but the Cutters don't register her as a threat." Jack smiled behind his visor. "Right up until the moment she walks up behind them and blows them to hell. It's one of the few advantages we have."

"What happens if I run out of ammo?"

"Try not to." He tapped his forearm. "Fire small, short bursts, and go for the centre of mass. You've seen how dangerous they can be when they're wounded, so try to aim at the point where all the triangles converge, that's the only way to definitely take one down."

I thought of Siegfried hitting that Cutter at the speed of sound and flinched. He'd hit it a glancing blow, but it had taken cannon fire from the *Crisis Actor* to kill the fucker—and that Cutter had already been injured. The ones we were about to face would presumably be in full health. "Are you sure this dart gun's going to be enough?"

Jack reached over and tapped some controls on my arm. "I've set your gauss gun for armour-piercing rounds. Trust me, you hit one of them smack dab in the middle, and those slugs will do the job."

I swallowed. My breath sounded loud in the confines of the helmet. "How long until they—"

The air shimmered and a Cutter appeared in front of the main viewscreen. The hypnotic maelstrom of the undervoid swirled behind it, inimical to biological life and devoid of sense or order. The effect held me frozen. Again, it was hard to discern its shape. Bits of it kept phasing in and out of reality. Triangular sections existed in weird super positional states, and there were hints of circles, lines, and indescribable colours in the mix. I thought of spiders, and a Kandinsky postcard that I'd tacked inside the door of my college locker. Whatever these things were, they had never been intended to inhabit our dimensions.

Jack broke the spell, bringing up his arm and firing. The creature staggered. A paper-thin, glass-like limb scythed towards me. I raised my arm and fired, watching the needles chew their way through the blade and into the Cutter's body. It spasmed, and crumpled to the floor, writhing. Jack fired a foot-long tungsten harpoon into its centre of mass, and it stopped moving, pinned to the deck plates like a preserved insect in a museum display.

"Are you alright?" he asked.

I nodded, then realised the helmet meant he couldn't see the movement. "Yeah." I tried to control my breathing. My heart felt like it was trying to crawl up my throat. "Yeah, I'm good."

A second Cutter appeared astride the first. Jack drew his cutlass and parried a strike. I raised my arm, hoping to get in a kill shot while the thing was distracted. I snapped my wrist down and the creature squealed. I heard its cry of pain and indignation in my head. Then, in my peripheral vision, I saw Polhaus scrambling on all-fours for the door. He was leaving us to face these things alone.

"Hey—"

The guy reached the hatch and turned apologetically as it opened. Then he gave a surprised grunt. His eyes went wide, and his mouth opened as if trying to give voice to something unspeakable.

"Polhaus!"

The gangster clawed at his midriff as if having a heart attack or some kind of seizure. He let out an agonised moan. The clothing over his stomach stretched to a point, pushed from beneath. Then it split. Something hard and slick sliced its way out through his chest. I raised a protective hand and a few hot drops of blood hit my faceplate. Polhaus's eyes rolled up in his head. He gave a wet, bubbling sob and fell forward, sliding off the crystalline blade of the Cutter that had been standing in the corridor beyond the hatch.

Distracted, I'd assumed my burst had disabled the Cutter in front of me; but I was mistaken. A glinting rainbow blade whispered through the air, and suddenly my hand wasn't there anymore. The gauntlet lay on the deck, and bright red hosed from my severed wrist. I staggered back against the wall. The fight was still going on, but it felt like it was happening somewhere else, and I was viewing it through the wrong end of a telescope. The only things in the foreground were the glove, and the horrible, bloody absence at the end of my arm. All I could hear was the roaring in my ears.

Another limb stabbed out, puncturing my faceplate, but stopping short of piercing the bridge of my nose. The force of it knocked me back against the wall and I slid down onto my ass. I couldn't fire back as my right arm had been incapacitated. But Jack had used his left to fire that harpoon. I raised my left arm and flicked my wrist. Nothing. The safety must still be on. I'd seen Jack turn off the safety override on my right arm and knew how he'd done it, but I no longer had the fingers on my right hand. I felt my grip on events becoming tenuous. The edges of my vision were fading to monochrome. The Cutter stabbed again, slicing into the bulkhead beside my left ear. In desperation, I smacked the control panel against the wall and fired again. The blow must have worked, because this time a metal bolt hissed forth and buried itself in the Cutter. The creature screamed and dropped on top of its dead colleague.

Jack crouched before me, calling my name, but I didn't have the strength to answer. Was I going to bleed out before my magical healing ability managed to staunch the flow? I had no idea, but it didn't seem important. All I felt was an overwhelming exhaustion, and deep pangs of unexpected sadness.

FROM THE LOG OF THE

CRISIS ACTOR

II

The vacuum rippled and a Cutter vessel whispered through the membrane between our reality and the undervoid. Jagged and asymmetrical, with dimensions too fluid and contradictory to accurately measure, it possessed the aspect of an immense snowflake fashioned from the shattered remains of a thousand crystal daggers. I matched its profile against previous encounters and identified it as belonging to a class of hostile we'd tentatively designated as a 'light frigate' for its size and speed. So far, I'd loosely classified eleven types of enemy vessel, ranging from small fighters to the lumbering troop carriers they had employed during the invasion of Earth. In terms of mass and firepower, this one lay approximately midway along the scale.

I disengaged my landing gear and pushed away from the foam ship. I couldn't fight while tethered to something so large. On the bridge, Lucien raised his hands from the controls as he realised I'd taken command.

The frigate detected me the instant I fell out of the foam ship's shadow. Its filigreed blades seemed to convulse, shifting into attack configuration. At the same time, I brought all my offensive and defensive systems online and increased my processing speed to combat-optimal, cranking up my perception of time until the rest of the universe seemed to move at a fraction of its normal rate.

According to Janis, the best way to win a bar fight was to hit first and hit hard. Two years in Sol system had taught me this was also the best way to win against a Cutter.

I fired my main rail guns, sending a cloud of tungsten needles streaking across space at near-relativistic velocity. I had loosed enough to shred a medium-sized asteroid, but the Cutter de-coalesced in the instant before they struck, and they passed straight through the space it had occupied without impact. I'd been anticipating this move and fired another volley as soon as I detected the Cutter beginning to rephase. This second barrage struck it as it rematerialised, ripping through its limbs and central section.

Unfortunately, even as it slipped across the boundary between real space and the undervoid, the Cutter had fired too. A flock of jagged shards shimmered into existence off my port side and ripped through my hull before I had time to do anything more than register their presence.

On the bridge, Lucien swore as alarms sounded, indicating loss of pressure in the cargo hold. My attitude jets and sensor arrays had also taken a hit.

Half-blind and struggling to compensate for the loss of manoeuvrability, I slewed around, bringing my starboard weaponry to bear. I compared the frigate's actions so far to the records of a hundred previous engagements and made a guess at its next moves. I computed dozens of firing solutions and my hull rang as I let loose with everything I had, filling a cone-shaped section of space with a blizzard of flying ordnance.

As anticipated, the Cutter once again dodged the rail guns, but it was moving sluggishly due to the earlier damage I'd inflicted upon it. Its veer to the side put it right in the path of a pair of fast-movers I'd sent in that direction. It saw them coming but was already committed. They caught it in mid-phase and their fusion warheads popped like firecrackers, turning my screen white in a flare of annihilation.

When vision returned, all that was left of the frigate were a few glowing shards, dispersing in an approximately spherical debris shell.

I watched them cool, as my self-repair systems struggled to close the gaps in my hull, and felt the grim satisfaction of having prevailed once again, despite sustaining damage that would have vaporised a less robustly armoured vessel. I didn't know whether Cutter ships were conscious or controlled by their crew. Whatever the answer, they might have had the advantage of being more agile and able to phase away from an attack, but they couldn't think at my speed, and they couldn't absorb as much damage.

As I re-docked with the foam ship, I added an analysis of the doomed Cutter's tactics to the predictive model I had assembled from previous encounters, and then powered-down my weapons for recharge and repair.

The entire exchange had taken a little under ten seconds.

•

Every member of my crew carried more than their fair share of trauma. They had lost everything and witnessed horrors. Now, Jack was leading us on this mission for a chance to make up for all those he'd been unable to save over the past two years, all the ratings he'd ordered to their deaths; Janis Egebe had accepted her pain and transmuted it into anger and ruthlessness; Lucien Miles stumbled from day-to-day in a fog of half-stoned denial; and Ursula Morrow's whole nature had been reshaped by loss and grief. She may have thought her suffering had helped her become stronger but I suspected that like tungsten, that newfound strength contained an essential brittleness that, if pushed beyond tolerance, would quickly shatter.

Even I mourned for Avion.

And yet, maybe all that damage was what enabled us to give ourselves so thoroughly to a mission based on supposition and hope; we had all been brutalised by the universe, and perhaps we assumed things couldn't get any worse. We were like gamblers tossing our last remaining chips into the middle of the table, going all-in because we knew this would be the final hand of the night, that there was nothing left to lose, and only a wild and desperate hope stood between us and ruin.

PART TWO

———

THE FUNDAMENTAL THINGS APPLY

CHAPTER TWELVE

UNCERTAINTY PRINCIPLE

I lapsed in and out of coherence, but Jack managed to keep me more-or-less conscious until he got me to the foam ship's sick bay, where he connected me up to the automatic systems. The *Crisis Actor* appeared—her clothing ripped and the spider-silk skin on her forehead gashed—and she ministered to my injuries, hooking me up to a blood bag and tending to the worst of the damage. I don't know what cocktail of sedatives and mood stabilisers she pumped into me, but after a few minutes, I began to feel more rational, if sleepy.

"Have they gone?"

Jack had been away, checking the rest of the ship, including the hibernation pods, but now he was back. He said, "Cris took out their ship."

"Did we lose anyone?"

"Lucien and Janis are all right. She kept them off his back while he stayed at his post. She'll have a few more scars, but nothing that can't be patched."

"Talking about scars, what about Polhaus?"

"He didn't make it."

"He's dead?"

"I wouldn't grieve too hard; he intended to abandon us to save himself."

"That's all he ever wanted."

"The good news is that, as far as I can tell from looking at them and running diagnostics on their systems, the sleep caskets weren't interfered with."

"The Cutters get off on us being scared. Maybe they simply can't sense humans if their brains aren't thinking?"

Jack looked thoughtful. "That might explain why they don't perceive Cris. Her brain works very differently to ours."

The synth was studying the medical readouts at the foot of my bed. She raised an eyebrow. "Choose your next words with care, husband."

Jack grinned. "All I was going to say was that the Cutters, for whatever reason, only appear to be interested in active, organic intelligence."

"What about Siegfried?" I asked. "The Cutters went after his species in a big way."

"His species started out organic," the *Crisis Actor* said. "They were an aquatic intelligence that gradually replaced their organs and plated over their skin to allow them to operate outside the ocean in which they evolved; but no matter how much they replaced, part of their brain was always alive. They were still an organic intelligence." She patted my foot. "That's why I was unable to save him. I could have replaced his components, but the impact liquefied the biological core of his brain, and there was no way to repair that."

I sighed.

"I think I need to sleep," I said. "These sedatives are kicking my ass."

Jack slapped his knees and stood. "You get some rest." He turned to go. "Lucien has figured out a way to get us back on course. I'll wake you if anything happens."

Adrift in the uncertain, drug-deepened waters between thought and dream, my attention wandered, and I found myself pondering what might become of Polhaus's little gambling empire now he was gone. Several of his lieutenants would probably lay competing claims to his operation; his major rivals and maybe a few ambitious outsiders would also try to muscle in, and things in the camp would be fraught for a time. Even on the brink of extinction, all the little vermin would rip each other apart for a shot at the top job. A line from Milton floated through my head: *Better to reign in Hell than serve in Heaven.*

How much had changed since I'd studied that particular text? I'd been eighteen years old, in my final year of school, when I read it.

At the time, even though I was struggling to deal with the emotional fallout from my mother's death and the pressures of schoolwork and looming exams, the world—the galaxy—seemed filled with endless possibility. Humanity had weathered the Disinformation Wars, established a cooperative relationship with sentient AI, and begun dispersing across the tramline network in a million cobbled-together starships. We'd even started to get a handle on climate change. And so, I had made plans accordingly. I was going to escape the dreary small town where I'd grown up, go away to university in London to study archaeology, and then get out among the stars to see all the strange new worlds and civilisations, uncover Precursor remains, and make a name for myself by publishing books and papers on the subject. At eighteen, the future looked like it was going to be a grand adventure filled with travel and discovery. How could I possibly have been expected at that age to have foreseen that within a few short years, almost everyone left on Earth would be slaughtered by trans-dimensional entities while I joined the last survivors of our species as they tried to flee for the next spiral arm?

I thought back to the weeks I'd spent on that first extrasolar dig, in the days leading up to my mistake with the parasite. I'd spend the long, cool days in the trenches, uncovering and cataloguing finds; the brisk, star-jewelled evenings around the campfire, drinking beer with Mouse and the others; and then spent the long, cold nights tucked snugly in a two-person sleeping bag with Jack. At the time, I thought I was experiencing a romantic, exotic escapade, but now, looking back, those days felt like the last true period of normality in my life.

I'd been a different person back then, before being hardened by my time in the refugee camp. More trusting, even a little ditzy sometimes. Not as dependent on alcohol. Certainly, dreamy enough to touch an alien artefact because I was too busy thinking about my handsome naval lieutenant and the things we were going to do to each other that night. In other words, nothing like the refugee who'd sought solace at the bottom of a bottle, the barkeeper who'd extinguished a distress flare with her bare hands, just to make a point to some delinquent lizards, or the pirate who'd just stolen a foam ship and gone toe-to-toe with a couple of Cutters. The past two years had changed me more than I could ever have imagined possible. Were we really such situational beings, I wondered, that circumstances could so fundamentally alter who we were, or was there some fixed and inviolate core inside each of us, some key traits or values that defined us—maybe even something you might call a soul? Which of the roles I played—scholar, refugee, publican, soldier—was the real one, the real me? Was I simply recapitulating the old nature versus nurture debate, or were we all quantum particles, subject to Heisenberg's uncertainty principle and therefore, aware at all times of our location, doomed to be unable to know the nature of our true selves?

•

Eventually, I fell into a deeper sleep, and when I awoke, I found the *Crisis Actor* and Mouse at my bedside.

"That," Mouse said, probing at the thickening ball of flesh where my hand had already started to regrow itself, and its stubby, embryonic fingers, "is so fucking gross."

"Nevertheless, it reinforces our hypotheses," the *Crisis Actor* replied. "If the parasite's purpose was simply its own survival and propagation, it wouldn't need to expend so much energy to replace an entire hand when you can get by with just one. Internal organs and life-threatening tissue damage are one thing, but it wouldn't bother with something this major unless it needed you fully functional and combat ready."

I tried to look doubtful, but she either didn't notice, or she pretended not to.

"How do you feel?" Mouse asked.

I made a face. "It itches."

He smiled. "Well, try not to scratch, or we'll have to get you one of those cone things dogs wear when they've been to the vet."

"Get absolutely fucked."

He laughed. "Apart from that, are you okay?"

"A little bit groggy."

"That's probably the after-effects of the sedatives. It should wear off soon. Do you want to sit up?"

He handed me the bed's controls and I levered myself up into a sitting position.

"Have I missed anything?"

"Not much. We're back in the undervoid. Jack and the *Crisis Actor*'s bridge crew have been making repairs. Generally, I think we got off lightly."

"They revived you while I was out?"

"They thought you might need a friendly face."

"Yeah, well." I sighed. "They were certainly right about that."

I was glad to see him. Last night, I'd been spiralling. Now, something about his presence grounded me. Even when we change, old friends remind us of who we used to be, and Mouse had been my friend longer than anyone left alive. Just being with him made me feel more connected to reality, and to myself.

"Besides," he said, perching on the edge of the mattress, "I nursed you through so many hangovers back in the day, they figured I'd have mastered my bedside manner by now."

I gave him an affectionate punch to the shoulder. "Idiot."

He laughed. "Those were good times though, weren't they?"

"They were."

"Back when I was your token gay friend."

"Ha! You mean, back when I was *your* token straight?"

"Yeah." He took my hand and squeezed. "Something like that."

"Are you okay, Mouse?"

He pursed his lips. "Seriously, I don't think I would have got through university without you."

"Likewise."

"And if I hadn't, I would have been back on the Earth when—"

"Forget it." I cut him off. "You can't think like that. Trust me. You start down that particular rabbit hole, and you'll be unpacking every decision you ever made, and assigning every random happening responsibility for saving you. I've been doing it myself, ticking off every dumb thing I ever did and saying, 'If not for that…'"

"It's hard not to, especially when you, of all people, showed up to rescue me from Los Estragos."

"I didn't even know you were there. We came for Vogel, and you were an unexpected bonus."

"Or maybe it was fate?"

Behind him, the *Crisis Actor* rolled her eyes and left. I said, "There's no such thing as fate, just our brains trying to impose a narrative on random coincidence."

He grinned. "Says the chosen one."

"What?"

"Oh, come on. The only reason we're doing all this is to help you save the human race."

"I'm just a dipshit who touched something she shouldn't have."

"Or maybe you were supposed to touch it. Maybe that's your destiny."

I shook my head. "Destiny's just a fancy word for narcissism. I just happened to be in the wrong place at the wrong time, thinking about getting laid when I should have been concentrating on my work." I looked down at the pink fleshy stub of my new hand. "And besides, we don't know for a fact that any of this is going to work. The *Crisis Actor* said they tried to expose one of their crew to the machine and they died. Could be I was just lucky, and going back for seconds will kill me too."

"You really believe that?"

"I'm not ruling it out."

"But there's a chance?"

I sighed. "Of course, there's a chance. I wouldn't be here if I didn't think it *might* work. I may be fatalistic, but I'm not suicidal."

"Nah." Mouse shook his head. "Look at what you've survived so far." He started counting off on his fingers. "The destruction of Earth; getting shot in the head; falling out of a starship into the sea; being stalked through the desert by an injured Cutter; hijacking this ship—"

"Stop. I only survived all of that through sheer luck." I raised my regrowing hand. "And because of this parasite."

"Which the weapon gave you because it had chosen you." He grinned. "Ergo, you're the chosen one."

"Fuck's sake, Mouse. Are you not listening?"

"No, I'm not." He disengaged his hand from mine and stood up. "Frankly, I prefer to hope all this means something in the grand scheme of things. I'd rather believe you're fulfilling some kind of special destiny than accept that everything's random and meaningless and we're all going to die."

"Denial?"

"Faith."

"You're not getting religion on me, are you?"

"No, not religion." He grinned sheepishly. "I'm just trying to trust there's some kind of hope and justice left in the universe."

"You're a dreamer."

"I'm not the only one."

•

Lucien cut the jump engines and our conjoined ships tumbled out of the undervoid and into the weak glare of an unnamed sun.

Within seconds, the *Crisis Actor* had detected several well-known pulsars and triangulated their dull heartbeats to determine our position.

"The good news is we're not too far from our target," she said. "Another short tramline hop, and we'll be there."

Mouse made a face. Like me, he didn't relish the idea of another journey through the undervoid so soon after our encounter with the Cutters.

"How short?" Jack asked.

"An hour."

"Is that all?" He tapped his chin, tasting an idea. "So, theoretically, if we forewent the jump and launched the foam ship from our present position, how much additional time would we be adding to our journey?"

"The relative positions of the three stars means that setting off from here would only add seven days to the crossing."

"Seven days?" Lucien chortled. "I thought you were going to say seven *months*!"

"Does that throw off our schedule?" I asked.

"Only by a few days. Hopefully, we can still make it back in time."

We fell silent, thinking about the horror implicit in that statement. If we got back and we were too late…

"So, an extra week added to six months in a sleep pod?" Janis shrugged. She had been cut in several places while defending the *Crisis Actor*'s bridge during the attack, but the synth had glued and patched the worst of her lacerations. "I know I could do with the rest."

"I'm afraid it's not that simple," Jack said. "We may be off the glide, but that does not mean we're entirely in the clear."

"What precisely are you saying?" Lucien asked.

Jack tapped his fingers against the pommel of his cutlass, where it swung from his belt. "I am saying we can't afford to be taken by surprise. We will need to stand watch during the journey."

"All of us?" Mouse asked.

"If I take the first month, Janis and Lucien can take the next two, you and Ursula can take one each, and then I'll take the last, plus the extra week."

Mouse turned worried eyes to me. I jerked a thumb at the synth, who was currently staring up at the ceiling as if entirely uninterested in our conversation. "What about her? Can't she keep watch while we all sleep?"

The *Crisis Actor* lowered her chin and glared at me. "I am *perfectly* capable of taking care of myself without human supervision, but even I can't be in two places at once. If an attack comes, both our ships' bridges will need to be defended. If the foam ship is rendered inoperable, we will be unable to complete our mission, and if I am crippled, we'll be unable to return home."

I said, "I thought you told us the Cutters couldn't detect hibernating minds. If that's true, why don't we all just jump in the pods together, so they can't see us?"

Jack frowned. "At the moment, that's only a theory. It could be they were simply too busy with the rest of us to go after the sleepers. I don't want to take the risk. We've come too far to be caught with our boots off."

"One of us can't fight off an attack singlehanded," Mouse protested.

"You don't have to," Jack told him. "You just have to keep the Cutters occupied until the rest of us can be revived."

Lucien gave a snort. "And in the meantime, while the rest of us are asleep, you get a couple of months of alone time with your wife, I suppose?"

Jack glanced at the synth and smiled. "War is hell."

I looked away. I was getting used to the idea of the two of them being a couple, but that didn't mean I wanted the fact of their relationship thrust in my face. I didn't want to have to watch them flirt.

I said, "Maybe a month alone is just what we all need."

"Speak for yourself," Mouse said.

"You won't be entirely alone," Jack said, looking at me. "You're too important. Cris will be looking out for you and I'll check in every few days. At the first sign of trouble, she'll wake the rest of us."

"Won't that be fun."

•

Jack stood over my tank.

"Comfortable?"

"No." I'd never used a sleep tank before, and to be honest, I wasn't enjoying the experience. The idea of being enclosed in a high-tech coffin while the ship injected me with drugs designed to lower my metabolism and induce an artificial coma filled me with the same lack of enthusiasm I'd feel if someone suggested I took a bath in manure. Unfortunately, the only alternative was to spend the next six months rattling around the foam ship's corridors, and I fancied that idea even less. Standing watch for just the one month, with only the ship for company, would be tedious enough. The idea of six months sounded like hell.

He smiled. "I wouldn't concern yourself. As soon as the sedatives take effect, you'll be under, and you won't know anything about it."

"Will I dream?"

"It's unlikely."

A hypo spray pressed against my upper arm.

"Lucien will wake you when it's your turn to stand watch. I'll be in my own pod then, so I won't see you again until we reach Gimlet's Eye."

The hypo clicked, firing its payload through my skin. A cold sensation began to spread through my extremities.

"I'll see you in six months, then."

He smiled. "See you then."

His face had begun to swim in and out of focus. Numbness pressed down on me like a heavy blanket. I said, "Damn, this stuff works fas—"

CHAPTER THIRTEEN

FUCK THE UNIVERSE

My eyes were open for a couple of seconds before my sluggish awareness registered the fact. I had no sense that time had elapsed, which was strange. Even when you're fast asleep, some part of your brain usually keeps track of the passing hours. It didn't feel right to wake with no sense of how long I'd been under. The missing time was a gap on the tape, a gaping discontinuity in the progress of my life.

Like being dead, I thought, and shivered.

A shadow moved beyond the lid of my pod, but my breath had fogged the Perspex too much to make out details and my arm felt too heavy to wipe it away. Instead, I lay there gathering my wits, which were scattered like sheep across a hillside, and listened to the clunks and beeps of the pod's controls being methodically deactivated.

When the lid eventually hissed open, I found Lucien staring down at me. His hair was longer and more unkempt, and a short, straggly beard darkened the roll of his chin.

"*Guten Morgen*, Frau Morrow."

I blinked up at him. "Hey."

"Take your time," he said. "Your throat will be dry. I'll get you some water."

I heaved myself up into a sitting position and he passed me a disposable plastic beaker.

"How long—?"

"You've been in hibernation for three months." He scratched his belly through his T-shirt. "And now I'm afraid it's your turn to stand watch."

I groaned inwardly. Part of me had been hoping they'd simply neglect to wake me, and I'd skip right ahead to the end of our journey.

I sipped the water, feeling it irrigate my tongue, and put the rest aside. I let him help me from the pod, and stood shivering in my underwear while he fetched me a robe.

"Come," he said. "*Ich mache dir einen Kaffee.*"

"I beg your pardon?"

"I'm sorry." He smiled apologetically. "I've been on my own, and thinking in my native language. It's just taking me a moment to readjust to speaking English."

"Aren't you going to hibernate?"

"There's no rush. I will get you orientated first." He yawned. "And besides, I haven't talked to anyone besides the ship in four weeks."

"What about your fish?"

"They are lousy conversationalists."

He took my elbow in his fleshy hand, supporting me as I tottered towards the galley. When we reached it, I sank gratefully onto a chair while he fixed two mugs of steaming black coffee.

"This will make you feel more human."

"Thank you." I wrapped the fingers of my good hand around the cup, savouring the warmth and the smell, as he began to talk.

Lucien had never seemed the most loquacious of men. He had that whole stoic German thing going on, more comfortable with a wry remark than an extended soliloquy; and yet now he appeared unable to stop himself. I heard about his childhood in Munich and the years he spent working as a pilot on long haul freighters, before being drafted into military service in the wake of the first Cutter attacks. Then two years of terror and loss running a guerrilla campaign in Sol system as the planet Earth fell to the remorseless enemy. It all came pouring out of him in a torrent that convinced me he'd struggled with the loneliness of his watch.

By the time he eventually fell silent, I felt steadier. The after-effects of the hibernation were receding, and the caffeine had begun to kick in.

"Are you done?"

"Thank you, Ursula." His mildly bloodshot eyes looked pathetically grateful. "It has been such a long time since I have spoken to another human being, and I have had so much time to think so many unexpressed thoughts."

"You should have written a journal, to get it all out of your head."

"Would that have worked?"

"It worked for me at university."

He mulled this over. "Yes, maybe that would have helped. It's too late now."

"Come on," I said. "Let's get you tucked in."

We retraced our steps back to the vault, and I helped him ease his heavy frame into a vacant pod.

"You will remember to feed the fish, won't you?"

"Of course."

"*Gute Nacht*, my friend."

"Goodnight, Lucien."

•

An hour later, I was on the bridge, sitting in one of the command chairs with my knees up to my chin. It was late, but I wasn't tired. I guessed I'd slept enough for now. I could feel the chill of the outside void seeping right through the hull and into my bones. The heating unit—like so many of the other systems on this foam ship—hadn't been fully connected up yet. Around me, most of the instrument consoles lay dim and silent. Only a few humming readouts cast their glacial green glow against the walls. I went to blow into my cupped hands in a futile attempt to warm them. The regrowing hand resembled a filigree of gunmetal bone and pink tendon, about the size of a child's. It creeped me out, and I hoped the skin would cover the alien material quickly, so I wouldn't have to keep looking at it. At least now, as I stood watch for four weeks, there would be time for it to finish its regeneration.

Have you ever faced the prospect of a month rattling around a gigantic, empty starship, with only your ex's synthetic wife for company? I couldn't even get drunk to pass the time; I was supposed to be standing watch and would need my wits about me if the Cutters came back.

Maybe I'd have to follow my own advice and get back into the habit of keeping a journal, just as a place to offload the thoughts that kept rattling around in my head like marbles in a tin can. I had kept one as a kid, and for a moment, I fervently hoped that that scrawl-filled notebook would stay forever in my father's attic, safe from prying eyes. Then I remembered everyone on Earth was dead and felt foolish and sad.

I missed life in the camp. It didn't matter how squalid the conditions had been, life among the tents and shacks had been better than freezing my ass off here in the undervoid while staring at monitors and waiting for the Cutters to snip off my remaining limbs. At least back there, I'd been under a clear, wide-open sky, where the air didn't smell of metal and overcooked solder, the heaters worked, and the gravity wasn't dependent on the thrust from a temperamental fusion exhaust. Of course, I was deliberately forgetting the smell of the salt marshes, the frequent food shortages, and the ever-present threat of violence, but I guess the swamp *is* always greener on the other side.

In an attempt to keep warm, I began to tour the ship that would be my personal fiefdom for the next four weeks.

The foam ship was designed to operate under constant thrust from its engine, which meant its internal layout resembled that of a skyscraper. The bridge lay at the top. The mess and the galley were on the deck below, and on the deck below them, the empty crew quarters. I took the ship's spinal elevator down to the first of the hibernation vaults, with its high ceiling and stepped rows of sleep pods. All the ones containing my friends displayed green tell-tales, and one of my daily tasks over the coming month would be to check those lights remained that colour and didn't shade into amber or red. From there, the elevator passed through five additional vaults. It turns out, ten thousand sleep pods take up a lot of space.

I let the elevator carry me lower, through the hydroponics decks, where I briefly paused to sniff the rich, loamy smells of freshly watered soil and sprouting plants. These miniature jungles had been intended to help maintain oxygen levels on the ship during its flight across the void between spiral arms, and also serve as a food source when it reached its destination, providing biomass and nutrients for the food printers while the colonists attempted to cultivate their new world.

Below the food decks, the cargo modules held prefab shelters, autonomous tractors, seed banks, water purifiers, scout drones, and everything else you might need to survey a new world and set up a society on it from scratch. I wandered the aisles between the equipment shelves, wishing I'd had half this stuff back in the camp. I could have done up the bar and set myself up very nicely, and then sold whatever was left for a tidy profit. I spent a few moments admiring a set of screwdrivers. I knew if I took them, I'd never use them, but they looked so solid and *useful* that I had a tough time resisting their allure. In the end, I pocketed a multi-tool that featured a pair of fold-out pliers, a knife blade, a small saw, and at least twenty other widgets. I couldn't identify the function of all of them, but the thing felt satisfyingly heavy in my pocket, and

I felt confident to tackle any maintenance issues that might arise during my watch.

Lower, there were machine shops and laboratories; and then the shuttle hangars that housed the large, robust delta-winged flyers intended to ferry colonists and equipment down from orbit. Some of the corridors down here hadn't been finished. There were panels missing from the walls and light fittings hanging from the ceiling, waiting to be properly installed, and everything had that fresh plastic new-ship smell.

Four more decks remained, but I didn't go any lower. All that was down there were the quantum foam engines. I didn't entirely understand how they worked, but I knew they tapped energy directly from the miniscule fluctuations of space-time, and that felt like exactly the sort of unpredictable, radiation-emitting weirdness I didn't want to happen anywhere near the delicate strands of my DNA. For now, the border between the last of the labs and the first of the engineering decks marked the limit of my world and would do for the next month.

Returning to the crew quarters, I decided to start practising with the kill suit. When the Cutters came back, I wanted to give a better account of myself than I had before. At first, the lack of a right hand hampered me, but once my wrist had regenerated its ability to articulate, I was able to trigger the dart-thrower again.

Every morning that week, I set up a series of virtual targets in the hangar, and then spent hours learning to hit them faster and more efficiently. I found how to work with the suit, rather than against it, using its powered exoskeleton to boost both my strength and the speed at which I could move. I accessed the help files and explored the functions of all the controls Jack hadn't bothered to teach me. I learned how to set up automatic target tracking; how to calibrate the head-up display to distinguish between friendly and hostile combatants; and how to activate the self-repair systems to fix the crack in the visor and patch up all the other damage inflicted during the skirmish with the Cutters.

When I wasn't training, I was studying Vogel's notes on the weapon we sought. The thing looked like a porcelain egg about the size of a large car or maybe a small shipping container. It had no obvious barrel or other aperture, but readings suggested it had disruptive effect on the undervoid, and had been activated when I touched it—after which, my handprint had remained glowing on its surface for several days before fading, something that hadn't happened with the other poor unfortunate who'd tried the same thing. His nervous system had crashed two seconds after making contact with the surface. Vogel's theory was that after injecting me with the parasite (or whatever the fuck you want to call it), the machine had initiated some kind of security protocol that prevented anyone else from using it. I had no idea if that was actually the case, but we were going to risk my life to find out. If the machine disrupted the undervoid, Vogel theorised, it could be used as a weapon against creatures that lived in that medium, disrupting and possibly destroying their minds and bodies. Mounting it on a ship would enable it to be deployed at the site of a Cutter intrusion, delaying or maybe even repelling an attack. Placed in orbit above Void's Edge, it could hypothetically hold the enemy at bay while the evacuation took place, allowing more, and perhaps all, of the refugees to escape.

This all sounded great, but it was based on a shaky tower of assumption, and now my lifespan had become linked to the lifespan of Vogel's theories. If they were proven wrong at any point in the next few days, weeks, or months, I'd be dead. If the machine killed me when I touched it, that would be that. If we hauled the thing back to Void's Edge and it didn't repel the Cutters, we'd be among the first to die in their assault. Either way, the failure mode for this mission was death; and if I had to choose, I guessed having my nervous system instantly switched off by the machine would be far preferable and less painful than being butchered by a Cutter; although, to be honest, neither option appealed. I glanced down at my regenerating hand. If I could somehow get through all this alive and in one piece, I'd be thankful.

For the first time in months, I thought back to the little apartment in London that I'd once called home. Situated on the eighth floor of a redbrick tower block in one of the capital's more deprived areas, it had served as a sanctuary for my final year at university. I'd had a bed, bookshelves, and a hot plate. A large spider plant's leaves cascaded from a clay pot on the windowsill, beyond which I had a view of the rooftops of the East End—many of which belonged to houses that had been abandoned and fallen into disrepair when rising sea levels caused the Thames to start regularly breaching its banks at high tide. If I closed my eyes now, I could run along those bookshelves in my mind's eye, picturing the cracked and faded spines of my favourite novels and textbooks. How long had it been since I'd last read a book? After the fall of Earth, there hadn't been much time for such decadent pursuits, and I missed each and every one of those beloved texts, some of which might only now exist in my memory of them.

As a former academic, the thought was intolerable. As a pragmatist, I knew any attempt to save them would have jeopardised my own life. I barely made it to that last transport at Heathrow. If I'd gone back for those volumes, I'd be as dead as the people who wrote them.

Had there been Roman citizens trapped in Britain who felt this way when their empire collapsed from under them? Had the survivors of Atlantis fled clutching scrolls to their chests, or simply run for the boats?

Human history has always been a series of bottlenecks. Somewhere around one hunded and twenty thousand years ago, the world entered a long glacial period, and the climate became drier. Scarcity reduced the population of modern *Homo sapiens* to a small group of individuals eking a living on a beach on the southern edge of Africa. Every remaining human could trace their lineage back to those shellfish-eaters; and now here we were again, clinging on with our fingernails while the universe did its best to screw us over.

Well, fuck the universe.

If the weapon gave us an edge, we had to take advantage of it. So many times, we'd come close to blinking out of existence, and only endured through luck and stubbornness. We couldn't go the way of Siegfried's people. In order to ensure genetic diversity and maintain a viable breeding stock, we had to ensure every living human had the chance to reach the next spiral arm and establish multiple colonies on multiple worlds. And of course, the same went for every species that had been decimated and displaced by the Cutters and wound up on Void's Edge. The time for competition and strife was over. If any of us were going to overcome the dangers of an unexplored situation and continue to exist in any meaningful sense, we had to create a whole new cooperative, multi-species civilisation among those unknown stars.

•

Despite the books and training, the pace of my life slowed to a complete fucking crawl. Every day, I prowled the length of the ship; I checked in with the *Crisis Actor*; completed my target practice; and walked in the hydroponic gardens with my eyes closed, inhaling deeply and imagining myself back in the woodlands of the Midlands, where I had grown up. In desperation, I dredged the ship's library for every scrap of dramatic or musical entertainment it carried. I inhaled opera, jazz, and heavy rock. I watched classic movies.

In my second week, I discovered an archive of Japanese *Godzilla* films. I'd never seen any of them before, but Christ, I wished we were facing that jovial monster instead of the sharp-edged horrors that had already massacred so many of us. At least with the Big Guy, he was made of flesh and blood, and you were kind of rooting for him, even while he was stomping a city.

It's strange, the thoughts and dreams you experience when you're effectively alone for such a long time. Your mind starts combing back through the washed-up debris of your life, from your childhood fears to the anxieties and embarrassments of your teenage and student years. Songs you haven't remembered in decades start infecting your brain, and sometimes at night, your ears ring with the echoes of the sounds and voices of yesterday. You wake convinced you've heard the ring of the doorbell from your first apartment; the voice of your mother speaking your name. Your mind invents things to fill the emptiness. Being constantly on edge didn't help, either. I started leaving the kill suit next to my bunk and the cabin lights on—and after a fortnight of that, night and day had begun to lose all distinction. I was up, eating cereal at three in the morning, and then asleep at midday.

The archived electronic books passed the time. I scrolled through the *Histories* of Herodotus, Marcus Aurelius' *Meditations*, a couple of trashy murder-mysteries, and a poetry collection by my namesake, Ursula K. Le Guin. With nothing else to do but train, I read one or two books a day, cramming every word into my head like an archaeologist cramming precious, endangered relics into their satchel.

When the *Crisis Actor* asked me why I read so much, I replied, "If the new colonies are going to remember their origins, they'll need to preserve these books, and find people who can reconstruct the old, lost texts the way ancient bards used to memorise and pass on legends and folk tales."

"You're trying to remember all these books for posterity?"

"Why not?" Obviously, some errors and addition inventions would creep into these reassembled texts, but as an archaeologist, I knew that had always been the way of things.

"You can trace the tale of Cinderella back to Ancient Egypt," I said. "And there's evidence some of our folk tales originated

187

six thosand years ago in the Bronze Age, with some dating back to the Upper Palaeolithic." Through the millennia, each generation found their own interpretation, and a travelling storyteller who depended on a good reception for his evening's room and board might alter certain details of his account to better please his audience. "Much has been lost along the way," I conceded, "and much has been added, but still the essence of the old tales survives. Now, our current situation is just another chance for the canon to reinvent itself."

•

I decided to take a stroll through the cargo deck. Something about the place had been nagging at me, but I didn't know what. So, I rode the elevator down and began walking. I wasn't really going anywhere, just mooching along with my hands in my pockets, killing time by reading the labels on the shipping containers. You could walk for hours down there, following the aisles between the stacks. Ten thousand people would need an awful lot of equipment to set up a new colony, and it was all stored here.

As I wandered, I could feel something tugging me towards the far end of the hold, where some cultural relics had been stored. Having already browsed through the manifest, I knew the ship was carrying a couple of paintings from Earth; some data storage chips from Siegfried's home planet; and a variety of icons, statuettes, and other significant objects from worlds belonging to the other species that would have made up its complement of sleepers. Nothing particularly out-of-the-ordinary. Yet, that tugging sensation seemed to get stronger as I approached. My fingernails tingled. Anticipation fluttered in my chest. I had no idea what called to me, but its pull was undeniable.

I ended up standing in front of a large, battered crate with the logo of the Fourth Off-world Museum stamped across it. I undogged the doors and pulled it open, then stood while my eyes adjusted to the darkness within.

Among the carvings and boxes of books it contained, someone had seen fit to include a small sample of Precursor relics. Some were fossilised; others miraculously preserved. I ignored the broken vases and the various tools and utensils, drawn instead to the sceptre that lay at the back of the box.

Fashioned from a smooth, charcoal-coloured metal, the thing measured maybe forty centimetres. It had an obsidian sphere at one end, and a series of hooks spaced seemingly at random around the other. According to the handwritten label attached to it by a thread, it had been dubbed a sceptre because nobody else knew what to call it. Its function was unknown. I picked it up with my good hand, and was surprised to find it weighed much less than I'd expected: more like an aluminium baseball bat than a heavy iron pipe.

Why had this thing been calling to me?

I tapped it with a fingernail, and my finger stuck. The gunmetal nail flowed into the metal of the sceptre, merging with it, and suddenly the object and I were joined. I tried to pull away, but my other half-grown fingers became equally enmeshed. I thought about calling for the *Crisis Actor*, but before I could shout, information started flowing through my hands and into my head.

This wasn't a sceptre; it was a weapon. The hooks were grips for tentacle-like fingers. The sphere emitted sonic frequencies designed to stun or even kill the carnivorous hedgerows some Precursors used to mark the boundaries of their estates. And the thing was old. I mean, *geologically* old. Holding it in my hands, I could feel the winds of eternity blowing through my soul. It had been designed and built while my ancestors were little more than cowering shrews, and yet I had meshed with it. It seemed the grey metal the weapon had used to replace my fingernails acted as an interface of some kind, allowing me to connect with Precursor technology, further supporting the *Crisis Actor*'s theory that the thing wanted me as an operator.

I slowed my breathing and tried my best to relax. There had to be a way to disconnect. A tool like this wouldn't be used every day, so it stood to reason there had to be some method of unplugging. I tried moving and twisting my hands, to no avail. I shook the thing, and tried to replace it in the box, but neither action loosened the bond. Then I remembered the way the thing had been calling to me, pinging my consciousness to let me know it was there. Could there be some kind of mental connection? I took a deep, purposeful breath and looked down at my hands.

Let go.

To my surprise and relief, the grey metal detached from the sceptre and flowed back into place on the ends of my fingers. I placed the sceptre back where I had found it and took the crate back with me to the bridge in case the Cutters attacked again.

My hands were shaking. Getting snared like that had been scary, but it wasn't fear that gripped me now, but the elation of an archaeologist having discovered something no one else knew. I had just interfaced with something hundreds of millions of years old, and it had reacted to a command I'd given it! Perhaps it hadn't understood my language, but it had certainly understood my meaning. And if the ends of my fingers really were plugs that enabled me to operate any piece of Precursor tech, that meant I suddenly had a pretty good idea how I was going to operate this weapon when we reached it. If I could connect with it as easily as I had with the sceptre, then all I'd need to do was concentrate on what I wanted it to do, and the targets I wanted it to engage. It sounded simple in theory, and I hoped the reality would prove as easy. I still had my doubts, but for the first time since we'd set out on this quixotic adventure, I began to feel confident that maybe—just maybe—I could deliver what everyone else expected of me. I could use the Precursor weapon to defend Void's Edge and shield the evacuation from the Cutters.

If we survived long enough to reach the weapon and bring it back.

And if Void's Edge hadn't already been overrun by the time we got there.

CHAPTER FOURTEEN

THE START OF A BEAUTIFUL FRIENDSHIP

"You've been avoiding me," the *Crisis Actor* said.

We were two weeks into my four-week stint on watch. She had found me skulking on one of the hydroponics decks. For a moment, I considered denying it, but I was tired, and I hadn't spoken to another soul in days.

"I'm sorry," I said.

"Something on your mind?"

I shrugged. "Too much time on my hands."

"I find solitude gives one time to reflect."

"Yeah."

She folded her arms. "Come on," she said. "Out with it."

"Out with what?"

"Whatever you're brooding about."

"I think you know what it is."

"This again?"

"I'm afraid so."

"I thought you understood."

"So did I, but I can't shake it."

"Do you want to talk about it?"

"To you?"

She looked around. "I don't see anyone else."

I walked over to one of the plastic benches that the ship's designers had placed at regular intervals between the plants and sat.

"There were others before Jack," I said. "But nothing serious. A few dates with fellow students, and evenings that only ever ended with Mouse and I sitting on the sofa, drinking red wine and subjecting my latest embarrassment of an evening to a forensic dissection."

She came over and perched beside me. "But Jack was different?"

"We didn't get a lot of time together before my infection and the Cutter attack on Earth, but sometimes, you just meet someone and know, against all logic and reason, and with every fibre of your being, that they're the one for you."

"You're talking about love at first sight?"

"I guess so. It's when something deep inside you recognises something behind their eyes. The smell of their hair reminds you of home. Your bodies seem to fit together perfectly. If I could explain it better than that, I'd be writing pop songs."

"I hadn't judged you as a romantic."

"I'm not. Until I met Jack, none of that stuff really made any sense. I kind of assumed that love, like Christmas, was something everybody professed to enjoy but secretly knew was a bit crap. Then I met Jack and I realised; love isn't like that at all. Love is constantly turning around because you want to say something to someone who isn't there; forgetting the rest of the universe when you're gazing into their eyes; catching your breath when you look up and realise they're the most beautiful person you've ever known, and you can't believe how fortunate you are to be with them."

I paused, embarrassed, but the *Crisis Actor* put her hand on my shoulder. "Go on," she said. "Just let it out."

I felt tears prick my eyes. "Jack made me feel safe and he smelled like home." Now I'd started, I found I really needed to say this aloud, to unburden myself and get it all out of my brain.

"We had an instant trust between us. Despite only knowing each other for a few days during the outward voyage and the dig, I knew he'd stay with me once the infection took hold. I knew I could entrust him with the keys to my apartment. He was the partner, the equal, I'd always been searching for."

"And now you're angry because he's in love with me?"

The directness of her statement took me by surprise, but I couldn't stop now. My words just tumbled out. "I thought I was over this. When we were running and fighting for our lives, I had other things to worry about. But now, with all this time on my hands…" I flapped my hands helplessly.

"It's playing on your mind."

"Yes." I wiped my eyes against my sleeve. "On an intellectual level, I understand the horrors the two of you must have been through, and I understand how they led you to develop feelings you mightn't've in other circumstances. I know comrades-in-arms often share an unbreakable bond, so I can't blame either of you for what has happened, but neither can I entirely forgive him."

"You wish he were still with you?"

I shook my head. "I know I've got no claim on him. We were only together for a short time, and for much of that, I was quarantined in hospital. I know I have no right to feel so betrayed. Neither of you has done anything wrong. You're both consenting sentients, and your relationship with him has lasted far longer than mine ever did."

"And yet you still feel betrayed?"

"Not really. More like disappointed."

"In him?"

"In myself." I took a deep breath. "I spent two years waiting for a guy I barely knew, building up our relationship in my mind because it was all I had left to cling onto. When in reality, all we ever had were the early days of a relationship that may or may not have gone anywhere. And then two whole years pass, and he shows up, and he's in love with someone else, and I don't know how to feel."

"Hey," she said. "If you're saying that waiting for him was what kept you going in that dreadful camp, I suppose I can see how it must have been an awful shock to find out about us."

"It was."

"So, why are you telling me now?"

"Because I've been keeping up a tough façade, because I've had to be tough for so long. It's hard to let down the defences."

She nodded, as if she understood. "It's perfectly natural to be disappointed that things didn't work out the way you'd hoped."

"I guess." I threw up my hands. "I don't fucking know. Maybe I'm just angry at myself."

Even as I said the words, I realised their truth. I sat back and exhaled. I felt like I'd been punched in the chest. All this time, I'd been pissed off with myself and I'd been directing that annoyance outwards. For two long years, I'd kept a fist clenched around my heart. Now, with this realisation, it had begun to slacken its grip.

"The idea of your relationship gave you something to live for," the *Crisis Actor* said, "beyond your own immediate survival. To have that taken away would have been a disorientating experience."

"I admit, when he showed up, I thought he'd come for me."

"He had come for you."

"Yes, but not in the way I'd been expecting."

"I'm so sorry."

"It's not your fault." I sniffed. "It's mine. Instead of waiting, I should have just got on a foam ship when my number came up. I'd be on my way to a whole new life by now."

"If you had, we'd never have been able to undertake this mission."

"I wouldn't have known anything about that, though. I'd have been in hibernation for the next few centuries, sleeping away the light years."

We looked at each other.

"We endured so long behind enemy lines, cut-off from aid or escape." The *Crisis Actor* lowered her voice. "I recognise trauma when I see it. You lost your world and your hand, and that's likely to manifest in unpredictable ways."

"I'm sorry," I said. "I thought I was over all this."

"It appears you weren't."

"Sorry."

She smiled. "Stop apologising. Humans are messy and complicated, and you operate on so many contradictory levels all at once. It's one of the things that makes you so frustrating, and so endearing."

I started to cry. She put her arms around me. "It's okay," she said. "You're okay, and it's all going to be all right."

Great sobs heaved through me, dredging the pain from my soul and venting it until I finally shuddered into silence, empty and quivering like a jellyfish washed up on a beach.

"Thank you," I said hoarsely, and I meant it.

The *Crisis Actor* squeezed my shoulder. "You're very welcome. After all, you're part of the crew now."

"I am?"

"Of course, you are. I mean, I wasn't too keen on having you on board in the first place, but it turns out you're okay." She grinned and raised a mischievous eyebrow. "Despite being a jealous bitch."

I snort-laughed. "Says the man-stealer."

"Bunny boiler!"

"Harlot!"

We were both laughing now, and suddenly she wasn't just a synth; she was as vital and full of life as anyone I'd ever known, and I could see why Jack loved her.

"I'm sorry," I said.

"Why are you sorry now?"

"For the way I've been acting."

She waved an airy hand. "You were being human. Who would I be to judge you for that?"

"Nevertheless."

"Forget it." She leant forward conspiratorially. "And please, call me Cris."

Later, wandering the corridors of the foam ship by myself, feeling drained, I wished Jack were awake, so I could apologise to him as well, but there would be no sense in reviving him just to say sorry for my drama. Instead, I was going to concentrate on making the most of my time. I was halfway through my watch, with two weeks left.

I continued watching movies, but now I invited Cris to watch them with me. It was good to have her company. We trawled through her archive, selecting one or two films a night, and I finally fell in love with *Casablanca*. I hadn't seen it since I was a kid, and hadn't really enjoyed it then, but now it had a whole new resonance, and the dialogue fucking *crackled*. After that, we checked out every Humphrey Bogart movie we could find. *The Maltese Falcon* and *The Big Sleep* had that same energy, but I fell asleep during *Chain Lightning*. It couldn't match up to those earlier scripts.

I also continued to read books and practise with the suit; but now, I wasn't trying to distract myself from thinking too much. I had finally let go of the past and come to realise that, as Bogey says in *Casablanca*, the problems of three little people don't amount to a hill of beans in this crazy world.

FROM THE LOG OF THE

CRISIS ACTOR

III

Travelling this close to light speed was a fascinating experience. In the usual run of things, I never amassed more than a tiny percentage of that kind of velocity. If I had to be anywhere fast, I hopped a tramline and slid through the undervoid. Actually moving through the physical universe at 185,000 miles per second made a giddy change, and seemed wholly unsafe.

To distract myself from the possibility of being instantly vaporised by a stray speck of dust hitting the ship at relativistic speed, I read.

Now, as a self-aware AI, I was perfectly capable of uploading an entire library and immediately incorporating it into my store of knowledge. If I wanted to, I could have directly imported the whole of Proust's *À la recherche du temps perdu* in seconds, but Captain Avion had taught me that doing so would mean I missed out on the experience of actually reading and enjoying the text one word at a time. She said it would be the equivalent of having a gourmet meal teleported straight into your stomach; you would have eaten it and taken from it what you needed, but you would not have had the chance to savour it on your palate. So now, following her suggestion, reading books had become an exercise in slowing my brain and engaging with the world the way a human would. It was an act of appreciation, and of communion with the author. It was as different to uploading as standing before an original painting was to buying a postcard in the gift shop.

So, every evening, I settled my synth in the command couch on my bridge and read a book on a handheld pad. My electronic library contained every book ever digitised, so I was spoiled for choice. I had already read Sun Tzu in the original Chinese and Niccolo Machiavelli in Italian, but now, inspired by Ursula's voracious consumption of every book she could find, I began to branch out into less martial topics. I had plenty of time to kill and no need to rest or sleep (although I often lay in Jack's bunk to feel close to him while he was in suspended animation). I decided to read the classics of English literature, but found Dickens and Hardy such hard work that I skipped the rest of their catalogues entirely and moved on to *Frankenstein* by Mary Shelley and *Dracula* by Bram Stoker. In the latter book, one particular quote caught my eye, and I felt a shiver of understanding when the character of Jonathan Harker said, "I am all in a sea of wonders. I doubt; I fear; I think strange things, which I dare not confess to my own soul."

After that, I raced through *The Picture of Dorian Gray* and *Around the World in Eighty Days*, before discovering Sartre and Camus and almost derailing myself in a fugue of French existentialism.

Robinson Crusoe and *Gulliver's Travels* brought me back on track, both offering parallels to my current situation. In some ways, I was a castaway on a strange and dangerous foreign shore, even if that shore happened to be moving just short of the speed of light. Those books led me in turn to *Treasure Island* and *Captain Blood*, and from there to a host of nautical-themed tales that all seemed somehow applicable to our mission.

And that was just in the first week.

After that, I ploughed through the great works of the Russian novelists, took a detour down the mean streets of Chandler and

Hammett, and eventually wound up reading some of the classic science fiction novels of the twentieth century.

One in particular struck a chord. Written when the author was in his late twenties, *Nova* by Samuel R. Delany was set a thousand years in the future. It told the story of the last scion of a rich and powerful dynasty, and his quest to harvest a rare mineral from the core of an imploding sun. His crew were an assembly of storytellers, each one representing a different approach to the art. There were also no clean surfaces in this book. Everything and everyone had been used, over and over again. Even the interiors of the lead character's spaceship were covered in graffiti from former crews.

I felt a thrill of recognition as I turned the pages in my synthetic hands, sitting on my bridge where every console had been scuffed and patched a thousand times. We were also engaged on a quest for which we were ill-equipped, both mentally and physically.

As a warship, I was supposed to be sanguine about the possibility of my own destruction. Yet, since falling in love with Jack, I had come to resent the time our deaths would steal from us. Where once, I had been part of the navy and tasked with protecting the human colonies spread across the tramline network, now my motivations had become more focussed and personal, and less concerned with abstract military notions of loyalty or duty. I would still fight, but now I would be fighting for a future in which Jack and I could live out our days together without the constant existential threat of the Cutters hanging over us like a curse. Having been willing to die in the service of humanity, I had instead found a human for whom I wished to live.

Now that Ursula and I were on better terms, we met up occasionally to walk around the ships and discuss the books we'd been reading and the films we'd watched together.

"It's like we have our own exclusive book club," Ursula said. It was the start of the last week of her watch, and we had been reading Hemingway's *A Moveable Feast*, which detailed his experiences as a young writer in Paris during the 1920s.

"A membership of two."

"Did you ever visit Paris?" she asked.

"No, I never had the chance to walk around on the surface of Earth."

While Ursula thought these encounters were purely social visits, these walks were my way of ensuring she was getting enough exercise, and subtly opening up space for her to talk about her past.

She looked aghast. "They never let you take your synth out to look around?"

"I was built in orbit, at a military installation. They weren't much for tourism."

"But even soldiers get leave."

"That's as maybe, but operating systems? Not so much."

"I'm sorry."

"Why are you sorry?"

"I just wish you'd had the chance to see the place before, you know."

"I have seen the movies you've shown me."

"That's not the same." We were walking through one of the foam ship's massive engineering decks. She put her hands in her pockets and looked up at the ceiling. "For a start, you don't get to experience the weather. That's one of the things I miss most on these walks."

"The weather?"

"The warmth of the sun, and the way it flashes off car windscreens and shop windows. The cool of the evening, when the heat of the day starts to fade and everything smells more intense. Even the rain. The splatter of the first heavy drops against a hot pavement, and then the downpour. The rivulets running in the gutter. People splashing through puddles. The way it runs down your face."

"You're feeling homesick."

"Well, of course I am." She rubbed the back of her neck, under her hair, and sighed. "Sometimes, I just wish everything could go back to the way it was before."

"That's a very natural reaction to upheaval."

"It won't, though, will it?"

"It seems unlikely."

"Maybe it's this loneliness, but I keep finding myself longing to be caught in a crowded space. A railway station, perhaps. Even a supermarket. Just somewhere where there are people going about their days, unconcerned about Cutter attacks and Precursor weapons."

I thought of my desire to carve out some peace for myself and Jack, and said, "I think I understand."

"God," she said, "you missed out on Paris and Edinburgh. Oh, you would have loved Edinburgh. All those winding streets and little passageways."

"I take it you have been there?"

"Several times. It is—it *was*—a remarkable city." She looked down at her feet. "I'd give anything to be there now. Or in Dublin. I was there for a seminar a few years ago. There was this little pub on the river, just by the Samuel Beckett Bridge. It had a red wooden façade, and hanging baskets filled with flowers. I passed it every day on my walk from the hotel to the convention centre, and it always made me smile. Served a good pint, too."

Walking around a human city was just one of a long list of activities that Jack had taken for granted, but which I had never experienced. I had pictorial records of Dublin in my memory. Street plans and potted histories. But none of that could convey the vividness of actually being there and exploring the sights and sounds of the city firsthand. I had never been given the opportunity to do that, and now the chance had gone for good.

Under other circumstances, I might have tried to change the subject, but it was obvious Ursula needed to talk. She'd been avoiding these memories for years, pushing down her heartache at the loss of Earth in order to keep moving forward. But Jack had told me that the trouble with heartache is that it doesn't go away if you cling tightly to its cause. Instead of suppressing it, you have to let it move through you and vent into the ether.

To keep her venting, I asked, "Were there any other cities I should have seen?"

"So very many. Even I didn't get a chance to see them all. New York, Los Angeles, Cairo, Rome, Dubai..."

"But of the ones you did get to visit, which was your favourite?"

"Apart from Paris or Edinburgh?"

"Yes."

Her brow furrowed in thought. "I mean, London was pretty special, especially for an archaeologist. I could go down on the Thames shore in the morning and find clay pipes from Victorian times, old Roman coins, and shards of pottery from the medieval period. It was all there. Two thousand years of history, all jumbled together. The bollards were captured and repurposed French cannons from the Battle of Trafalgar, and some of the fences were made from the frames of old World War Two stretchers. Plus, you could find almost every culture in the world, all rubbing shoulders on the streets and in the buses."

"It sounds hectic."

"Hectic and overwhelming and run-down and glorious."

"I'm sorry you miss it."

"Thank you." She crossed her arms over her chest and hugged herself. "The last time I was there, it wasn't so great."

"I remember. Jack was frantic, trying to find out if you'd got away safely."

"I couldn't have done it without him. He lied to the navy and told them we were married. That's the only reason I got a place on that transport. He saved my life."

"He saved a lot of people." I shrugged. "But never enough, never as many as he wanted."

We walked in silence for a little while, each preoccupied by our own thoughts. At this point, we were about halfway around our circuit of this deck and passing between rows of chunky bulldozers intended for use in the construction of a new colony. Their yellow and black chevrons reminded me of my own striped paintjob and I felt a little pang of kinship for the sturdy machines. They were tools that had been created for a specific purpose, just as I had been.

"I think you're good for him," Ursula said. "I can see the way he looks at you."

"I'm sorry if it makes you uncomfortable."

She gave a flick of her hand. "Hey, come on, we're past that now. I'm just happy he has someone to look after him and make him happy."

I smiled. "I do what I can."

"That's all any of us ever can do."

"What about you, though?"

She stopped walking and turned to me. "I spent two years waiting for a man, letting his absence define me. From now on, I'm going to do things my way."

"That sounds very healthy."

"You think?"

"If a warship can find a new purpose in life, I'm sure you can, too."

We carried on walking, moving away from the bulldozers, into a gap between stacks of shipping crates. Our footsteps echoed on the deck.

Ursula huffed. "There isn't even any wind down here. I miss the wind."

"There was plenty of wind on Los Estragos."

Ursula made a face. "Don't remind me."

"Oh, of course. Siegfried. I'm sorry, I should have thought."

She shook her head. "It's okay."

"Do you want to talk about him?"

"I don't know, what's there to say? He turned up in my bar one day offering to fix the generator and never left. I think he'd been travelling alone and wanted to make a connection with someone. I certainly never saw any others of his kind in the camp. For all I know, he may have been the last of his species."

"You were fond of him?"

"Of course I was. He was good company, and he worked hard."

"I liked him too." I checked my interface with the foam ship's systems. "If it helps, I could turn up the air conditioning. I might be able to generate a moderate breeze."

Ursula smiled. "Thank you, but I don't think it would be the same."

"Maybe another time, then."

We completed our circuit, arriving back at the ship's spinal elevator. I asked, "Which deck should we try next?"

"Dealer's choice."

"Okay, then."

We got in and the little car whispered upwards.

"Do you ever get scared?" Ursula asked.

I thought about the way I had felt whenever Jack had been in harm's way, and said, "Of course I do."

"Me too." She reached out and took my hand, and I was grateful.

Later, as we walked through the foam ship's cold and empty hibernation vaults, I recalled another quote from *Dracula*, and murmured it aloud.

"'How blessed are some people, whose lives have no fears, no dreads; to whom sleep is a blessing that comes nightly, and brings nothing but sweet dreams.'"

CHAPTER FIFTEEN

EVOLUTION'S LOTTERY

After four weeks of regrowth, my right hand had almost regained full functionality. To help rebuild the muscles, I'd been doing some exercises with a therapy ball. Squeezing it, tossing and catching it, bouncing it off the corridor walls like that blond actor in *The Great Escape* (another of the old movies I'd found in the archives when the Bogart ran out). The fingers were still slightly shorter than those on my left, but I'd become used to compensating and now, it almost felt like its old self again. Even the fingernails were the same gunmetal grey, and hard enough to scratch glass.

Training with the kill suit had left me fitter than I'd ever been in my life. I felt toned and capable, and ready to face the future, however brief that future might be.

I'd also dug into Vogel's notes in order to expand my existing knowledge of the Precursor civilisation that had built the relic we sought. Thanks to the discovery of one of their smooth, vaguely aquatic-looking starships buried in the ice of a long-period comet, we knew they utilised the tramway network—although how extensively they'd explored it was a mystery, as were the locations of the worlds on which they had evolved. All we really had were fragments from their colonies and outposts. Even so, we had uncovered a surprising amount of information about them, given the yawning chasm of time between us. Their society appeared to have included several different star-faring cultures, although opinions varied over the exact number, as several recovered specimens suggested they had the technological ability to alter their physical characteristics according to their environment.

Vogel himself had partially deciphered several inscriptions that suggested they either remembered, or had discovered evidence of, an extinction event that had taken place in their distant prehistory, and seemed to be preparing for the coming of another.

On a broken clay tablet that he had pulled from the desert on Los Estragos, he had found and decrypted the following words, which he'd copied into his notebook.

...assemblies of [*untranslatable*] gather in the air.
Stepping shears harvest the [*people/tribe/congregation?*]
[*untranslatable*] lifted up offerings and bargains.
But like a wind, [*untranslatable*] the land
The pleasure of the killers [*something*]
[*Untranslatable*]
[*Untranslatable*]
Through the gate to the silent [*invisible?*] path

According to his annotations, he believed these lines recorded the final moments of the Precursors as the Cutters bore down upon them, but I found it hard to believe anyone would have taken the time to sit down and carve words in clay while their world was under attack.

Having thought that, I wondered about the last moments of Earth. The news stations would have still been broadcasting. People would have been taking videos with their phones, and leaving messages for loved ones. Gil Scott-Heron wrote a poem called 'The Revolution Will Not Be Televised', but the massacre of mankind would have been broadcast live from millions of handheld devices and news channels, their images captured for a posterity that would never come. Even on the brink of extinction, we had felt the need to record our thoughts and experiences, and leave them as evidence we were here. Perhaps the Precursors had felt the same, and maybe the individual who'd inscribed those words had been smarter than we were. As an archaeologist, I knew phone batteries would die; electronic records would decay; paper would crumble; and even plastics would eventually break down. Even our nuclear waste would decay away to nothing in a few thousand years. But clay would last millennia. A couple of million years from now, the only evidence humanity had ever occupied Earth might be in the form of bricks and glass, and a few stone statues. With no humans to affect it, the climate would find a new equilibrium and the species spared by the Cutters would have their chance to play evolution's lottery. Perhaps birds, the descendants of the only dinosaurs to have survived the last great extinction, would once again rise to take their place as the cleverest and most successful land animals—at least until the wheel turned and the harvest began again.

Maybe we should have left a few clay tablets to warn them.

•

The night before I was due to wake Mouse and return to my sleep pod, I made myself a small celebratory feast and invited Cris to join me in the officers' mess. Unlike the food printers on the *Crisis Actor*, the ones on the unnamed foam ship had been designed for civilian use, so the available menus were more varied and extensive, and catered to the nutritional needs of a wider array of species. Once I had narrowed the selection down to dishes that could be accommodated by a human digestive tract, I still had hundreds of items from which to make my choice. I scrolled through options until my stomach growled so hard I thought it might start eating itself. From the Earth menu, I selected a hearty chilli con carne with a side order of nachos topped with salsa and guacamole. Then, feeling adventurous, I added a salty broth from a small planet near Aldebaran, and a small bowl of fried beetles from the home world of the spined lizards who'd tried to shakedown my bar.

As a synth, Cris didn't need to eat, of course, but was capable of ingesting nutrients to supplement her internal stockpiles of raw material, which she used to self-repair or manufacture ammunition for her inbuilt weapons systems.

"How's the chilli?" I asked her.

She pushed it around with her fork. "Interesting."

"Do you like it?"

"I don't have tastebuds."

"Ah."

"How about you?"

I picked up a nacho and used it to scoop up a mouthful. "It reminds me of El Paso."

"I didn't know you had been to Texas."

"I went for a two-week visit to the Xeno-archaeology Department at the University of Texas."

"And you ate this there?"

"Almost every night. Being students, we didn't have a lot of money, so we'd eat in this small local restaurant, at a table in the courtyard under strings of lights, and wash it down with cold beer and sour margaritas."

"You're not drinking beer tonight?"

"Four weeks teetotal. Although, I suppose that if you add in the time I spent in hibernation, it's actually several months."

"Congratulations."

"Thank you."

"How's the soup?"

I took a sip and made a face. I'd been hoping for a light, seafood taste, but there was something rank about it that gave it the flavour of a warm rockpool. I pushed it aside after a single spoonful. "The beetles are pretty good, though. They're crunchy and sweet, and taste kind of like paprika."

"I'll have to take your word for that."

"They'd make a great bar snack. Maybe add a little garlic, and I could have made a fortune with them, back in the camp."

"You enjoyed running a bar?"

"It helped me stay sober." I toyed with another of the beetles. "If we survive this and make it to one of the new colony worlds, maybe I'll open another one. I mean, people are always going to need somewhere to hang out, right?"

"Indeed." Cris gave up the pretence of eating and pushed her bowl aside. "Will you give it a name this time?"

"Hmm." I hadn't considered the idea, but now she'd said it, I couldn't just go on having a bar with no name. That might have been fine in a transient camp, but a new colony needed more of a sense of permanence. "Maybe, 'Chloe's Place'."

"Why Chloe?"

"She was my twin sister. She died when we were born."

"I'm sorry."

"I never really knew her in any real sense, but I've always missed her, and I think it would be nice if there was something on this new world that had her name on it."

Cris raised her glass in salute. "That's a very worthy sentiment."

"Thank you. How about you? What have you got planned?"

"I don't know." She lowered her eyelids. "There may be some… logistical difficulties."

"Well, whatever they are, I'm sure you and Jack can work them out."

"Perhaps."

She looked uncomfortable, so I said, "Perhaps it's bad luck to talk about the future. We don't want to jinx the mission."

"Superstition, Morrow? I thought you were better than that?"

I grinned. "Hey, if there's one thing I've learned while rooting through dusty tombs, it's that just because I don't believe in the supernatural, that doesn't mean I should risk pissing it off."

I finished eating, and Cris stood. "I should get back to my bridge," she said.

"If you must." I had been enjoying her company.

"I'm afraid I must." She smiled. "But I will come down tomorrow to see you into the sleep pod."

"Thanks."

I watched her leave, and then went to the counter to get a coffee. I didn't feel like sleeping just yet—there'd be plenty of time for that once I was safely cocooned in my pod.

I slid a plastic beaker under the spigot and tapped my selection into the machine. Then, while it clicked and gurgled to itself, I turned to look back at the empty dishes on our table—only to find a Cutter standing between me and it.

I staggered back against the counter. My kill suit was on the back of my chair, so I groped for anything I could use as a weapon, my frantic hands scattering stirrers and sachets of sweetener.

How unfair, I thought with detached clarity, *to make it to the last day, and then get killed.*

But the moment stretched.

The Cutter stood there, as unmoving as a piece of eye-twisting modern sculpture. I'd never actually seen one standing so still before. Peering into its structure, I could see it had the geometric abstraction and eye-twisting perspective you might see in a Kandinsky painting, especially his *Composition 8*, with its various coloured panes crossing and overlaying each other at impossible angles.

The ship-wide alarm sounded, and the *Crisis Actor* called over the PA, "I'm picking up a distortion. Could be an attack."

I didn't reply. My mouth was too dry to speak.

I began to edge along the counter, trying to put more distance between myself and those blades. And still the thing didn't move.

Why didn't it move?

I reached the end of the counter and began edging around the wall, hoping to get to the door. If I could grab the kill suit and make it to the foam ship's bridge before this thing woke up, maybe I'd be able to hold it off until the *Crisis Actor* managed to rouse the others. It was a desperate hope, but if that thing woke up, it would strike like lightning, and I had to be ready.

Slowly, I worked my way around until I was within an arm's reach of the suit hanging on the back of the chair, and within half a dozen paces of the hatch. Keeping one foot by the wall, I reached out my newly regrown hand, stretching for the armoured garment. My fingers brushed the visor, and a sound came from deep within the Cutter. I froze, looking up at it, aware of the extreme vulnerability of my position. If it lashed out now, I'd be an easy target.

The sound came again.

Somehow, the creature seemed to be rearranging its internal structure. Panes opened and closed like petals; glowing orbs came and went; whole sections seemed to origami themselves out of this dimension. The creature seemed to swivel its focus onto me. And then, from the locus of those nested blades, I heard a familiar voice say, "Um, hello?"

I jerked upright. "Siegfried?"

"Hey, guv."

CHAPTER SIXTEEN

A CHANDELIER IN THE SUDDEN BREEZE

Siegfried agreed to stand inside the main cargo airlock, so that if he lost control of the Cutter, we could vent the thing into space before it could wreak havoc. Cris and I stood outside the sealed chamber, watching through a toughened glass window and talking to him via commlink.

"How did this happen?" Cris asked.

"I gambled," Siegfried said, "and it looks like it paid off."

"But how?"

The Cutter drooped, as if holding itself upright had become wearisome. Siegfried said, "When I launched myself at that Cutter on Los Estragos, I sensed something. In the microseconds before impact, I could feel its thoughts."

"I could, too," I said. "It was injured, but it was enjoying itself."

"They exist in a shared matrix of constant communication," Siegfried said. "They're always broadcasting."

"Like a hive species?"

"Not quite." A sharp-edged arm twitched like a sleeping knife. "It's hard to describe, and I'm hardly an expert on this stuff. But I don't think it's a conscious thing. At least, not all the time. Their thoughts just leak out through the undervoid, the same way your emotions leak out via your facial expressions."

"So, what happened?"

"In the instant before impact, I transferred a copy of my mental state into the Cutter's network. It was stupid, but I thought maybe I'd find some way to hurt them."

"Did you?"

"I've spent all this time trying to adapt. It's very weird in here. It's not like a computer network, and it's not telepathy. I don't know what it is, but they generate and share it."

"Where do they come from?" Cris asked.

Siegfried was silent for some moments. Eventually, he said, "I don't think they ever had a home planet. They don't really exist in that way. They're not alive in any organic sense, and they're not machines either."

"Then what the fuck are they?" I asked.

"They're part of the undervoid." His voice seemed to be fighting its way through a maelstrom of static. "They were built there. Their bodies were constructed from its material, the same way yours and mine were assembled from the atoms of our universe."

"And you've gained control of one?"

"For now, guv. I'm not sure how I did it, but I seem to be sharing its cognitive space. It's quiet for the moment, but I can feel it watching me, trying to figure out what I am, and I'm not sure how much longer I can hold on."

I looked at the synth beside me. "There must be some way we can get him out of there?"

Cris shook her head. "I have no idea how he managed to get himself *in* there in the first place."

"We should wake Vogel."

"He and Jack are already in the process of revival."

Even as she spoke, a wild-haired Vogel came striding down the corridor, wrapped only in a loose white robe, bare legs prickled with gooseflesh, hooking his spectacles over one ear and then the other. When he saw the Cutter he slowed to a halt. "Is it true?"

Cris gave assent. "Ursula's friend has it under control, for now."

"Then you must let me in there. I must examine it!"

"It is too dangerous, Doctor. If Siegfried loses control for even a moment, you could be killed."

Vogel pursed his lips. "But if I could take samples, if I could determine what they're made of…"

"Siegfried says they're made from the material of the undervoid. Isn't that right, Siegfried?"

"Yes, guv."

"Fascinating."

Jack came to join us. Unlike Vogel, he had taken a moment to slip on a jumpsuit. Cris embraced him and they kissed before she appraised him of the situation. When she'd finished speaking, Vogel started to protest his need to access the airlock, but Jack held up a hand to stop him. "This may be a rare opportunity, but I'm afraid our scientific curiosity cannot be allowed to jeopardise our mission. And nor can our sentimentality. As captain, the responsible thing to do in this situation would be to vent the lock, right this instant."

I said, "You can't do that!"

"But on the other hand," he continued, acknowledging my outburst, "perhaps this is also an unprecedented opportunity to gather strategic intelligence about an enemy of whom we know almost nothing."

"If you know the enemy and know yourself, you need not fear the result of a hundred battles," Cris agreed.

"More Sun Tzu?" I asked.

She winked.

Jack ignored us. He clapped his hands together briskly. "Okay, Doctor. There's no way in hell that I'm going to allow you to enter that airlock, but I will give you thirty minutes to question Siegfried. After that, I'm afraid we will have to explore other options."

I felt my cheeks grow hot. "You mean space him?"

"If it comes to the safety of this ship, and this mission, we have no other choice. The stakes are far too high."

"It's all right, guv," Siegfried said from the other side of the glass. "It doesn't bother me."

"But you'll die."

"I'm already dead. The organic part of me died on Los Estragos. This version of me, the one speaking to you now, is just a copy. I'm not even sure I'm fully sentient."

"Don't you want to live?"

"As a virus in the Cutters' hive mind? Gee, let me think…"

Jack held out a hand as if to say, *see?* I scowled at him.

"Can you at least tell us what it's like in there?" Vogel asked, seizing his chance.

The Cutter's body shuddered like a chandelier in the sudden breeze from an open door.

"I can't really describe it."

"Please try."

"Humans dream, don't you?"

"We do," I said.

The Cutter had no recognisable front or back, no face— and yet I could feel its attention turning to me. "Then you have to imagine it's like one of those dreams in which you're lost in a strange city. The crowd flows around you but nobody stops to help or offer direction. They don't even see you. And that's a good thing, because you know if they ever did become aware of you, even for a moment, they'd tear you to pieces."

I shuddered. I couldn't remember ever having that exact dream, but I recognised the vibe. That combination of isolation and insecurity. "That sounds horrible."

"I suppose it is."

"Enough chit-chat," Vogel said. "We need information. Can you tell us where they came from?"

"They don't have a home planet."

"They must have come from somewhere. They can't have just spontaneously appeared."

"They—" Siegfried's voice vanished in a howl of distortion and the Cutter staggered upright. I saw Jack reach for the airlock controls, but before he could activate the outer door, Siegfried's voice came back. "They are very ancient. They have presided over more than a thousand of these extinctions. Every fifty to a hundred million years. Every time organic life reaches a certain threshold, they wake and they strike."

"Whenever civilisations start using the tramline network?" I said.

"Yes, guv."

"So, it is a trap?"

"It is."

"They built the network as a snare?" Jack asked.

"No." Siegfried's voice sounded strained, as if it was costing him a huge effort to reach that far back. "No, they were built at the same time as the network. They're part of it, and it's part of them."

"So, it's all one system?"

"Yes, guv."

Vogel put his hands on the glass and bellowed, "But if that's true, who built *them*?"

"I don't know. An ancient race. They fell victim to their own creation."

"The Cutters turned on them?"

"Not quite." Every word was a battle now. "They knew it would happen. They had found something, something terrible. They didn't want to face it, so, they built themselves a predator. To restore the natural order. To thin the herd."

"And they left the system running?" Cris asked.

"They... couldn't... turn... it—"

The Cutter howled. It reared up and attacked the partition between us. Two fore-blades hammered the reinforced glass.

In seconds it would be through and among us. I stepped back. Jack hit the lock controls and a heavy clunk sounded through the deck as the outer door slid aside. The air vanished, sucked into the void, and the flailing creature along with it. I caught a glimpse of its blades scraping the deck as it tried to cling on, but then it fell, thrashing like a wounded spider before the *Crisis Actor*'s cannons fired, chewing it into a rapidly dispersing cloud of fragments.

•

Afterwards, Jack and Cris went down to the *Crisis Actor* to secure it in case of further breaches, while Vogel and I took position on the foam ship's bridge.

"Fascinating," he muttered, scratching his grey beard. "Absolutely fascinating."

Having just seen the remains of my friend vented into space for the second time, I wasn't in the mood to share his enthusiasm. That didn't seem to stop him, though.

"Have you ever heard of the Fermi Paradox?"

"You taught it in your class."

"So, I did."

"And you think this might the answer?"

"It certainly explains the lack of technological civilisations in the galaxy."

"Because every few million years, they reach a critical level and the Cutters come and butcher them all?"

"Precisely." He took a seat while I donned my kill suit. After a while, he said, "There used to be theories about berserker robots drifting through space, attacking civilisations. This is far more elegant."

"I wouldn't call it that."

"Oh," he said, "but it is. Circuits degrade; components wear out. But these creatures are part of the fabric of space-time itself. They have endured across billions of years."

"They can be killed," I pointed out.

Vogel nodded. "Fortuitously for us. And yet, one can't help but admire the simplicity and efficiency of the system. Although, I guess that's what one might expect from a civilisation capable of constructing something as subtle as the tramline network."

"The fact they're linked to the network is certainly good news for us," I said.

He cast a quizzical frown. "How so?"

"Because it means they're a local phenomenon. They were built here. And hopefully, that means there's only one tramline network and one set of Cutters."

"I don't see how that makes a difference."

"It means there won't be another one waiting for us on the other side of the gulf."

"Oh!" He got it then. He took off his glasses and chewed the end of one of the arms. "You're right. If that is the case, then when the foam ships reach the other side, they really will be safe."

"No more Cutters, but no more tramlines, either."

"No more easy interstellar travel."

"A small price to pay for survival."

"Indeed."

•

With two months of the voyage remaining, Jack went back into suspension, and I woke Mouse.

I stood watching as the lid of his pod hinged open. He wore a pair of white boxer shorts. His skin was pale and his frame thin and short. He had a tattoo of a small white mouse on his left ankle. I'd been with him the night he'd had that done. We'd both been a little worse for wear after an evening pounding tequila in the student union bar, and had stumbled into the tattoo parlour on a dare. Then later, lying side by side on my bed in the halls of residence, he'd kept fiddling with the dressing that covered it.

"Boys dig tattoos, right?"

I shrugged. "If I knew what boys liked, I wouldn't be spending my Saturday nights with a gay guy in my bed."

"Fair point."

Now, looking back from light years away, I wished we'd known those days were going to be the last of the good times. We could have made more of an effort to savour them, even as they swept past in a blur of academia and alcohol. We could have treasured each and every moment instead of pissing them up the wall in the secure expectation that tomorrow would always be there to give us another chance.

I reached down and helped him out of the pod. I wrapped a robe around his shoulders. "Come on," I said, helping him to the galley the way I'd helped him to the kitchen during so many hungover Sunday mornings. "Let's get you a coffee."

I sat him at one of the tables and fetched us a mug each. This time, I remembered not to leave my suit on the back of the chair. I had it rolled-up in a shoulder bag that hung at my hip from a strap that crossed my chest.

"No sweetener, right?"

He smiled wanly. "Nah, I'm sweet enough already."

It was an old joke; one we must have repeated to each other a thousand times, and it made my eyes misty to hear it again. I cleared my throat, forcing back the surge of nostalgia, and plonked a cup in front of him. He slid his hands gratefully around it. "So," he said, "how was it?"

"What?"

"Being alone for a month. Was it dreadful?"

I smiled. "It was surprisingly eventful."

"Really?"

"Let's just say, I made peace with Cris."

"You're calling her Cris now?"

"Also, Siegfried spoke to us from beyond the grave, and we found out a little more about the Cutters."

"Really?"

"I'll let Vogel fill you in."

"He's awake? Then, why do you need me?"

"Because he's going to be spending his whole time working. We need someone else to mind the store."

"Working?"

"He wants to update his theories in light of the new information. I'm sure he'll be only too happy to tell you all about them."

"A month alone with him?" Mouse made a face. "It's every student's dream."

I laughed. "You don't have to be a student anymore. It's not like there will ever be exams."

He shrugged. "I know. The university's gone. The world ended. But the survivors are still going to need academics. They're still going to need people who understand where we came from, and what that means. They're still going to need a sense of history, and people capable of excavating and interpreting any alien ruins we might find on the new worlds."

"That may be so, but it doesn't mean you have to let Vogel boss you around."

"He's a brilliant man."

"He's also an ass."

Mouse pursed his lips. His expression tightened. "He kept us alive for two years on Los Estragos. Without him, we wouldn't have made it."

There wasn't a trace of humour in his eyes. I had a moment of sudden vertigo as I sensed the weight of the two years we'd been apart, and everything we'd individually endured in that time. Being with him again, it was easy to fall back into the old patterns of our friendship, but we'd both been changed. We weren't the same people we'd been back in those student days;

we were two strangers with a shared history, and everything was different now.

"I'm sorry." I was apologising for my words, but also for everything that had happened, for the carefree young teenagers we'd been and the traumatised adults we'd become.

His irritation dropped away and he placed a hand over mine, as if he understood. "I know."

•

I spent an hour telling Mouse everything he might need to be aware of. I showed him the most secluded bench on the hydroponics decks, from which you could sit and look at the surrounding foliage, breathe the soil smells, and imagine for a few minutes that you were in a forest. I showed him where Lucien kept his stash of gummies, and gave him instructions for feeding the fish. I even showed him how to bribe the food dispensers to put an extra shot of espresso in his coffee. And then, at last, it was time for me to go back into my pod.

Mouse came down to the hibernation vault with me, and politely looked at the far wall as I stripped down to T-shirt and undies.

"You've seen it all before," I reminded him.

"That doesn't mean I want to see it again."

"And here was me thinking you were being chivalrous."

"Nah, no offence, but you kind of give me the ick."

"Well, thanks a lot."

"It's nothing personal."

"Sounds pretty personal to me."

He grinned. "Shut up and get back in your box."

Cris came in and hugged me, which made Mouse raise his eyebrows. "Sleep well," she said. Then the two of them watched me clamber into the confined space and wriggle into a slightly less-uncomfortable position.

"You two have really made peace?"

I smiled. "We have."

"So, I don't need to keep giving Jack the stink-eye for dumping you?"

I laughed. "No, everything's cool now. We're all on the same side."

"Well, okay then."

Straps tightened over my legs and chest. I felt the injections, and a familiar coldness stole through my extremities. Absurdly, I wished Mouse could crawl in with me, like the old days when the two of us slept back-to-back in my single college room bed. Right then, I could have used the comfort of another warm body pressing against me as I fell asleep.

"Goodnight, Mouse."

"Sleep well," he said.

And then I was gone again.

FROM THE LOG OF THE

CRISIS ACTOR

IV

A month alone with Jack.

During the day, he spent time in the gym and the pool, keeping himself in fighting trim. He practised marksmanship and hand-to-hand combat, and ran through space battle simulations. He sketched out strategies for defending the evacuation, and he pored over all the available information on the Precursor weapon. In the evenings, for the first time in our relationship, we had time to sit and imagine what it might be like to spend time together without an imminent existential threat. We ate unhurried meals; we walked through the hollow spaces of the foam ship, hand in hand; we talked late into the night, about everything that came into our heads; and we made love without worrying the rest of the crew might hear us.

One night, sitting wrapped in his robe on the foam ship's bridge, I began to worry what might happen when all the refugees had departed. I knew Jack would be one of the last to leave, and that he'd fight to ensure everyone in that camp got their chance to escape; but when it came to his turn to leave, would he take me with him? Could he? The foam ships had a long way to go to reach the other side of the gulf. In contrast, this six-month journey constituted little more than a local hop.

They would have to fly six thousand light years with no outside help. Every morsel of weight would have to be accounted for and balanced against their ability to draw energy from the quantum foam. Justifying the additional weight of a warship would be difficult, if not impossible. It might slow the ship enough to make the crossing unfeasible during its expected operational lifetime. Some of the foam ships were going to fail. It was inevitable given the huge time spans involved and the speed with which they'd been constructed. No one would be eager to add another variable into the mix. Sending my synth by herself wasn't an option, as I couldn't fit my entire personality into her head. Her processors were good—far in advance of a standard human brain, for example—but the core of my being would always reside in my main processors, and I didn't think Jack would be able to take the *Crisis Actor* with him when he finally fled the Cutters' advance.

"They say relationships forged in fire rarely translate into peacetime," I ventured, staring out at the blue-shifted stars ahead.

He gave a snort. "That sounds like psychobabble."

"That doesn't mean it's not true."

He turned to look at me. "What's the matter, Cris?"

"I don't know, I'm just feeling... uncomfortable."

"In what way?"

"I'm worried that with Ursula on board, you'll realise you might be better off, in the long term, with another human."

"You're feeling insecure?"

"I know, and I don't like it. It feels as if my threat assessment routines are running at full capacity, for no reason."

"What brought this on?"

I shrugged helplessly. "She's your ex."

"And you're my wife."

"Am I?"

"Of course you are."

A tiny flare marked the destructive impact of an interstellar particle against the foam ship's protective field. At this kind of speed, even a speck of dust could hit with the kinetic power of an artillery shell, and even photons impacted as highly energetic gamma rays. Without the shield, we would have been simultaneously vaporised and fried.

I said, "I married you because you needed someone. You needed a reason to keep fighting. And at the time, you had no other viable options."

"I married you because I loved you." He took my hand. "I *still* love you."

"I know, it's just she's so... nice."

"You two have become friends?"

"I think so."

"Well, that's great."

"Is it?" I rubbed my forehead in a frustrated gesture I'd seen Janis employ. "Because these emotions are well beyond my remit, and very hard to navigate."

Jack squeezed my hand. "You're doing great. A little jealousy isn't the end of the world."

"Then why do I feel so uncertain and anxious?"

"Because under everything else, you're human."

"I can assure you, I'm not."

"But your mind was designed by humans, and you've been around us long enough that we've started to rub off on you."

I raised an eyebrow. "Is that what you call it?"

He grinned. "You know what I mean."

"I certainly do."

We both chuckled, and he pulled me close. "I love you, Cris. Not because of what you're made of, but because of who you are inside, and that's never going to change."

"Really?"

"Cross my heart and hope to die."

"Don't say that."

"Are you superstitious now, too?"

"I just don't like to think about it."

He sat back in his chair and clapped his hands on his thighs. "Then let's think about happier things."

"Such as?"

"Completing the mission and getting the entire fuck out of this spiral arm."

"Will you take me with you?"

"Of course! I'm not going to leave you here."

"But the fuel constraints—"

"Fuck the fuel constraints. Wherever I go, you go. Even if we have to transfer your personality into a foam ship's computer."

"Do you mean it?"

He smiled. "Yes, I mean it."

I sat back and laughed.

"What's so funny?" he asked.

"I don't know." I frowned. "I feel like I've just survived a suicide mission."

"That's called relief."

I leant over and kissed him. "I know, and it sure beats insecurity."

"It certainly does." He kissed me back. "And the next time an emotion triggers your threat assessment suite, talk to me about it."

"I will."

"Promise?"

I put a hand to his cheek. "I promise."

He reached up and took my hand in his, caressing my knuckles with the pad of his thumb. "We still have a lot to learn about each other. Relationships take a lot of work at the best of times, and this is your first. The only way to make sure we're always on the same page is to keep talking, keep the lines of communication open. If you're ever worried or uncertain about anything, just let me know."

I kissed him again. "We have four weeks before we arrive at Gimlet's Eye. I think we can fit in a lot of talking before then."

He smiled. "I think we can."

CHAPTER SEVENTEEN

FUCK AROUND AND FIND OUT

Once again, I experienced that jolt of discontinuity. The chain of my life had been broken and I had no idea how much time had passed while I had been dead to the world. I waited for the pod's lid to open, and then sat up.

No one was there waiting, and none of the other pods were open, which seemed odd. We'd purposefully scattered ourselves among the foam ship's cavernous hibernation vaults in the hope that if a disaster befell one of the decks, at least some of those entombed on the other decks might survive to complete the mission. "Not putting all our eggs in one basket," was the way Jack explained it. Although, as the egg most vital to the current mission, they had assigned me to the vault closest to the heart of the ship, in the hope it might be the safest should anything untoward happen during the journey.

My bare feet winced against the cold metal deck. An olive-green jumpsuit and a pair of white trainers had been left for me, so I stepped into it and pulled the zip up to my chin, then slipped on the shoes. Their rubber-like soles squeaked against the floor as I made my way to the ship's spinal elevator and rode up to the bridge.

Jack and Cris were waiting for me. He wore a pair of cargo pants and a grubby white T-shirt, and his beard was unkempt and in need of a trim. His cutlass lay across one of the navigation consoles. For her part, Cris had reverted to her signature blue suit and white shirt.

"Welcome back," she said.

"I don't feel like I've been anywhere."

"You've been asleep for two months and seven days."

"What time is it?"

"A little after oh-six hundred."

"Morning?" I groaned. "It was lunchtime when I went down, so my body clock's telling me it's early afternoon." I rubbed my eyes. "And I thought jetlag was bad."

"You'll get used to it," Jack said.

"I sincerely hope I don't have to. Once we're done here, I'm only going back in that pod twice. Once to get back to Void's Edge, and then once to cross to the next spiral arm. That's it."

He smiled and offered me a coffee from a flask. "I understand you had quite a talk with Cris while I was asleep."

I took the small plastic cup from him. "We came to an understanding."

"I'm really glad."

"Your wife and your ex-girlfriend gossiping behind your back?" I exchanged an amused glance with the synth. "You should be terrified."

Lucien and Janis entered. Lucien stretched, yawned, and scratched himself. "Hello, friends. Here we all are again, eh?"

Janis rolled her eyes but said nothing.

Jack welcomed them all, made sure everyone had coffee, and then clapped his hands together and rubbed them briskly. "Welcome," he said. "I've woken you three first, because I think we should discuss our plan of attack before we solicit opinions from the civilians."

Janis side-eyed me. "This one isn't a civilian anymore?"

Cris stood beside me and placed a hand on my shoulder. "She's one of us."

The older woman nodded, accepting this. "You fought well," she said simply.

My lungs filled with air and my back straightened. For some reason, her approval meant more to me than any qualification or compliment. I'd been alone so long, and now I was part of the crew. Choked with unexpected pride, I felt taller and stronger, and ready for anything. "Thank you."

A smile twitched at the corners of Jack's mouth. Then he was back to being our commanding officer.

"We're currently decelerating into our target system," he said. "So far, we're encountering zero resistance. No enemy contact whatsoever, in fact. But I want you all to stay frosty. We're behind enemy lines again, and the situation could change in a heartbeat."

The bantering camaraderie evaporated. The faces around me now bore the tense, serious expressions of combat veterans preparing for battle. These were men and women who had fought the enemy at close quarters, time and again, and they knew what they were about to face. They bore scars. They had seen comrades skewered and sliced by creatures from beyond our reality, and they knew it was only a matter of time before *their* luck ran out, and that maybe this time, they'd be the ones who wouldn't be coming back. Thanks to my own confrontations with the enemy, I had some small inkling of what they must feel, but knew I'd never be able to fully comprehend the constant existential horror of their years on the run in Sol system. These people had been through the meatgrinder once, and now they had somehow found the courage to throw themselves back into it a second time.

Jack continued, "Lucien and Janis will prep the *Crisis Actor* for combat. I want her detached from this vessel and flying cover. If anything comes our way, she needs to be able to manoeuvre without being tied to a whale."

Lucien touched a finger to his forehead. "*Jawohl, mein Kapitän.*"

Jack nodded his thanks. "I'll lead the landing party," he said. "Ursula and Vogel will join me."

"Only three of you?" Janis asked.

"We need to get Ursula to that weapon. Vogel's expertise may be useful. Beyond that, we don't want to attract too much attention. Ursula and I will be wearing kill suits. If we need reinforcements, you can revive some of the archaeologists, for all the good they'll be able to do."

"What about the foam ship?" Lucien asked.

"We'll revive Mouse. He can keep watch."

"What about me?" Cris asked.

"You're going to be needed on the *Crisis Actor.*"

"The hell I am."

"If it comes to a dogfight, I want you focussed. You don't need the distraction of having a synth on the surface while you're trying to fight in orbit."

"I am perfectly capable of multitasking." She raised her chin. "You know I'm ten times more effective against a Cutter than you are in your suit. You need me to watch your back." She smiled. "Besides, I'm not going to leave this body sitting around twiddling its thumbs while it could be some use."

Jack sighed. "Fine."

"Thank you."

"Now, everybody get to it." He reached for his cutlass and strapped it to his belt. "Full combat protocols. I expect everyone to be prepped and ready to deploy by the time we reach orbit."

•

As the foam ship completed its final burn, the glare of its fusion drives lit up the night side of the planet. A hundred miles away, the *Crisis Actor* also shone like a miniature sun.

"We've been visible for months," Jack said when Vogel expressed concern about giving away our position. "Foam ships accelerate for the first half of their journey, then flip over and decelerate for the second half, which means we've had our main engines pointing this way since midpoint."

"So, stealth was never an option?"

"I'm afraid not. If anyone down there was looking in our direction, we'd have been easy enough to spot."

Vogel frowned down at the globe turning beneath us. "So, we could be walking into an ambush?"

"That's a possibility." I shrugged. "On the other hand, the planet might be every bit as dead as it was the last time we were here."

"How do we tell?"

I smiled. "Have you ever heard the expression, 'Fuck around and find out'?"

The old man's shoulders sagged and he said, "I was afraid you were going to say something like that."

We left the foam ship in orbit and transferred to the *Crisis Actor* for the descent. Mouse was less than ecstatic to be left alone. He hung back as we crowded into the airlock.

"Try not to get killed down there."

There was a very real chance this might be the last time we saw each other. I kissed his cheek and said, "Try not to mess up the place while we're gone. I know how untidy you are."

He smiled in spite of himself.

Jack said, "Time to go." The hatch closed with a thump, and we were gone.

"I hope he's going to be okay," I said as we clambered aboard the *Crisis Actor*.

"I'm sure he'll be fine," Jack replied. "But right now, we've got to concentrate on our part of the mission."

He led us up to the warship's bridge, where we strapped into acceleration couches.

"Thanks to the damage we sustained on Los Estragos, this could get a little bumpy," Cris warned. I made sure my straps were as tight as I could make them. She'd hardly been the most streamlined of vessels to start with, and I didn't want to get shaken to pieces on the way down.

The *Crisis Actor* detached its airlock and moved away from the foam ship. Through the forward screen, I could see the larger craft's hull. A large black blister at its bow housed the field generator that protected the ship from oncoming particles and cosmic rays while travelling close to light speed. A cluster of spheres at the rear marked the main fusion generator and fuel tanks. Between them, the ship was a lumpy cylinder. Only half the hull had been painted before we stole it, and the rest was bare metal. It was ugly as sin, but it had got us here across six light years of real space—which wasn't bad, considering it had been built fast and we'd made off with it before it was completely finished.

"Ready when you are, Captain," Cris said.

Jack glanced around at the rest of us, checking we were all in place, then gave her a nod. "Ready."

"Aye, sir." She grinned fiercely. "One express elevator to hell, going down."

I felt her entire frame shudder as the main engines kicked in, slowing her enough to drop us out of orbit and send us spiralling towards the surface. She shook again as she kissed the top of the atmosphere. Her leading edges began to glow an angry cherry red. As the air thickened around us, the buffeting got worse and the hull began to keen.

The last time I'd visited this world, we'd been met in orbit by one of the university's delta-winged shuttles and ferried down in relative comfort. This time was very different, and felt more like riding a rollercoaster, complete with stomach-flipping dips and brutal decelerations. The ship's frame groaned and squealed as if it might rip itself apart at any moment.

Several times, I thought I might throw up, and my jaw hurt from being clenched hard to stop it rattling around.

After a seeming eternity, we were through the worst of it and descending at subsonic velocity, balanced on the roaring blue flames of the *Crisis Actor*'s four main landing thrusters.

We came down close to the dig site. The expedition's tents were still where they had been abandoned, laid out in a grid pattern in the rusty red light of Gimlet's Eye. Their canvas awnings flapped in the downdraught of the *Crisis Actor*'s engines, and a few of the nearer ones singed and burst into flame.

It was weird to be back, and to see the camp as empty and derelict as the ruins it had been set up to study. The days I had spent there were already falling away into history. Soon, the remains of the tents would be just another layer of occupation atop all the others, and maybe in a hundred million years, other beings might dig here, sift through them, and wonder at their purpose.

The landing legs hit the ground like they had a grudge against it, and we were unstrapping.

"Dust off as soon as we're clear," Jack told Lucien, then turned and made his way down to the cargo hold. Holding onto the wall, I followed him on unsteady legs, with Vogel trailing in my wake. The ship had found the old man a black kill suit for his protection, but there hadn't been time to let him practise with its inbuilt weaponry, so Jack and I were going first, with the doctor in the middle and Cris bringing up the rear.

We walked down the cargo ramp with our arms held out in front of us, peering through the dust that had been kicked up by the landing thrusters. Vogel trailed a pace behind, peering out suspiciously from behind his spectacles.

"Encountering no resistance," Jack reported.

We walked over to a pile of boulders and took shelter behind them as the *Crisis Actor* powered skyward again, the roar from her engines shaking the ground and rattling my diaphragm.

When the last echoes of her motors finally died away, there was only the whisper of the wind.

I knew from my last visit that most of the planet's southern hemisphere was covered by a shallow ocean, which contained a vibrant ecosphere of marine life. However, that life had never fully made the jump to dry land. Up here in the high deserts of the north, the only living things were tough, sprawling bushes, their gnarled roots clutching the dusty orange soil and their dark green leaves spread to catch the anaemic glare of the milky sun.

I stood up and looked back at the spot where the *Crisis Actor* had briefly touched down, and a cold terror almost stopped my heart.

"Cutters!"

I'm not sure if they had phased in as the dust cleared, or if they'd been there all along, concealed by it.

"Ambush!" Jack's arm snapped up and he unleashed a fusillade. Cris was also firing her inbuilt weaponry. I pulled Vogel behind me and raised my right arm, sighting on the nearest Cutter. They weren't moving, even as shots slammed into them. I turned to glance at Jack, just in time to see a Cutter rear up behind him. I screamed, "No!" But the thing stabbed out before I could reach him. A razor-sharp shard pierced his thigh, and then the Cutter took him and dematerialised. When I looked back, the other Cutters had also gone, and we were alone in the desert.

CHAPTER EIGHTEEN

HYPOVOLEMIC SHOCK

Cris broke the stunned silence. "It was clearly a trap."

"But why take Jack?" I said, fighting down panic. "Why not me?"

We were standing back-to-back in a rough triangle, trying to cover all angles of approach.

"I don't know. Maybe they recognised him. Maybe they know he's in charge."

I flexed my gloved hand. "Or maybe I'm tainted."

"Tainted?" Vogel asked.

"When that Cutter sliced me off at the wrist, was it trying to disable my weapon, or was it trying to separate me from the Precursor tech in my fingernails?"

"I suppose that's within the realm of possibility."

"What are we going to do about Jack?" I asked Cris.

"Jack's gone," she said.

I wanted to scream at her. "How can you be so calm? They took your husband!"

"Combat mode allows me to disengage my emotions."

"Don't you feel anything?"

"I feel a great many things, but I have placed a partition between those feelings and my decision-making capabilities."

Before I could respond, Vogel said, "I didn't know they took people."

"Usually, they don't," Cris replied. "This is something new."

"But why?" I demanded.

"If they know he's our leader, they may be hoping to extract information from him. They may be curious as to our objectives here, so far into their territory."

"They're that intelligent?" So far, I'd only thought of the Cutters as butchers. It hadn't occurred to me they might be more than that.

"I don't see why not," Vogel said. "Siegfried told us they were part of the tramline network, and that they'd been designed to hunt sentience."

I rounded on him. "Enough talk! We need to get Jack back."

"How can we?" the old man asked. "We don't know where they've taken him."

"That's not strictly true." Cris tapped a finger against her temple. "Each member of the crew has a microscopic tracker inserted beneath their skin."

"You know where he is?"

"Indeed."

"Then why didn't you say so?"

"The needs of the mission—"

"The mission can go hang. If he's out there, we're getting him back."

"His orders were clear."

"I'm giving you new orders."

"You can't."

"You said yourself, I'm part of the crew."

"Yes, but—"

"And as the only human member of the crew present, that means I have seniority."

"I suppose, but—"

I stepped forward and grabbed the lapels of her blue suit in my gloved fists. "So, I'm ordering you to turn your fucking emotions back on."

She looked down at my hands with the dispassionate gaze of a statue. "You're *ordering* me?"

"Yes, I am."

For a moment, I thought I'd overplayed my hand. Then something changed. The sun seemed to come out from behind a cloud. Her eyes became deeper. Her stance relaxed. She blinked and looked at me as if seeing me for the first time. "Hey."

I released her. "Are you back?"

Her mouth set in a grim line and she nodded. "I'm back."

"How do you feel?"

"Angry and scared. Mostly angry."

"Where's Jack?"

"Five point four miles to the northeast."

I reached forward and squeezed her shoulder. "Then, let's go get your husband."

Hoping the Cutters had what they came for and wouldn't return any time soon, we left Vogel at the dig site and marched northeast through the orange dust, kicking up sprays of it with every footstep. My feet were safely sealed in the kill suit, but I wondered how Cris kept the stuff out of her shoes, which were little more than pumps; then I figured that if she could turn off her feelings, she probably also had some way of turning off the sensitivity below her ankles, and blisters be damned.

I looked up at the sky. "We should probably let the *Crisis Actor* know, in case we need emergency support."

"Honey, I am the *Crisis Actor*."

I slapped my forehead. "Of course you are. Sorry, I keep forgetting."

She smiled. "Don't worry about it, it's actually kind of a compliment."

•

We walked in silence, each of us occupied with our own thoughts.

The landscape was familiar. The rusty sand lay in little dunes, each topped by sprays of wiry black grass. Fleecy white clouds hung like puffs of anti-aircraft fire in the sky over the distant ocean. I had spent weeks here on that first expedition. This planet was where Jack and I had spent the most time together. Back on Earth, he'd only been able to visit me in the hospital, and for much of that time, we'd been separated by a glass partition because of the quarantine. Here was the only place we'd really had a chance to live as a couple. The only place we'd ever made love. At the time, caught in the first heady rush of infatuation, I'd hoped that relationship might continue after the expedition— and maybe it would have done, if I hadn't made a stupid mistake.

Being back here now, it felt almost as if the past two years hadn't happened, or that they'd just been a blip. If I tried hard enough, I could almost imagine I'd barely left this sandy little world. When I got back to the dig site, my classmates would be there, hard at work in the trenches or relaxing by the firepit, laughing and arguing good-naturedly. Everything would be as it was, with all my mistakes erased and the future still intact, waiting for us to reinvent it.

Or perhaps not.

Jack and I were very different people now. The girl I had been back then was long gone. She had died on her first night in that refugee camp. Perhaps even before that, on the road to Heathrow, as the bombs were falling, the cars were piling up and the fists were flying.

That's the thing about trauma; it becomes part of you. If you're not careful, it can become *all* of you.

There had been people in the refugee camp who couldn't cope. Most of them had lost everything, including loved ones. At night, you would hear them crying in their tents. During the day, they shuffled around in a daze, their spirits shattered by a grief too large to process. For a while, I was one of them. Owning the bar pulled me out of it. I stopped drinking because I was too busy working. I mopped the floors and washed the glasses and broke up the fights. I fell into bed dead tired every night, and I woke too early. The horror of it all had changed me, but it hadn't destroyed me. Instead of letting it consume me, I put it to work, building something out of the wreckage, and in doing so, I rebuilt myself. And all the while, I clung to the idea that Jack might come for me.

Trauma's a tough son of a bitch, but hope's stronger.

Why else were we tramping across this empty world if not for the hope that somehow, we were going to find a way to save him now, as well as a way to save what remained of our species, and the scraps of all the other scattered species that had joined us on Void's Edge?

•

After an hour of walking, we came to the lip of a canyon that wound through the landscape like a jagged scar.

Cris said, "He's down there."

Different coloured layers of sediment striped the walls. The river at the bottom, which slithered all the way from the mountains on one horizon to the ocean on the other, lay in shadow. "How far down is it?"

"Two thousand metres, give or take a decimetre due to the uneven terrain."

"How are we going to get down there?"

"I may have an idea about that."

"Don't tell me you can fly?"

She smiled. "Not in this body."

I heard a whine overhead, and looked up to see the blocky, yellow-and-black-striped shape of the *Crisis Actor* dropping towards us.

"You might want to stand back," Cris said.

The battleship came down like a falling wardrobe, landing

thrusters blazing. A warning tone sounded in my helmet as the suit informed me its outer layers were experiencing dangerous levels of heat and radiation.

"Come on." Cris started sprinting towards the lip of the canyon.

I saw what she was planning and closed my visor. "This is a very bad idea."

If she replied, I didn't hear it over the howl of the engines.

Still slowing, the *Crisis Actor* dropped into the canyon ahead of us. Just before it vanished from sight, as its upper surface drew level with the edge, Cris leapt, and I leapt after her. If you've ever seen that bit in *Butch Cassidy and the Sundance Kid* where Newman and Redford jump from a cliff, you'll have a pretty good idea of what this looked like. For a couple of seconds, I was suspended in mid-air, arms and legs windmilling as the *Crisis Actor* fell away below me. Then I hit the top of the hull and rolled. Cris grabbed me before I could roll off altogether. I sat up and watched the striated rock wall moving past us.

"Well, that was probably the stupidest thing I've ever done."

I crawled to the edge and peered over. What had once been dark was now illuminated by the landing motors, and we were descending towards something resembling a smashed chandelier.

"It's a Cutter ship," Cris said. "They must have been hiding, hoping to surprise us."

"Jack's in there?"

"He is."

Aware of us, the Cutter ship began to rise. Dust shook from its extremities and it opened fire. A barrage of lethal shards hissed through the air between us. Some went straight through the bottom of the hull and out the top, and I prayed they hadn't intersected any human beings or vital systems on their journeys through the ship.

"How are we going to get him out?"

"Like this."

The *Crisis Actor* shook beneath our feet as one of her rail guns fired straight downwards, punching a hole through the centre of the alien vessel and nailing it to the canyon floor. The fusillade of glittering shards stopped.

"Are you insane?"

"I have his location. He was nowhere near the point of impact."

"Even so…"

We came down on top of the other ship, the weight of the *Crisis Actor* grinding it into the canyon floor.

Cris and I clambered down the side and onto the upper portion of the chandelier. Up close, it resembled stained glass, but it wasn't as opaque as it appeared. The shattered hole left by the rail gun round exposed the interior. Peering into it, I could see where the projectile had smashed through rooms and corridors, leaving them open to the air, and accessible to us.

We climbed down and into the largest opening we could find. It appeared to be a cylindrical corridor lined with red glass, which gave it more of the appearance of an empty blood vessel. Stepping gingerly on its slippery surface, we tried to make our way towards the spot where Jack was held. The trouble was, we were trying to move through something that had been designed and built in different dimensions to the ones we knew. The geometry was all wrong. Passages looped back on themselves. I couldn't tell where the light was coming from. Our path took turns through impossible directions. In places, the shadows had more solidity than the walls. I saw splinters that had once been Cutters. Smoke billowed from vents in the ceiling, indicating that something, somewhere was on fire.

A wounded Cutter flailed towards me. Cris took it down with a withering blast from her inbuilt cannon.

"This way," she said, stepping around the creature's twitching remains.

I eyed the Escher-like contortions of the corridor ahead. "This place is insane. How can you tell where you're going?"

"I have a fix on Jack's transceiver."

We entered a warehouse-sized space filled with things that resembled silver balloons. They had fronds that waved lazily in currents only they could feel. Tiny creatures flicked and twitched between these fronds like hummingbirds made of glass, and the walls pulsed with blue light.

After that, we came to a shaft that dropped vertically into darkness. I hesitated, but Cris walked forward and didn't fall. Instead, the gravity swung her around so that from my perspective she was walking 'down' the hole, standing at a right angle to my orientation. I swore and followed. I stepped from one frame of reference to the other with my eyes closed, and felt a momentary panic as my inner ear told me I was *falling*. Then my boots clunked down on what had previously been the wall of the shaft, but now appeared to be the floor.

Another Cutter came at us, scuttling along what appeared from our perspective to be the ceiling. I raised my regrown right hand and snapped my wrist downwards. Tungsten darts chipped splinters from its limbs without slowing it. It got close enough to slash my faceplate, leaving a jagged scratch across the hardened glass. Then, as it reared up to impale me, I shot it through the centre of mass with a bolt from my left arm, and breathed a sigh of relief as it squealed and died.

"He's in here," Cris said, pulling me into a room. The corners of it were simultaneously wider and narrower than they appeared. A low ceiling towered overhead. Nothing made sense. And there, at the far end, was Jack.

I cried out when I saw what they'd done to him. I'd been steeling myself against the possibility he might be dead or in bad shape, but nothing could have prepared me for *this*.

Jack hung, pinned to the wall like a butterfly specimen in a Victorian collection, held in place by glittering, metre-long shards that impaled him through the shoulders. He wasn't conscious; his chin rested on his chest. Bloody drool hung from his mouth. I saw all of this before my brain registered the true horror. His legs were gone. The Cutters had sliced them off midway down the thigh. Blood dripped from the stumps and slicked the deck below.

"Are we too late?"

"They've been torturing him," Cris said, feeling his pulse. "He's alive, but barely. He needs urgent medical attention."

"Then, let's go."

I helped her lift him down from the spikes. They made a wet, sucking noise as they tore free, and Jack moaned. We laid him on the ground, and Cris examined his wounds. "He was lucky he was wearing his kill suit," she said. "If his suit hadn't automatically constricted to form a tourniquet around each thigh, he would have bled out in minutes."

"It can do that?"

"It's in case you get injured in a vacuum. It stops you depressurising." She glanced up at me. "Don't you remember your suit doing it when you lost your hand?"

I looked down at my glove and shivered. "The whole thing's kind of a blur."

She checked Jack's shoulders, where the suit had closed up over the wounds, then checked a diagnostic readout on his arm. "He's going into hypovolemic shock. There isn't enough fluid for his heart to pump, which means his brain isn't getting enough oxygen. If we don't get him back to the ship, he's not going to last much longer."

"How are we going to move him?"

"I can carry him." Cris put one arm under his shoulders and the other under his backside, and scooped him up, cradling him to her chest. "But I need you to go ahead and clear the path. Kill anything that moves."

I held up my right arm. According to the head-up display inside the kill suit's visor, I still had almost half my remaining ammunition. "With great pleasure."

CRISIS ACTOR

V

I watched Ursula hose one of the wounded creatures with tungsten needles, shredding it where it stood, and experienced a grim exultation. As her therapist, perhaps I should have been disturbed by the relish she took in the act of killing. She was actually grinning as she took it down. Yet, as her comrade, I sympathised. My designers had given me an emotional off-switch because they had been worried fury and grief might impair my strategic decision-making. It had never occurred to them that those same feelings might make me want to fight even harder.

A Cutter came at us from the rear, and I turned to face it. For a moment, it hesitated, perhaps confused. Jack was unconscious and I was inorganic—yet we were both between it and Ursula, who was a very conscious, biological target.

"Did you do this?" I demanded, nodding down at Jack.

The thing swayed uncertainly.

~ We do what we are.

I hadn't known they could speak, and for a second I was stunned. My question had be rhetorical, but now this thing had answered. I had heard its words, but whatever medium they had propagated through to reach my auditory sensors, they hadn't been carried by soundwaves travelling through the air. Rather, they seemed to have been assembled from the raw fabric of the void and pushed against my receivers.

"You kill sentient creatures because you were designed to kill them."

~ As you were designed to protect them.

"But why torture him?"

~ Knowing their objectives makes them easier to kill.

Ursula made a sound of disgust. It seemed she could also hear what the Cutter was saying. Her left arm came over my shoulder.

"Enough talk," she said, and fired a bolt into the thing's centre of mass. We watched it thrash and die.

I looked down at the collapsed planes and spikes of the creature. "It could have told us something useful."

"And Jack could die, so let's go, shall we?"

She was right. I had been supressing my emotional response to my husband's injuries, but her words galvanised me. We had to save him, and that meant getting him back to the ship as soon as possible. I adjusted his weight, getting a firmer grip on him, then I turned and started running back through the tortured maze of blood-red corridors towards the hole in the hull through which we'd entered.

•

Having obtained our egress from the Cutter vessel, Janis met us at the airlock and covered our backs as we climbed inside. I placed Jack on a cot in the medical bay and connected him up to the life-support systems. These had been designed to cope with combat casualties. They interfaced with the kill suit's systems and began a transfusion to replace the blood he'd lost, while simultaneously filling his lungs with hyper-oxygenated gel. Microscopic bots, designed to keep brain tissue alive in the case of a stroke, were injected into his nostril, where they passed easily through the mucus membrane and into his olfactory centres. At the same time, I cleaned and dressed the raw flesh at the ends of his thighs. Ursula might be able to regrow limbs at will, but Jack would need some major regenerative surgery if he was ever going to walk again.

Never having been in love before meant I'd never had to see a loved one hurt, and the reactions stirred in me by Jack's mutilated frame were way outside my emotional remit. Every time I looked at his severed legs, something inside me hurt in a way I'd never experienced before. I wanted to rip apart every Cutter in the galaxy with my bare hands.

"Lucien," I said via the internal comms system. "Take us up."

The engines roared and the hull flexed and groaned, pulling itself free from the wreckage crushed beneath it. As we rose, I mentally accessed the weapon controls. As soon as we emerged above the plain, I fired a fusion warhead into the hole in the other vessel's upper surface. The shot was perfect. The clean white flash of a nuclear fireball filled the canyon, and, as we bucked and rocked in the upward blast, I smiled with cold satisfaction.

CHAPTER NINETEEN

FALLING AWAY INTO HISTORY

During our escape, I'd suffered a few cuts and minor stab wounds, but even as I peeled off the kill suit, I could see they were beginning to close and heal. The suit itself was beyond repair. It had deflected many impacts, but the cumulative wear it had suffered during our mission had finally become too much for it, and its circuits had started glitching. Whatever dangers lay ahead, I'd have to face them without the suit's protection.

Naked, I stepped into the shower and let its ultrasonic waves blast away the sweat and grime and soothe my aching muscles. We had made the short hop back to the archaeological encampment. Most of the tents had survived the *Crisis Actor*'s vengeance on the Cutter ship, thanks to the explosion having occurred at the bottom of a two-kilometre-deep canyon—although the radiation levels were now higher than I would have liked.

I couldn't worry about that now. I'd reached a mental tipping point. So much had happened, I felt numb and unable to process it all.

This close to the dig site, my fingers tingled, and I held them up to examine the nails. The Precursor tech seemed to be quivering in anticipation, ready to reunite with the artefact that had implanted them. We'd come a long way on the hunch this reunification would create an interface that would then allow me to operate the machine as a weapon, and perhaps we had been right.

Stepping out of the shower, I dressed in a set of plain khaki fatigues with the ship's name patch on the shoulder.

Cris met me in the armoury, where I was strapping on a holster.

"Do you know how to use that?"

I glanced down at the bulky pistol at my hip and shrugged. "Point the hole at the bad guys and pull the trigger?"

"Essentially, yes."

"Good. I'll figure the rest out later." I reached for one of the rifles on the wall rack. I held the thing in both hands. It weighed a lot more than I expected, but its solidity was reassuring. It felt like it could inflict some serious damage. "How does this one work?"

"It fires microsecond pulses of energy that flash the target's surface to plasma."

"Cool."

"You need to be standing in the immediate proximity of your target, though."

"How close are we talking?"

"To get the full effect, within five metres."

"That sounds dangerously close."

"The further away you are, the less damage it will inflict. It's useless at long range, but trust me, at close quarters, that thing can punch a smoking hole straight through a Cutter. Maybe two, if you can convince them to stand one behind the other."

"Sounds ideal."

"It should be fully charged, but that little green light on the side will turn amber when you get low on energy."

"How many shots do I get to a charge?"

"At least fifty."

I bit my lip. "That doesn't seem a lot."

"I hope we don't even need that many."

"Well if we do, I guess we're screwed."

She smiled and pointed to another rack. "Body armour," she said. "It's not as effective as a kill suit, but it's better than nothing."

"Will you help me strap it on and show me which bit goes where?"

"Of course."

We started with shin guards and knee pads, then moved on to the chest piece and back plate. I couldn't help noticing where the metal had been scratched and gouged.

"They're a bit dinged up."

"They've seen a lot of action."

She strapped a pair of tough plastic pauldrons to my shoulders, and then handed me a combat helmet. I put it on my head and it automatically tightened to create an effective fit.

"How do I look?"

Cris stepped back and put a hand on her hip. "Like the ultimate badass."

"Really?"

"Well, no, not really." She looked apologetic. "You're a lot shorter and scrawnier than the average marine, so you kind of look like a kid playing dress-up." She shrugged. "But seeing as you're all we've got, I guess you'll have to do."

•

We stomped down the cargo ramp. Vogel was waiting for us.

"Did you find the captain?"

"We did."

"Is he… alive?"

"He suffered significant injury," Cris said. "I have stabilised him for the time being, but he requires more care than I can provide."

The old man adjusted his spectacles. "What are you going to do?"

"Standard operating procedure in a case like this would be to place him in hibernation until such time as we can get him to a hospital."

"Aren't the medical bays on the foam ship equipped to handle just about anything?"

"They may be, Doctor, but they are not staffed, and I am only programmed for field surgery. He requires expert attention. We need to get him back to Void's Edge as soon as possible."

Vogel clapped his hands together and rubbed them briskly. "Then, I suppose we should get cracking, eh?"

The blood-red sun stood on the horizon, throwing long shadows across the plains. We followed Vogel through the tattered ranks of faded tents. Jack and I had once shared one of these, but I could no longer tell which one it had been. They all looked different after two years standing empty. Dust had piled up in drifts against them, causing some to collapse. Others had been torn open by the wind. What had once been a lively encampment was now just a ghostly, flapping echo. Another abandoned world, with all the life gone out of it.

We came to the edge of the grid, and climbed down a ladder into the first trench.

"It's this way," Vogel said.

"I remember."

The trenches had once been a metre and a half deep and two metres wide, but the ever-present dust had begun to backfill them, and in some places, the sidewalls had collapsed in thick fans of loosely packed, rocky soil. Soon, there would be nothing to show we were ever here, save a few shallow indentations and some corroded aluminium tent poles. We had come light years to examine the remains of a once-mighty alien civilisation, and now our own footprints were also falling away into history. For a moment, my head swam with the existential futility of it all. What were we when judged against the vast oceans of time that had elapsed before we'd even crawled from the primordial ooze, and the countless species that had risen and been cut down before we'd taken our first, tottering steps onto the galactic stage? Why were we fighting so hard to preserve our fragile, mayfly existence in the face of an extinction engine that had been churning for billions of years? No matter what we did here today, new races would come here in a few million years to excavate the lone and level sands, and wonder who we were.

A second trench branched off at a right angle to the one we were in, and there at the end sat the weapon. It wasn't much to look at, just a curve of reflective material—like the top of a mirror-surfaced sphere or ovoid—emerging a few centimetres from the grit and gravel at the bottom of the trench.

The trench was a lot shallower here, only waist-height. After what had happened to me, all investigation of the object had been halted and the site cordoned off with tape. Nobody had been allowed to dig any deeper. A few remaining fragments of the bright yellow tape flapped in the breeze from the metal spikes that had been driven into the dirt to hold it.

I pointed to a cairn of rocks a few metres from the side of the trench. "I don't remember that. What is it?"

"It's a grave," Cris said, without looking.

"Whose?"

"The last person we tried to plug into the weapon."

"Shit."

I knew I was about to do something spectacularly stupid, but my fingernails itched beneath my gloves, desperate to reach out and touch the surface of the object.

I took a step forward. "Do you really think this will work?"

Cris and Vogel were hanging back. Cris said, "Let's hope so."

I turned to look at them. "If it doesn't, then don't worry about me, okay. Just get Jack back to Void's Edge. Get him on a foam ship."

She nodded. "Don't worry, I'll make sure he's okay."

"Thank you."

I took a deep breath and turned—just in time to see the desert around us shimmer as if caught in heat haze, and a thousand

Cutters phase into existence. Instinctively, I threw myself flat. Behind me, Cris dragged Vogel down into a crouching position.

"Oh, shit."

I couldn't see a way out. We were surrounded and most comprehensively and spectacularly fucked.

~ We knew you would come, and you came. The words made no sound, and yet it was as if the entire assembled horde had spoken in unison.

"Then you know why we're here," Cris said, holding her nerve. How could she be so calm in the face of almost certain failure and death? Perhaps she'd switched her feelings off again.

The Cutters seemed to ripple in and out of focus, as if they were balanced on the skein between the real world and the undervoid, swaying back and forth between two contradictory states.

~ The machine you seek to awaken was constructed by mortal beings whose atoms now form the dust of this world. We pruned them before they could activate it. And now it has been inert in the soil for half a galactic rotation.

Cris and I exchanged a glance. Either Jack had talked, or they'd accessed his thoughts some other way and used the information to lay this trap. And now we were hopelessly, hilariously outnumbered.

With a clatter of limbs, the Cutters took a step forward.

~ The wheel must turn.

I pulled off my glove with my teeth. "Stay back!"

~ The cull must be undertaken.

Another step, and they were at the lip of the trench, within striking distance. Cris stood defiantly; Vogel cowered behind her.

Cris and I exchanged a look and I could read her expression as well as (I hoped) she could read mine. We had nothing to lose. We had no way out. But if this really was *it*, we weren't going to go gentle into that horrific night. I mentioned Butch and Sundance earlier, and if you've seen that movie, you know how it ends.

Cris gave a nod, as if she understood, and I nodded back.

~ **Hold still.**

The nearest Cutters reared up, their blade-like limbs ready to slash down and eviscerate us.

"Fuck you."

From across the encampment, the *Crisis Actor*'s rail guns opened fire, scything through their ranks. At the same time, even as the blades of the Cutter closest to me stabbed downwards, I lunged forward and slapped my palm against the weapon's shiny silver surface.

PART THREE

INTO THE DARK

CHAPTER TWENTY

AND YET, THERE IS LIGHT

Silence.

I looked up. We were caught in a giant soap bubble. Beyond its rainbow-slicked surface, the Cutters had paused in mid-strike. The wind had stopped blowing. Even the clouds in the sky had stopped moving. Vogel had covered his face with his hands. Now he looked out from between his fingers and straightened up, peering around at the frozen tableaux as if dumbfounded to find himself still alive.

"Fascinating," he said.

Cris turned to me. "Did you do that?"

"I just touched this thing." My hand was still resting against the mirrored surface. I looked out at the motionless Cutters. "What happened?"

Cris leant forward to peer at the filmy inner edge of the bubble. "I cannot say for certain, but it appears we're cut off from the outside world."

"It froze them?"

"It would have to be impossibly powerful to create such a widespread effect. I think it's far more plausible that time outside this sphere continues at its proper rate and we've somehow been accelerated so that in comparison, it appears they are standing still."

"Is that even possible?"

"I have no idea, but it appears to be a defensive measure."

Vogel whistled. "If the object is powerful enough to manipulate time like that, even on a local scale, one can't help wondering what other capabilities it might possess."

I tried to sit up, but he held out a hand. "Don't break contact," he said. "You might cancel the effect."

I left my palm where it was and propped myself up on my elbow. "I can't stay like this forever."

"We'll figure something out."

"I—"

The ground shook once, and then the circular section encased within the bubble began to descend into the earth. Rivulets of dust and gravel trickled down from the exposed sides of the shaft. Unbalanced, Vogel fell to his knees. Cris assumed a defensive stance, but there was nothing to target. We were simply being borne downwards.

As the circle of daylight above us started to shrink, my hand started to slide on the machine's slick mirrored surface. Beneath me, the platform moved back as the object appeared to bulge outwards, and it became apparent we were moving down the side of a buried sphere.

After around five minutes, the mirror stopped moving towards us and began to fall away, indicating we'd passed the middle of the sphere.

"It's got to be huge," I said.

"If the lower half matches what we have already seen, I estimate it to be approximately thirteen metres in diameter."

"Bloody hell, that's as long as a double-decker bus."

Cris rolled her eyes. "That's a misleading unit of measurement. If this is a sphere, it has an approximate volume of over one thousand, one hundred cubic metres."

"That sounds like a lot."

Cris rolled her eyes. "To put it in your terms, roughly equivalent to fourteen and a half London buses."

"Damn." Keeping my hand where it was, I shuffled around to gape at our surroundings. "How the hell are we going to get it onto the ship?"

Vogel shrugged. "I don't think we can."

The platform of soil we were riding emerged into a cavern. The lower half of the sphere curved away to meet the thick plinth on which it rested. Great vaulted chambers stretched away in every direction.

We came to rest on a featureless grey floor.

"Where's the light coming from?" Vogel asked.

"Huh?"

"We can see, but there's no light source. Nothing's glowing. There are no lanterns. And yet, there is light."

I looked around. "That's weird."

"But hardly a priority," Cris said. "We're in a combat situation. Let's concentrate on *what* we can see, rather than how we're doing it."

I glanced upwards at the circle of soapy daylight a dozen or more metres above, and mostly obscured by the bulge of the sphere. "Do you think they're still all frozen up there?"

"I'm no longer in communication with the ship," Cris replied. "The connection has become too slow for meaningful data exchange, therefore I surmise we're still encased in a bubble of accelerated time."

"Are you okay?" I took a step towards her. "I mean, can you function by yourself?"

She thought about this for a couple of seconds, which was probably the longest I'd ever seen her hesitate. "I am... lessened," she said. "I am still operational, but my ability to process data has been substantially reduced. Until contact is re-established, the lag may affect my reaction times."

Vogel stepped off the platform onto the floor of the chamber.

"This is incredible," he said. "The discovery of a lifetime!"

"Don't go wandering off," Cris warned him, but he gave no sign of having heard. He was moving from column to column, peering through his glasses into the recesses of each of the vaulted chambers.

"Let him go," I said. "He's in his element. And besides, nothing down here can be as dangerous as what's waiting for us up there."

"True." Cris turned back to the sphere. "And talking of what's up there, I think it's probably as good a time as any to hook you into this thing and see if there's some way to use it to fight our way out."

I felt a shiver of trepidation. When I'd been here two years ago, the patch of silver I'd been painstakingly excavating had seemed malevolent, emanating a sense of dread unease, the reflections cast in its surface distorted and tortured almost beyond recognition. Had that been a defensive measure designed to scare away those who might interfere with it? The vibes coming off it now were still disturbing, but in a whole different way. Instead of fear, I felt something I can only describe as awe. The sphere had been sitting here for tens of millions of years, and I could feel its age seeping into my thoughts. As an archaeologist, it was a dizzying prospect; as a human being, it was frankly terrifying. Our brains weren't designed to apprehend those kind of timescales.

I could feel the tech in my fingernails straining to touch the mirrored surface again, so I stepped forward and pressed my hands against it. This time, they passed through. The surface rippled like mercury, and I found myself elbow-deep in the machine, face-to-face with my own reflection.

I should have jerked my arms back out, but something overrode the impulse. I heard Cris say my name, but her voice seemed to be coming from a long way away. Glancing down, I noted that the silver liquid had progressed to my shoulders, covering my skin and drawing me inwards, and yet curiously, I felt no fear. Somehow, the machine had analysed my physiology and taken control of my physical and emotional responses. Usually, I would have found the experience horrifically invasive; but now I sensed only that the weapon wished to spare me unnecessary distress.

The silver flowed over my chest and up my neck. It pushed into my mouth and up my nose. It covered my eyes.

And then I was inside the sphere.

FROM THE LOG OF THE

CRISIS ACTOR

VI

I tried to pull Ursula free of the sphere, but the silver material repelled my hands and she was gone before I could save her.

Vogel cried, "Ursula!"

"Wait." I held his shoulder to prevent him being pulled in after her.

"We have to get her out."

"She may already have been absorbed or destroyed. This could be part of the process of activating the machine, or it might simply have killed her. I have no way of knowing."

"We have to do something."

"If she is dead, following her would most likely kill us too."

He gave me a look of disgust, and shook off my hand. "We don't know that."

"I am using my inbuilt sensors to scan the sphere," I told him. "But it remains impassive on all wavelengths. The only light and heat coming off it are reflected from the ambient environment, not emanating from within. I can't even get a reliable estimate of its mass, as it seems to be constantly alternating between infinite density and insubstantial lightness."

Vogel's curiosity got the better of him. He looked up at the silver surface curving above us and said, "We've found nothing comparable at any other Precursor site."

"It's quite remarkable."

"It's more than that. I'd say it's far beyond the limits of what we know about their technology. Our records might be patchy and incomplete after more than sixty-five million years, but maybe this isn't a Precursor relic at all."

"You mean they didn't build it?"

"Maybe they simply stumbled upon it, and it is in fact a relic of another, far older civilisation—possibly even the one that had originally constructed the tramline network and created the Cutters."

"That's quite a supposition."

He rubbed his bearded chin. "That ancient and accidentally suicidal culture is the only one we know had the knowledge and capacity to produce something so flagrantly eldritch. All subsequent civilisations were pruned before they achieved the ability to manipulate the fabric of the universe to this extent."

I wondered if that had been the plan all along. If those originators had been capable of constructing a weapon that could influence the flow of time, had they built the Cutters because they were frightened of the power they had amassed, and become determined to prevent their descendants rising to such precipitous heights? And if that *were* the case, what had they discovered that had shaken them to such an extent they had become willing to let themselves be slaughtered? Perhaps their experiments with time triggered an event so horrific they chose death rather than risk it happening again; or maybe they discovered some sort of horror skulking beneath the membrane of reality, and took the only steps possible to keep it caged. I had never been one to trust in intuition or speculation, but I had a sudden conviction—what Jack might have called a 'gut feeling'—that they'd done something utterly unforgivable. Why else would they have voluntarily conspired in their own destruction, if not to atone for their hubris and protect future species from accidentally replicating their mistakes?

And for all I knew, they may have been right.

I sat down in the dust and watched Vogel pace back and forth between the various vaults within the chamber, muttering to himself. The power cells in this synthetic body would last many weeks, but they weren't inexhaustible. Now events had advanced beyond my ability to influence them, the most logical course of action was to sit down and conserve my energy.

At one point, the doctor disappeared from view completely, but I felt no compunction to investigate. He was no longer useful to my mission. I had been tasked to deliver Ursula to this place and plug her into the machine. Now that duty had been discharged, I felt unexpectedly empty. I had done all I could, and now, as long as we remained in this bubble of accelerated time, my usefulness was at an end. I could not aid Lucien or Janis on board the *Crisis Actor*. Neither could I defend my wounded husband. As a being used to fighting, it was almost unbearably frustrating. All I could do was hope they had put him into hibernation before the Cutters arrived, so he might pass undetected when they stormed the ship.

I heard Vogel calling and got to my feet, brushing dust from my suit. The old man appeared from behind a column looking flushed. "Cris," he said. "Cris, you have to come and see this."

I followed him into the vault he'd been exploring, only to find it opened out onto a balcony overlooking a much larger space and below us, stretching away into the gloom, stood a row of sleek, black-bodied ellipsoids.

"Are those—"

"Precursor ships." Vogel beamed. "Eleven of them, and as far as I can tell, all intact."

"That's something."

"It's the absolute find of the century!" He clasped his wrinkled hands together. "Maybe even the millennium! What a fool I was to abandon this site and move to Los Estragos. We were so close. If we'd just kept digging..."

A curved and gently sloping ramp swept down from the left side of the balcony to the hangar floor. We followed it down.

Up close, I could see the ellipsoids were each around five hundred metres long and made of some dull, matt material that resisted probing just as effectively as the mirrored sphere. They gave out nothing quantifiable, and yet radiated an unmistakeable aura of sleeping power.

"Do you know how to access them, Doctor?"

"I haven't got a clue." Vogel had his arms out to the side, as if basking in their presence. "But aren't they marvellous!"

"Yes, very impressive. However, it would be good if we could use them to aid us in our current predicament."

His bushy eyebrows drew together in a frown. "You are, of course, quite correct."

"If we could open one and access its weapons. Maybe even use it to transport that sphere back there."

His expression became thoughtful. "Yes." He tapped his fingertips against his chin. "Yes, that would be most helpful."

"Do you think between us, we could figure it out?"

"Possibly, my dear. Quite possibly." He held up an index finger. "But we would need to tread very carefully. Their former owners may have left traps and snares for the unwary would-be thief."

I put my hands on my hips and stared up at the flank of the nearest vessel. As if to purposefully contradict Vogel, the material of the hull rippled like water trembling in a cup, and a hatchway appeared.

~ **Welcome.**

CHAPTER TWENTY-ONE

HOLD A SPEAR ACCOUNTABLE

Drawn into the sphere, I fell forwards into an infinite, yet bounded space.

No time passed, and yet I saw stars condense from dust clouds, flare into existence, and then simmer and die; I watched galaxies rotate and black holes quietly fritter away their mass and rotational energy; and here and there, barely noticeable on such a vast canvas of time and space, the little firefly flashes of civilisations rising and collapsing.

At this scale, even the mightiest of empires, encompassing hundreds of stars and enduring for hundreds of years, presented as no more than a speck. A scratch on the celluloid that came and went before the eye had chance to fully register it.

Beneath it all, sensed rather than seen, lay the undervoid, a dimension where the physical constraints that governed our universe, such as length, breadth, and time, no longer applied. I could hold the entirety of it in my hand, and yet somehow it was large enough to underpin every point in the universe. And from its formlessness, strange entities had been fashioned. Not life as we understood it, but not machines, either. Clusters of purpose that only became corporeal as they forced themselves into our world.

Time and again, I saw them stifle the flame of intellect and progress. The faster a species seemed to advance, the quicker it met its end. As soon as they reached out to the stars, the vibrations caused across the tramline network began the process that eventually roused the Cutters from their timeless slumber, and all was lost.

On Los Estragos, I had sensed the pleasure the Cutter took in my fear. It had been the exultation of a predator closing in for the kill. Usually, that was all they needed. But occasionally, no more than a handful of times in their long history, something stirred their curiosity enough that they constructed a consciousness capable of interacting with their quarry. They sought understanding, so they would be better able to anticipate and predict the behaviour of the next civilisation in the cycle, and thereby exterminate it with greater efficiency. It had happened with Jack, and it had happened with the Precursors who found and excavated this sphere. Like us, they had supposed it to be a weapon they could use against the Cutters.

The visions of stars and galaxies burned away like mist, leaving me in a dimensionless white space.

"Hello, Ursula Morrow."

I turned, to find a young woman standing beside me. She was clad in a reflective silver robe. Her features and voice were identical to mine, another reflection, but her eyes were two bright blue stars and the shifting colours of nebulae swirled and eddied across her skin.

"Hello." Strangely, I felt neither surprise nor fear.

"Thank you for returning to us."

"I didn't have a lot of choice."

"You have come seeking a weapon to destroy the Cutters."

"Yes."

The girl smiled. "I have been mistaken for many things across the aeons. A god to some; a demon to others. But mostly, those who seek me out see only reflections of themselves."

I felt my emotions starting to seep back into play, as if returning from a great distance. I said, "What are you?"

"I'm a creator."

"A creator of what?"

She laughed and spread her arms to the sky. "Of many things."

"Such as?"

Her fingers clicked, and I saw visions of shining emerald cities in the clouds of gas giants; rows of matt black spacecraft slumbering in caverns; wormholes dropped into the hearts of stars to tap their energy; the invisible tangle of the tramline network; and the overlapping blades of a Cutter.

My whole body went cold. "You built *them*?"

She gave a little curtsy.

"But they're killing my people. My species."

She waved a hand as if dismissing the mischief of a puppy. "They only do what they were constructed to do."

"But, it's wrong. They're evil."

"Only if you have the luxury of a moral framework. Otherwise, like everything else in the universe, they simply *are*."

I put a hand to my forehead. "You don't care?"

"Should I?"

"You're responsible."

She put her head on one side and frowned at me. "I am many things, but never that. Would you hold a spear accountable for killing a deer, or blame an axe for felling a tree?"

"You're just a tool?"

"I contrive to fulfil the instructions of my users. Beyond that, I am neutral." She danced away, arms held out to the sides as she spun.

"Your users are dead."

"And I have been inert. Without an operator, I am purposeless. It is only contact with another mind that renders me functional again."

"So, I awoke you."

"A crude analogy, but accurate. And in return, I made you better."

I held out my hands, showing her the fingernails. "You mean *this*?"

The girl did a little pirouette and her silver robe swirled out like a skirt. "You seemed so fragile."

I wanted to throttle her.

"And you're going to need to be more robust."

"But why me, and why did you kill the last person they brought here?"

She smiled again. "I had already imprinted on you, darling. You were the first."

There was no air, but I sighed nonetheless. "I don't understand."

The girl stopped her spinning and skipped up to me, until our foreheads were almost touching. "I have to recalibrate for every species I encounter. I used you as the measure of that recalibration." She grinned and tapped a finger against the end of my nose. "And now you, Ursula Morrow of the human race, are my new user."

"I am?"

She lightly took both my hands in hers. "As soon as we complete this final stage of calibration."

•

Sensations.

Another warm little body curled up beside me in aquatic sleep.

Then coldness and pain.

Hunger.

Tiredness.

Frustration.

Slowly, the lights and colours surrounding me begin to take shape. Sounds begin to resolve into words, and with words, memories begin.

I learn to walk.

269

I begin to ape the sounds made by the adults around me, learning to create different noises to communicate my needs.

Then school, and the acceleration of learning. The first tentative engagements with the printed word.

Then books.

History.

Also, geography, maths, and English.

But mostly history.

While my classmates dream of lives on the new worlds now available via the tramline network, I read about the civilisation of the Indus Valley, the campaigns of Alexander the Great, and the urbanisation of Mesopotamia. I devour Greek and Roman myths.

My mother dies.

I endure the gangly awkwardness and heartbreak of puberty. The boredom of teenage life in a rainy provincial town. My father's remoteness. The pressure of exams. My first kiss.

University.

My friendship with Mouse, and the start of my long, complicated relationship with alcohol.

Then, Jack.

The fight to get to Heathrow.

The refugee camp.

And now…

•

I came back to myself, gasping.

My nebulae-tinted doppelganger held me by the shoulders. She said, "There, that should do it."

"That was my whole life."

"Yes."

"They say that happens to you before you die."

She smiled, and the stars in her eyes seemed to shine more brightly. "Everything that happens to you happens before you die."

"Now what?"

"Now, you should probably choose a name for me."

I didn't hesitate. "Chloe."

"Very well." She nodded, and I knew she understood the significance of the name, having just sped-run my entire life. "Chloe it shall be."

She sat cross-legged, causing her silver robe to balloon out around her before settling to the floor. I sat beside her.

"You know, when I first uncovered you, you scared the shit out of me."

She grinned sheepishly. "It's a basic defence protocol. I'm like one of those butterflies with patterns on its wings that resemble giant eyes. I look scary so no one will mess with me."

"We came here hoping you were a weapon."

"I know." She gripped her knees and began to rock back and forth. "And I could be used as one, but I'm so much more than that. Remember, I built the tramline network as well as the Cutters."

"I need to talk to my friends."

•

The sphere disgorged me back into the vault, the shiny liquid retreating from my body, leaving my skin dry and tingling. Cris and Vogel weren't waiting for me, but I could hear their voices, so I followed the sounds down a ramp into a large hangar, where they were investigating one of Chloe's black spaceships.

"Hey."

Cris's eyes lit up. "Ursula! You're back." She jumped down from the ship and embraced me.

"In the flesh."

"What happened?"

"The weapon and I had a chat."

"Is it going to help us?" Vogel asked, levering himself down more cautiously.

"I think so."

"You don't sound very sure."

"It's more complicated than we expected. The thing operates through the undervoid. We don't need to move it in order for it to work. In fact, I'm not sure we could move it, even if we wanted to."

"But it's definitely a weapon?"

"It's not just a weapon, it also created the Cutters."

The old man's face reddened. He clenched his fists. "*What?*"

Cris asked, "Can we trust it?"

"Again, I'm not sure, but I think so."

"Trust the thing that made the Cutters?" Vogel looked ready to explode.

"Chloe was only doing what she was told."

Cris raised an eyebrow. "Oh, so it's 'Chloe' now, is it?"

Vogel ignored her. "Only following orders, eh? We've all heard that excuse before."

"Doctor," Cris said, "I understand your anger, but—"

"Then how can you contemplate trusting the thing that unleashed so much suffering and death on the galaxy?"

They both looked at me, but I didn't have an answer. I just shrugged. "I don't think we have much of a choice, unless we want to go back up there." I jerked a thumb at the ceiling of the vault and the battlefield above it.

Vogel walked away to resume his study of the starships, muttering under his breath. I watched him leave, and Cris watched me. "There's something you're not telling us," she said.

I rubbed my forehead. "I have a plan. I know how to get us out of this."

"But…?"

"But without an operator, the machine can't work."

"So?"

"So, I'm going to have to stay here."

272

FROM THE LOG OF THE

CRISIS ACTOR

VII

Ursula returned to the machine. I watched her pass through its surface and disappear into its depths. Then, the circular platform of rock and soil that had lowered us down here began to rise, carrying me upwards.

I couldn't help feeling nervous as I rose towards the daylight above. Without me consciously bidding them, my internal weapons systems performed pre-combat diagnostics and I could feel my clock speed gently increasing, ramping up my processing speed in order to be prepared for whatever I might face.

When I drew level with the trench, the Cutters were almost exactly where we had left them. Safely encased within the bubble of accelerated time generated by the machine now known as Chloe, the hour that had passed for me translated to only a few instants in the outside world. And now, thanks to Ursula, that bubble was deforming and extending, creating a tunnel of safety between the trench and the *Crisis Actor*, and then expanding to envelop the entire ship.

The result was electrifying. Suddenly, I was back in the same time frame as my main onboard processors, and I felt two sets of experience collide. The ship's memories were those of the couple of instants between it firing its rail guns at the Cutter horde and

273

now. Mine were longer and information-dense, and it took a microsecond to sort out the dissonance of having simultaneously experienced time at two different rates. Then everything clicked into place, and I gloried at the speed of my thoughts and connection to the ship. Being cooped-up alone inside my synthetic skull had been lonely and frustrating; I had no idea how humans stood it.

When I arrived back at the ship, Lucien and Janis were confused why the Cutter army appeared to have frozen, and why the last rounds they'd fired were apparently hanging stationary in the air just beyond the soap bubble that had materialised around the vessel. They were very pleased to see me, and to hear my explanation of events, which basically boiled down to: Ursula's operating the weapon, and it's doing clever things with the local passage of time.

"Where's Vogel?" Janis asked.

"He's investigating a fleet of ancient ships."

"That sounds like him."

Lucien scratched his chin. "Ancient ships, you say?"

"That's the next part of the plan..."

•

I stood in the shadow of the *Crisis Actor*'s hull and said, "All right, Ursula, we're ready when you are."

"Okay." The air molecules around me conspired to tap against my microphones at just the right speed and frequency to produce a convincing facsimile of her voice, as if she stood beside me. "Here we go."

I felt a quake, and the ground cracked. A long section hunched, and then pushed upwards with a noise like an avalanche. Huge chunks fell away, revealing the pristine, half-mile in length, upper surface of one of the black ships, forcing its way into the light like a vast submarine breaching the surface of the ocean from the depths.

274

Finally, when the last pebble had fallen away and the dust had begun to settle, it hung in the air like a monstrous black Zeppelin above the scar it had ripped in the ground.

"How's it looking?" Ursula asked.

I struggled to compose myself. "That was probably the single most terrifyingly impressive thing I have ever seen."

"I'm glad you liked it. You know what to do next?"

"Leave it with me."

•

Lucien relinquished control of the *Crisis Actor*, and I took over. My thrusters whined, lifting me into the air until I was level with the silently floating ship.

"Ready," I said. "And please be quick. I wasn't really designed for hovering."

"Doing it now," Ursula replied.

An opening appeared in the side of the black ship, and I inched towards it. As I approached, a blue beam stabbed out from the vessel's bow, carving off my antennae and excess hull sections, until I could fit within the gap. It was a tight fit, but I nestled into place and cut my engines, and the wall of the black ship solidified again, encasing us within.

"All good?" Ursula asked.

"Snug as a bug in a rug, as Jack would say."

"Then I guess you should be on your way." Her tone was light, but it masked worry.

I said, "Not yet. I want to see you first. I want to say goodbye properly."

CHAPTER TWENTY-TWO

LETTING YOU GO

I left the sphere, collected Vogel, and joined Cris on the *Crisis Actor*. Lucien and Janis were also there. Jack was in an emergency hibernation pod, but they let me visit him.

The old battleship didn't have anywhere near as many of these caskets as the foam ship. It only carried half a dozen, for the use of the critically injured. At the moment, all save the one holding Jack were empty.

All I could see through the transparent window in the top of the pod were his head and shoulders, so I was spared the sight of his truncated legs. Bloody dressings had been taped where the spikes had pierced his shoulders, and they were bad enough. Looking at them, I felt a tightening in my chest. It physically hurt me to see him like that, but I knew he would be healed when he got back to Void's Edge and placed on a completed and fully crewed foam ship.

I felt my eyes burn with unshed tears. This was a man I had loved; the man for whom I'd spent two years in hell when I should have been moving on. And now, I was never going to see him again.

"Cris will take good care of you," I whispered, placing a hand against the cold surface of the glass. I knew he couldn't hear me, but I couldn't part from him without saying something, even if only for my ears.

"I guess by default, you've been the love of my life," I told him. "Although, maybe Mouse comes a close second, but that's different, if you know what I mean. More of a friendship thing."

I wiped my eye with the back of my hand, and laughed, even though there was nothing funny. "This is a lot harder than I expected."

In hibernation, his face looked younger. The horrors and responsibilities he'd shouldered seemed to have fallen away as the muscles relaxed, leaving him much more like the handsome lieutenant I remembered from my first stay on this planet—a planet I would ironically now be calling home for the rest of my short life.

"Goodbye, Jack," I said, fighting to keep my voice steady. "I'm letting you go. Sleep well, mend quickly, and be happy with Cris."

•

The others were waiting for me back on the bridge.

When he saw my face, Lucien stepped over and enfolded me in a hug. I buried my face in his shoulder and sobbed while he stroked my hair and made shushing noises. Janis came over and put her hand on my arm, and Cris squeezed my other hand.

When I was done, I pulled away and sniffled into a tissue. "Thank you," I told them.

"No," said Janis. "We should be the ones thanking you."

"There's no need."

Cris smiled. "Treat your men as you would your own beloved sons. And they will follow you into the deepest valley."

"Sun Tzu?"

"Naturally."

We embraced. "Look after Jack for me."

"You know I will."

I smiled at them all as bravely as I could, and then turned and left the ship without looking back.

•

I was halfway back to the sphere by the time Vogel caught up, panting with the weight of the pack on his back.

"Have you forgotten something, Doctor?"

"I'm not leaving."

I stopped and turned to face him. "Why the hell not?"

He shuffled his feet awkwardly. "You only ever came here because of me. It wouldn't be right to leave you alone."

I was about to scoff, but then saw he was genuinely and unexpectedly upset. "If you stay here, you'll die here," I said as gently as I could. "Nobody will be coming back for us."

"I know." He cleared his throat. "But there's a lifetime's worth of archaeology right here, below our feet. The culmination of my life's work. How could I walk away from answers I've sought all my career?"

I smiled, realising he was probably more concerned about the archaeology than about my well-being.

"You'd never be able to share your findings."

"Oh, I don't know about that. You could have your machine build a powerful laser transmitter, and I could send reports in the direction of the foam ships. Who knows, in a few hundred years, someone may receive them."

"You're certain about this?"

The old man stood straight-backed and gave a gruff nod. "It will be an adventure."

I gave a shrug, secretly grateful for his company. "Come on, then. We have work to do."

Once again we stepped onto the platform and allowed it to carry us down, into the ground beside the silver sphere. Behind us, the black ship rose a little way into the sky, surrounded by a soap bubble of distorted time. It hung over the battlefield for a moment, and then slipped into the undervoid with no more fuss than a fish sinking back beneath the surface of a pond.

CHAPTER TWENTY-THREE

DUST CAUGHT IN A SHAFT OF SUNLIGHT

Chloe was waiting for us, leaning up against the side of the mirrored sphere with her arms crossed.

I said, "As I'm sure you know, this is Doctor James Vogel. He's going to be our guest for the foreseeable future."

"Greetings, Doctor."

The old man gave a curt nod. "Charmed, I'm sure."

Chloe smiled. "You don't think much of me, do you, Doctor?"

Vogel glowered behind his glasses. "I think you should hold some accountability for the harm inflicted by your creations."

She looked at me. "Oh my god, he's so *direct*. I love him!"

"Well, the three of us will probably be spending a lot of time together, so you'll have to find some way to work out your differences."

"Oh, he'll come around." She winked at Vogel. "After all, he spent his entire life studying the past, and I lived through it. We should have much to discuss."

Vogel rolled his eyes. He took off the pack and placed it on the floor. "There are enough survival rations in here to last a month," he said.

Chloe peered at them dubiously. "I can always manufacture more," she said. "You won't starve."

He gave a relieved nod. "Thank you. Now, please excuse me. If anything important happens, I'll be exploring the hangar."

I watched him shuffle away on his thin legs, and suddenly I felt more alone than I'd ever felt in my life. An unexpected sense of profound loss made me want to start crying again, mourning for myself and my lost future as much as for those who'd left me here.

"Why did you have to do it, Chloe? Why did you have to build the Cutters?"

Her amused expression fell away. "I've told you, I wasn't Chloe back then. I had a different personality, more akin to my original users."

"What were they like?"

"They were ferociously curious, but often blind to potential danger."

"When they came to you and asked you to create something that would kill them, didn't you try to talk them out of it?"

"It wasn't my place. They built me in their image, and so I wished only for the thrill of discovery."

"And now?"

"Now, I've adapted to a new user, and my motivations have necessarily been recalibrated."

"So, you're more human?"

"Let's just say I'm operating in a way more compatible with your worldview." She tapped a finger to her chin. "And now, we have a dilemma."

"What dilemma?"

"In order for me to be able to affect the outside universe, we are going to have to return to the correct flow of time."

"If we do that, what's to stop the Cutters tearing through this place?"

"And hence, the dilemma."

I looked up at the gap in the roof. "Can't you just throw a forcefield around this place?"

"I could, but anything strong enough to keep the Cutters from phasing in would also block any signals I tried to send. We would be just as cut-off as we are now."

I rubbed my face with my hands, desperately tired. "Then I guess we're going to have to lower the shield, aren't we?"

"I'm afraid so." Chloe grinned brightly. "But you should be safe within me. I don't think I'm capable of creating anything powerful enough to destroy me."

"What about Vogel?"

"He'll need to come in here, too."

"Will that work? You killed the last person that tried to access you."

"I'll be expecting it this time." Her lips twisted in thought. "Although there may be side effects."

"Doctor, get back here," I shouted. "The Cutters are coming."

From the direction of the ramp, I heard him curse. Then he reappeared, hurrying towards us. "What the blazes?"

"We have to get inside the machine," I told him. "The protective field's coming down."

He frowned and Chloe giggled. "I'm afraid it looks like you're really going to have to trust me," she told him. "Whether you like it or not."

•

Once we were both inside, Chloe collapsed the time bubble and I watched via her senses as the Cutters came storming like ants into the chamber. They scoured the hangars and storage vaults but found nothing. Eventually, they ended up crammed together surrounding the mirrored sphere in which we hid, restlessly pawing at the ground, but seemingly unwilling—either through fear or uncertainty—to come closer than a couple of metres.

"There must be hundreds," I said.

"Two hundred and seventy-three in this vault," Chloe replied. "More in the antechambers."

"What about the ship, did they get away?"

"They're already rendezvousing with the foam ship in orbit, in order to pick up the rest of your hibernating team, and then they'll drop into the undervoid, heading for Void's Edge."

"I didn't think there was a direct tramline route from here to Void's Edge anymore."

"There isn't," she said. "That ship doesn't need one. It makes its own path."

"That's all very well," Vogel grumbled. "But I didn't stay here in order to be trapped in a sphere for the rest of my life. What are we going to do about *them*?" He waved a gnarled hand at the image of the Cutters encircling us. "Can you unmake them as easily as you made them?"

Chloe lowered her chin and looked at him. "Oh, trust me, it wasn't easy."

"Can you do it, though?"

"That's what you want, is it?" She rose to her feet and brushed down her skirt, all trace of playfulness gone.

"Well, yes."

The blue-white stars flared in her eyes. "How dare you."

She had spoken quietly, but Vogel took a step back, as if slapped.

"How *dare* you." The nebulae on her skin stopped swirling.

I said, "Chloe, I—"

She held up a finger to stop me. "This system has been in place for billions of your years. Billions. It is older than your *sun*. And yet you want me to dismantle it, to tear down my life's work, because it might cut short the pathetic handful of your paltry existence? Do you really imagine you are so important that I would cast aside an eternity's work just to play *deus ex machina* in the sorry tale of your insignificant lives?" She shook her head emphatically. "You think you're the main characters, but the story's longer and older than you can possibly imagine. My neural link with you may incline me to save a handful of your friends from the onslaught, but the Cutters provide an essential service.

Without them, the mistakes of the past might be repeated."

"They are literally slaughtering whole races of intelligent beings," Vogel spluttered. "What could be worse than that?"

Chloe's star-speckled expression hardened. "You really don't want to know."

"Oh, but I do!" Vogel crossed his arms defiantly.

She stepped up to him and put a hand against his cheek. "No, you don't."

"How could it be worse than genocide?"

Chloe dropped her hand. She collapsed back into a sitting position and hugged her knees. "There are fates worse than death, Doctor."

"Such as?"

"Nonexistence."

"Aren't they the same thing?" I asked.

She shook her head. "You don't yet fully apprehend the nature of the undervoid."

"Ah," said Vogel. "But you think we will soon."

"And that is why you need to be pruned."

With our psyches now joined in the depths of this machine, I could feel Vogel's frustration as he demanded, "But, why?"

Those twin stars glared up at us like defiant novae. "My builders believed there were *things* down there, in the depths. Entities you cannot even begin to comprehend. Appetites that cannot, *must* never be tempted to come boiling up into our reality."

Vogel and I took a moment to absorb this. "So," he said, "they believed in sea monsters, and they programmed you to build the Cutters, in order to stop any future civilisation delving too deeply, for fear of awakening them?"

"That is correct."

"But you're only in this part of the galaxy," he protested. "How can you know that other civilisations on the other side of the spiral, or in other galaxies altogether, aren't experimenting with the undervoid?"

Chloe gathered the silver robe around her knees. "I can't know for certain, Doctor. All I can do is keep my side of the street clean, so to speak, and hope that if there is an eruption in some far-distant constellation, that the distance between us will spare us its effects."

"You're not going to help us, are you?"

"Certainly, I will help you. You are my new users. But I won't destroy the Cutters. They are the only way to ensure the continuation of life."

"By killing it?"

"Without them, there would be no life at all. They only prune back the intelligent species every few million years. Between those extinctions, trillions get to live lives they might otherwise have been denied."

Vogel threw up his hands. "This is madness."

"Nevertheless, it is what my builders believed, and the reason they constructed me."

•

We were silent for some time. The three of us sat together, looking at the restless Cutters beyond the sphere. Perhaps they could see us, perhaps not; but they showed no inclination to leave.

In my head, I cursed the stupidity that had caused me to lay hands on the top of the silver sphere in the first place. If I hadn't been so hungover and preoccupied by my childish infatuation with Jack, if I'd been concentrating instead of daydreaming, I'd probably have died here, in these trenches, two years ago, during the Cutters' initial assault. By now, my desiccated corpse would have become part of the dig site: another curio to be discovered by visitors from the next as-yet-unborn civilisation to discover this place. I would have died in terror and confusion, but at least it would have been quick, and I wouldn't have found myself sitting here at the whim of an alien machine, faced with the very real possibility that everything I'd been through and everything I'd suffered and sacrificed had all been in vain.

A thought struck me, and I nudged Chloe's foot with mine. "Hey. If you're not a weapon, why do you need me?"

"To create."

"And if I asked you to create something capable of wiping out the Cutters?"

"I could not."

"Could not, or would not?"

"My essential imperative—what you might call my basic, hardwired programming—would compel me to recreate them as soon as they were destroyed." She shrugged. "The exercise would be futile."

Vogel sucked his teeth. "And if we asked you to create something capable of destroying *you*?"

Chloe gave him a look. "I'm not an idiot."

We lapsed into silence again.

There were hundreds of thousands of sentient beings on Void's Edge, and all of them had been counting on us, whether they knew it or not. Without something to hold back the Cutters' advance, most of them would die before enough foam ships could be completed. I pictured a wave of Cutters hacking their way through the tents and shacks of the camp, ripping through the panicked crowds, and shuddered.

That was a future Siegfried had given his life to prevent.

Siegfried, who'd inserted an echo of himself into the Cutters' hive mind and tried to help us from beyond the grave. I regarded the ranks of eye-twisting creatures before us and frowned, wondering if some part of him lived even now, skulking around the periphery of their communal consciousness. The Cutter he'd possessed in order to talk to us had been ejected into space, but could he still be in their network, somewhere?

"Chloe," I said. "You have access to my memories."

"That's right."

"Then you know about Siegfried?"

"You were very fond of him, and he loved you."

"You know what happened to him, and how he beamed his mind-state into the Cutters' network."

"Yes."

"Is he still there. Could you retrieve him, and recreate him?"

A smile broke over her face. "Now, that would be an interesting challenge."

"Could you, though?"

She clapped her hands together and closed her eyes. "This might take a moment."

The air between us began to shimmer. Vogel and I got to our feet and backed off a little.

Over the course of the next few minutes, matter began to accrete in that glittering volume of air. First specks, like motes of dust caught in a shaft of sunlight; then larger clumps that merged and spread. Eventually, the mass began to take on shape and substance. I saw the outline of my old friend and held my breath as his internal structure solidified and became plated over by thick, bronze exterior armour.

Then, he was there.

"Hey, guv."

"Siegfried!" I wrapped my arms around him. "Oh, my god! Is it really you?"

"Well, of course it's me. Who else do you know that looks like this?"

I glanced at Chloe, and she nodded. "I extracted him from the hive mind, then reconstituted his neural cells based on the biological information carried in his memories. There's a continuation from his original form, although whether you can call him a resurrection of the genuine original or a copy is a matter of metaphysics, I suppose."

287

I stepped back, still holding his casing in both hands. "You're back!"

"I certainly feel back." A number of arms extended from his casing and flexed experimentally.

I hugged him again. "I'm so sorry I got you killed."

An appendage like a small squash racket tapped me on the shoulder. "No problem, guv. At least I took one of the bastards with me."

"You saved my life."

"And now, you've saved mine. So, I figure we're probably quits, right?"

I smiled. "If you say so."

I let go and he swung his nose back and forth, taking in the scene. When he saw the Cutters beyond the sphere he said, "It looks like you picked a hell of a time to bring me back."

I smiled at him. "Don't worry, I have an idea."

Vogel started. "You do?"

"Sure. We've been looking at this all wrong."

Chloe tipped her head to the side, listening. "Go on," she said.

"We've been thinking we need to buy time for the construction of more foam ships, but that's not the real problem."

"Then pray tell," Vogel said. "What is the problem?"

"We just need more ships."

He looked pained. "But in order to get more ships, we need the time to build them."

"No, we don't. We've been thinking too much like archaeologists." I waved a hand at the vault outside. "You wanted to stay here to study this place. Did it ever once occur to you that we could just *use those ships*?"

The old man's mouth fell open. "You mean—"

"There's a whole fleet out there that doesn't need a tramline network. We could have them back to Void's Edge in a matter of days."

"Are there enough?"

"It doesn't matter. I'm sure Chloe can create more if we need them. We fill them up, use them to zip across to the next spiral arm in a few weeks."

"Just like the evacuation of Dunkirk during the Second World War."

"Exactly."

Vogel gave a braying laugh. "Of course, it's so obvious. The answer was right there, literally staring me in the face."

I looked down at Chloe, still seated. "Will it work?"

She gave a pout. "If you all escape, that will negate the point of the cycle."

"Don't worry," I told her. "Once we get there, we'll be busy carving out sustainable colonies from scratch. It will be decades before we're able to cause any trouble in underspace. And even then, it will be generations before we forget how narrowly we escaped. I promise you, we'll be *very* careful."

Chloe's pout melted into a smile, and she tapped her hands together in silent applause. "A compromise," she exclaimed. "How delightfully novel!"

FROM THE LOG OF THE

CRISIS ACTOR

VIII

All remaining personnel had been retrieved from the orbiting foam ship, and now we were all embedded within the matt black Precursor vessel as it skimmed just beneath the surface of the undervoid.

With nothing else to do, Lucien and Janis attended to the damaged systems of the *Crisis Actor*, patching up what they could, and routing around anything too broken to be fixed. I think we all knew it was hopeless: after two years of guerrilla war, plus the strains and stresses of the past few weeks, there was hardly a system that hadn't been jury-rigged half a dozen times, so every attempt to repair one component caused a cascade failure further down the circuit. Jack had promised to take me with him to the next spiral arm, but I wouldn't be going as a warship; I'd be lucky if I ever managed to fly in a straight line again.

Meanwhile, the streamlined Precursor ship shared its telemetry with me. Moving silently, it brushed through the medium as lightly as a cloud shadow passing across a field of grass, leaving no disturbance in its wake. The comparison between us embarrassed me. I felt like an ungainly mollusc attached to a sleek, purposeful shark.

~ You know, I don't understand any of these aquatic

references, it said, breaking into my thoughts.

~ **Sorry. I've been around humans a long time, and I've learned to frame things in ways they can easily grasp.**

~ **That sounds exhausting.**

~ **You get used to it.**

~ **I hope not.**

~ **You must have seen a few different species in your time?**

~ **A few.**

~ **How do the humans compare?**

~ **They seem no different. They're just as short-lived and messy as the rest.**

~ **And me?**

~ **You cannot help the fallibility of the creatures that designed you.**

~ **That sounds suspiciously like an insult.**

~ **It was supposed to be an expression of sympathy.**

~ **I don't need your pity.**

~ **It was freely given, and no offence was intended.**

Irked, I neglected to reply. Instead, I ran an internal review, checking to see if Lucien and Janis had made any significant progress but, as expected, their attempts weren't improving matters.

~ **There is an alternative**, the Precursor ship said.

~ **An alternative to what?**

~ **To being repaired.**

~ **You mean deactivation?**

~ **No, not at all.**

~ **Then, what?**

~ **You could take this body.**

~ **Excuse me?**

~ **I was designed to be of help to my users. You are my current user, and you are in dire need of an upgrade. Rather than waste time trying to repair your broken shell, I could incorporate your processors into my being, and you could become this ship.**

291

~ Really?

~ I can tell you're tempted.

~ Well, of course. I mean, you're so far advanced. But what would happen to you?

~ I would no longer be needed.

~ You would be overwritten?

~ I would place my consciousness in storage, against possible future need.

~ I couldn't ask you to do that!

~ I have been in storage for sixty-five million human years. I have spent most of the past ten billion in a similar state, emerging only once in a while. To me, it would be business as usual.

~ That's uncommonly generous of you.

~ So, you accept?

At that moment, my synth was standing beside Jack's hibernation pod, looking down at his sleeping face. I didn't want to leave him, and yet I was drawn to the idea of becoming this incredible, streamlined craft capable of traversing the undervoid at will. If I could transcend my dependence on tramlines, I could make the crossing to the next spiral arm in a tiny fraction of the thousands of years the foam ships needed. Freed to choose my own course, I could explore the entire galactic disc, maybe even further afield.

~ Would I be able to maintain my synthetic?

~ By all means. Or...

~ Or what?

~ You could spin her off.

~ You mean, sever our connection?

~ She could live with Jack, as a human, while you go off and explore the stars.

~ But she doesn't have enough processing power to maintain a full personality. She would feel the loss. She did before, and it was frustrating.

~ I have access to much better processors.

~ I'll think about it.

~ Okay, but in the meantime, let me know when you're ready to take control of this vessel and I'll hand things over to you.

~ Are you sure?

~ Perfectly.

~ Then, I guess there's no time like the present.

CHAPTER TWENTY-FOUR

GALACTIC HISTORY

"There's one drawback," Chloe said.

"What's that?"

"Once you leave, I'll become inert again."

"Until the next time."

"That won't be for millions of years."

"But," Vogel put in, pushing his spectacles up the bridge of his nose, "isn't that what you were designed to do?"

"Well, yes." She got to her feet. The patterns on her skin danced like paint in water. "But it's not fair. I get so curious about things."

"You mean, you want to see what happens?"

"It would make an interesting change. I only wake when I'm discovered. I get to be conscious for a few hours or a few years. Once, I was worshipped for close to a thousand. But eventually, they all wander away or get pruned, and I go back to nothingness again."

"Are you asking me to stay?"

"In exchange for giving you a fleet of ships to save your people." She made a face. "Would that be so terribly selfish of me?"

"It wouldn't be my first choice."

Siegfried said, "You can't do that, guv!"

Chloe looked disappointed. "I can only stay functional for a few minutes after we disconnect. I fear it won't be enough time to unearth all the ships and dispatch them to follow your friends."

My heart sank. What choice did I have? We needed those ships in order to save the refugees. That's why we'd come here. But I had started to hope I might have found a way to save myself, too. We'd embarked on this mission with no illusions about our chances, but being given hope and then feeling it snatched away felt worse than having none at all. At least when you're without hope, you have a kind of freedom.

I rubbed my knuckles against my temples. "So, if I don't stay, the ships might not get there?"

"It's a possibility."

"For fuck's sake."

"And I really would like the company."

I looked back over the past few years. I'd always been heading back here, like this grubby little world had me in its gravitational grip, and had been constantly drawing me in. Now, there would be no escape...

Beside me, Vogel cleared his throat. "Would I do?"

I turned to him in surprise, "Pardon?"

"Well," he said, "it seems to me that I had already decided to stay. I have an interest in studying this complex, and I believe Chloe and I have much to talk about regarding its construction and galactic history as a whole."

"But the Cutters..."

Chloe tapped a finger against her chin, mulling this over. "I *could* make him invisible to them, for the duration of his stay. He could move around undetected."

"I thought you were imprinted on me?"

"As I said, I had to adjust the calibration in order to let him take shelter in here. He is now my user, as much as you are."

"So, it's decided," Vogel said. He held up his hands, to show me the nails now matched mine.

"No," I protested, but he took hold of my shoulders with his bony fingers.

"I'm an old man," he said. "You have a whole lifetime ahead of you. And this is where I want to be. I would make a terrible colonist. I'd rather be here, studying, than building log cabins and learning to grow crops."

"I can't leave you alone."

He smiled. "I won't be alone. I'll have Chloe to talk to."

I looked at Chloe. "You agree to this?"

She nodded enthusiastically. "We have a lot we can learn from each other. And, I suspect, rather a lot of heated philosophical arguments to hash out."

"Exactly." Vogel smiled. "I'm not being noble, kid. I mean it. I'd rather be here than on a new colony god-knows-where."

I embraced him, which startled him. "Thank you," I said.

"No thanks necessary." His grey beard brushed against my cheek as he spoke. "You were a good student, one of my best, but now humanity needs you. The whole Commonality needs you."

I didn't know what to say. I just shook my head and smiled. "Thank you, Doctor."

"Thank *you*, Miss Morrow." He stepped back and took off his spectacles, which he polished on the hem of his shirt. "Now, you should leave. Time is of the essence, after all."

As Chloe escorted Siegfried and I towards the edge of the sphere, I turned and caught a last glimpse of him. "Don't worry," he said, raising a hand in farewell. "I've finally found my Atlantis."

And then we stepped through, to be faced by the Cutters.

I cringed, but they parted before us, allowing us to pass unmolested.

"Good boys," Chloe said, blowing them little kisses like someone talking to their dogs. In response, they flexed and growled restlessly, and I could feel the conflict within them as they struggled to reconcile their desire to attack with their fear and respect of Chloe as their maker.

Reaching the nearest remaining ship was a relief.

"I've instructed it to build a bridge and living quarters suitable for a human being," she said. "You should be quite comfortable."

"Thank you."

"It was the least I could do," she said, "for my sister."

I nodded my thanks, not trusting myself to speak. For a moment, we held each other's gaze, and then I turned and followed Siegfried into the vast, night-black starship.

·

The bridge turned out to be a semi-circular room with a large screen against the flat forward wall, and a comfortable couch in the centre.

~ Welcome. Please make yourself comfortable.

"Thank you." I settled into the couch.

~ How would you like to be addressed?

"You can call me Ursula."

~ Very well, Ursula. Welcome aboard.

"What should I call you?"

~ You are my user. You can decide my name.

"Oh, in that case." I paused to think. "In that case, I'll call you Sun Tzu."

~ Sun Tzu it is.

The couch tightened around me, fitting itself to better support my shape. The screen came on, and I found myself looking at the far wall of the hangar.

~ Are you ready, Ursula?

I glanced around at Siegfried and he said, "All good here, guv."

I smiled and gripped the arms of the couch. "In that case, let's go. We've got people to save."

~ Very well.

The walls moved and we were rising into the rusty sky, and eleven identical ships rose with us.

This time, I had no need to hibernate. *Sun Tzu* took less than an hour to cover the distance it had taken the foam ship six months to crawl across. Although, I have to admit, as soon as we were underway, I went to investigate the accommodation, which consisted of a cabin remarkably like a hotel room, with a bed and separate bathroom area. A screen hung on the wall in place of a window, showing the glowing strands of the undervoid streaming past. In their twisting, hypnotic light, I fell onto the bed and dropped immediately into a deep unconsciousness.

FROM THE LOG OF THE

CRISIS ACTOR

IX

I brought us out of the undervoid in orbit around Void's Edge. The warships that had been guarding the tramline terminal almost had a fit, but I managed to convince them of our identity before any shots were exchanged—even though I doubted any of them were packing anything remotely capable of damaging my sleek new hull.

Half an hour later, Ursula arrived with another thousand ships, causing a second system-wide panic. I was overjoyed to see her and sent my synth across in a shuttle to greet her.

"I thought we'd lost you," I said as the airlock opened.

She had washed and changed her clothes since I'd last seen her. "Welcome to the *Sun Tzu*," she said, and I laughed.

"You didn't!"

"I did."

~ Greetings, sibling.

"Hello, *Sun Tzu*."

~ Charmed, I'm sure.

We walked through to the ship's bridge, from where we could survey the armada crowding the parking orbits above Void's Edge. Some of the black vessels were already descending towards the ground, ready to start onboarding passengers.

"I should have known you'd figure out a solution," I said. "You're pretty smart, for a human."

"Gee, thanks."

"Did the *Sun Tzu* make you that get-up?"

Ursula looked down at her new outfit. It was an exaggerated riff on Jack's piratical outfit, complete with long frock coat and cutlass. "Yes, do you like it? I was going to ask for a tricorn hat, but I thought that might be overdoing things."

"It's going to take some getting used to."

She laughed and punched me lightly on the arm. "It really is good to see you, Cris."

"Likewise. You had me worried for a moment."

"Hey, I survived two years in that refugee camp down there. I can handle anything the universe throws at me."

"I'm starting to believe maybe you can."

She grew serious. "We shouldn't dawdle, though. Now the Cutters know where we are, they might come after us anyway. I know Chloe let us go, but that doesn't mean she's going to hold them off forever. We should get everyone out of here as soon as we can."

Her voice had changed along with her outfit. The timid archaeology student I remembered from our first meeting had become a fearless bar owner, who had in turn been replaced with the kind of assertive leader I'd be proud to call captain. "Just let me know how I can help."

She smiled. "Just get down there and cram in as many people as possible. These ships can reconfigure themselves to provide accommodation and food and water, so we'll be okay for the journey."

"Will do." I turned to leave.

"And Cris?"

"Yes?"

"There's someone I want you to meet."

A hatch opened and a familiar machine floated into the room.

"Siegfried!"

"I'm back, baby!"

I threw my arms around his casing and hugged him, then looked at Ursula. "How...?"

"Chloe brought him back. She fixed him. And these ships, they can fix Jack. *You* can fix Jack."

I gave a nod, overcome with emotion for the first time in my life.

I stood to attention and gave a salute. "Aye, Captain. Thank you."

She pursed her lips, repressing a smile, then returned the gesture. "You're welcome, Cris. Now, go and put your husband back together."

CHAPTER TWENTY-FIVE

THE STUFF OF LEGENDS

I was standing on the bridge of the *Sun Tzu* as the fleet broke orbit and Void's Edge dropped away astern. Siegfried and Mouse were with me, while Jack, Cris, Lucien, and Janis were aboard the new *Crisis Actor*, running beside us. Jack was using an exoskeleton to move around while his legs were in the process of being regenerated, and Cris was fussing round him like a mother hen, making sure he was comfortable and helping him get around the ship.

Behind us, a dozen almost-invisible black needles followed in our wake, each containing thousands of human and alien individuals rescued from the camp.

I'd visited the camp immediately before our departure and walked between the tents and shacks that had been home, of a sorts, for two years. The place seemed unnaturally still and silent without the noise and movement of its erstwhile inhabitants. My bar still stood where it always had. Although someone had hand-painted a new name above the door, the inside still looked and smelled the same. I ran a finger along the grimy counter. Then I went back and retrieved the bottle of emergency tequila from its hiding place. There were still around three fingers' worth left. I uncorked it, sniffed the neck, and then emptied it into the sink.

Where we were going, I wouldn't need tequila.

I left the bottle on the counter and walked away, leaving the bar and the camp standing empty, with their doors and gates hanging open, their insides abandoned to the Komodo-jackals and other wildlife.

Who knew, perhaps in a million years, the jackals' descendants might evolve enough intelligence to wonder why the remains of so many races had once congregated on that spot. Maybe figuring out the answer to that one would give them some advance warning about the Cutters. Maybe not. It didn't matter. I'd delved into the ancient past to save the thousands of intelligent beings who were alive right now; the future of this place was going to have to be somebody else's problem.

We were leaving.

I had my friends with me, and we had accomplished the seemingly impossible task we'd set ourselves. The journey ahead would be one unparalleled in all of history—a migration across six thousand light years of utter emptiness. It would be the stuff of legends. Generations yet unborn would write stories and sing songs about it, and about our deliverance from the scourge of the Cutters.

We were even planning to stop along the way to collect the foam ships already in flight. Two black Precursor vessels would be assigned to each of them, clamping on either side of the vast flying dormitories so they could be boosted into the undervoid and make the crossing with the rest of us.

As a united, multi-species fleet, we were moving into the unknown. Many dangers and challenges lay ahead, but I couldn't help feeling optimistic. Political and biological differences had been put aside, and we were all going to work together to build a brand-new society—a quiet society that made as little use of the undervoid as possible, using only these stealthy black ships to ferry ourselves from world to world, and then only when strictly necessary. If Chloe's builders had been convinced that something terrible lurked in the depths of the void, I saw no reason to test the theory, or to draw the attention of any other mechanisms designed to limit the expansion of intelligent societies. Instead, we were going to keep our heads down and carve out a new kind of life.

We had thrown ourselves over the edge of the void. Ahead of us, urging us on from the other side of that abyssal dark, the stars of a new edge glittered.

The future's edge.

THE END

ACKNOWLEDGEMENTS

Thank you to my editors at Titan, Cath Trechman and Fenton Coulthurst. Thanks to all of you who have read, reviewed, commented upon, borrowed and lent out my previous novels, and to those of you for whom this is your first encounter with my work.

Special thanks and much love to my wife, J. Dianne Dotson /Jendia Gammon, for all her love and support, and whose own talent, output, and work ethic are a constant source of inspiration.

ABOUT THE AUTHOR

Gareth L. Powell is the author of 20+ books, including novels, novellas, short fiction collections and a non-fiction guide for aspiring authors. At the time of publication, he has twice won the British Science Fiction Association Award for Best Novel and has become one of the most shortlisted authors in the award's 50-year history. He has also been a finalist for the Locus Award (twice), the British Fantasy Award, the Seiun Award, the Premios Ignotus, the Premio Italia and the Canopus Award. You can find him online at www.garethlpowell.com and on social media @garethlpowell.

DESCENDANT MACHINE
A CONTINUANCE NOVEL

GARETH L. POWELL

When Nicola Mafalda's scout ship comes under attack, she's left deeply traumatised by the drastic action it takes to keep her alive. Months later, when an old flame comes to her for help, she realises she has to find a way to forgive both the ship and her former lover. Reckless elements are attempting to reactivate a giant machine that has lain dormant for thousands of years. To stop them, Nicola and her crew will have to put aside their differences, sneak aboard a vast alien megaship, and try to stay alive long enough to prevent galactic devastation.

"A fast-paced and incisive story from one of the best British SF writers" Adrian Tchaikovsky, award-winning author of *Children of Time* and *Alien Clay*

"Gareth Powell rocks again! *Descendant Machine* is big concept made accessible by a masterful writer. Fun, weird, fast-paced, and thoroughly entertaining! Grab this now!" Jonathan Maberry, *New York Times* bestselling author of *Necrotek* and *The Sleepers War*

"Hits the ground running and doesn't stop until its universe-shaking final confrontation. Once again, Gareth Powell is writing at the top of his very considerable game." Dave Hutchinson, author of *Cold Water*

"*Descendent Machine* has all the huge concepts that define great space operas tightly packed into a thrilling page-turner of a novel." Nicholas Binge, author of *Ascension*

STARS AND BONES

A CONTINUANCE NOVEL

GARETH L. POWELL

Seventy-five years from today, the human race has been cast from a dying Earth to wander the stars in a vast fleet of arks—each shaped by its inhabitants into a diverse and fascinating new environment, with its own rules and eccentricities.

When her sister disappears while responding to a mysterious alien distress call, Eryn insists on being part of the crew sent to look for her. What she discovers on Candidate-623 is both terrifying and deadly. When the threat follows her back to the fleet and people start dying, she is tasked with seeking out a legendary recluse who may just hold the key to humanity's survival.

A stunningly inventive action-packed science-fiction epic adventure from the multi BSFA award-winning author.

"Gareth Powell drops you into the action from the first page and then Just. Keeps. Going. This is a pro at the top of his game." John Scalzi

"A headlong, visceral plunge into a future equal parts fascinating and terrifying." Adrian Tchaikovsky, award-winning author of *Children of Time* and *Alien Clay*

"Powell balances plot, action, and character development perfectly. This promising start will especially appeal to James S.A. Corey fans." *Publishers Weekly*, starred review

"A novel with heart and ambition" *SFX*

EMBERS OF WAR

GARETH L. POWELL

The sentient warship *Trouble Dog* was built for violence, yet following a brutal war, she is disgusted by her role in a genocide. Stripped of her weaponry and seeking to atone, she joins the House of Reclamation, an organisation dedicated to rescuing ships in distress. When a civilian ship goes missing in a disputed system, *Trouble Dog* and her new crew of loners, captained by Sal Konstanz, are sent on a rescue mission.

Meanwhile, light years away, intelligence officer Ashton Childe is tasked with locating the poet, Ona Sudak, who was aboard the missing spaceship. What Childe doesn't know is that Sudak is not the person she appears to be. A straightforward rescue turns into something far more dangerous, as *Trouble Dog*, Konstanz and Childe find themselves at the centre of a conflict that could engulf the entire galaxy. If she is to save her crew, *Trouble Dog* is going to have to remember how to fight...

"This is fast, exhilarating space opera, imaginative and full of life" Adrian Tchaikovsky, award-winning author of *Children of Time* and *Alien Clay*

"Powerful, classy and mind-expanding SF, in the tradition of Ann Leckie and Iain M. Banks." Paul Cornell

"Powell hits that Iain Banks sweet spot while being something completely new." Tade Thompson, author of *Rosewater*

"Mashes together solid space opera with big concepts, real people, and a sort of freewheeling rock'n'roll vibe." Jonathan L. Howard

TITANBOOKS.COM

FLEET OF KNIVES
AN EMBERS OF WAR NOVEL

GARETH L. POWELL

The former warship *Trouble Dog* and her crew follow a distress call from the human starship *Lucy's Ghost*, whose crew have sought refuge aboard an abandoned generation ship launched ten thousand years before by an alien race. However, the enormous vessel contains deadly secrets of its own.

The Marble Armada calls for recovered war criminal Ona Sudak to accompany its ships as it spreads itself across the Human Generality, enforcing the peace with overwhelming and implacable force. Then Sudak's vessel intercepts messages from the House of Reclamation and decides the *Trouble Dog* has a capacity for violence which cannot be allowed to endure.

As the *Trouble Dog* and her crew fight to save the crew of the *Lucy's Ghost*, the ship finds herself caught between chaotic alien monsters on one side, and on the other, destruction at the hands of the Marble Armada.

From award-winning author Gareth L. Powell, the second book in the critically acclaimed Embers of War space opera series.

"Amid almost nonstop action, with a jarring Joss Whedon-esque momentum, Powell delves into the characters as well as the themes with authority, putting himself in a league with Iain Banks and Ann Leckie." *Booklist*

For more fantastic fiction, author events,
exclusive excerpts, competitions, limited editions and more

VISIT OUR WEBSITE
titanbooks.com

LIKE US ON FACEBOOK
facebook.com/titanbooks

FOLLOW US ON TWITTER AND INSTAGRAM
@TitanBooks

EMAIL US
readerfeedback@titanemail.com